EASY KILL

The door came off its hinges and blew inward. Horn turned toward Winger and saw him do a somersault. Then the lights in the hall blinked out.

Horn pulled his 9 mm and activated the laser, scanning the darkness. Winger's machine pistol erupted somewhere across the room, and strobelike muzzle flashes flared briefly as bullets ricocheted off the tanks. Dartt's big Mag roared, sounding like an elephant gun.

Something slammed into Horn's chest. He was propelled backward and upended over one of the tanks, knocking the breath from his lungs. A sharp, clipped voice cut through the darkness. "Kill them all." It seemed to come from the hallway, and Horn forced himself up from the floor.

He was feeling his way across the room when he suddenly remembered his built-in IR sensor. He ripped the patch off his eye and blinked several times. A burst of light exploded before him like a sunspot. Then everything was bathed in a green alien luminescence, as though he were viewing the scene through emerald water. His E-mods flexed, and letting the weapon follow his line of sight, he squeezed off three quick shots.

HORN
ULTIMATE WEAPON
BEN SLOANE

A GOLD EAGLE BOOK FROM
WORLDWIDE.

TORONTO • NEW YORK • LONDON • PARIS
AMSTERDAM • STOCKHOLM • HAMBURG
ATHENS • MILAN • TOKYO • SYDNEY

First edition July 1991

ISBN 0-373-64004-8

Special thanks and acknowledgment to
Stephen R. Cox for his contribution to this work.

ULTIMATE WEAPON

PROLOGUE

TWITCHELL HIT one in the stairwell. He was coming down as Twitchell was heading up, and had made simple eye contact. Twitchell felt it was better to take him out than have to worry about him later. His black-gloved hand grabbed the man's throat, crushing his windpipe. The gurgling death rattle echoed in the stairwell.

Twitchell hardly broke stride. He felt good. The low, dull pain in the back of his head seemed to lessen the more his body was utilized, the more he *worked* it. The correlation made no sense to him, but it really didn't have to. He had a mission, and everything else was secondary.

He knew the strange pain in his head was somehow controlling him, willing him to track down and kill a man he'd never met. His conscience had been replaced by the offbeat throbbing in his brain. A small arsenal was strapped in the webgear crisscrossing his chest: a 12-gauge autoloader, a .44 Supermag, a Stigler Arms 9 mm composite machine pistol. All great weapons for close work, but Twitchell doubted he would need them. His body seemed a weapon unto itself. Indeed, Twitchell felt charged, as though someone had plugged him into the chamber, cocked the hammer and was about to squeeze the trigger.

He reached a landing and examined the steel door. Below the stenciled 66th Floor, a sign had been taped to the wall: Floor Temporarily Closed For Security Reasons. He felt something like electricity pulsing through him. He pulled open the door, and a loud buzzer erupted. An overweight uniformed guard, apparently surprised, was struggling to rise from a folding chair.

"Hey, can't you read the goddamn sign?" the guard queried. "This is a private..." He fell silent, seeing the weaponry hanging from Twitchell's chest.

Ignoring the guard, Twitchell looked down the hall. A crowd of formally dressed people was milling about in a ballroom at the far end. He knew that was where he'd find Senator Jack Merrifield, his target. The man's image hung in his mind like a hologram.

"Just back out the door, Mac. You don't belong here."

The guard's voice snapped Twitchell back. He was aiming a large-caliber automatic straight at Twitchell's chest. The weapon shook in the guard's hands, and sweat glistened on his forehead.

"Certainly," Twitchell said, taking a step backward. But then he slammed his right knee into the guard's groin like a pile driver. The guard moaned, crumpled. Twitchell slapped the gun from his hand, then grasped his head. With one quick twist, he snapped the guard's neck as though it were a stick of rotting wood.

A scream echoed down the hall. Twitchell saw a woman covering her mouth as she stared at him. As he dropped the guard's lifeless body, she raced back to the ballroom. His hands moved automatically to the Stigler 9 mm, flipped up the smooth knob on the slide, jacked a shell into its chamber, slapped the bolt assist into ready position. The double-sized rectangular clip held 300 rounds of soft-tipped ammunition.

He moved into the ballroom, scanned the crowd for the senator, the 9 mm at his side. Seeing the weapon, the crowd retreated in panic. The woman who had screamed in the hallway now emerged from a door with two black-suited men and pointed at him, her face a mask of fear.

"Drop it right there, buddy," one of the men yelled. Both men produced large revolvers from their coats.

Twitchell swung the machine pistol around and fired. Screams erupted as bullets plowed through bodies. A refreshment cart exploded in a shower of glass and shredded metal.

The muzzle of one of the men's weapons flashed and Twitchell felt something slam hard into his chest. There was no pain, only the sensation of being knocked forcefully backward. He suddenly laughed crazily. "I'm goddamn indestructible!" he exclaimed.

Twitchell was hit again, this time in the back. He fired at a man who was crouched just beyond a door that was swinging closed. He caught a glimpse of a gray-headed man in the room beyond and smiled, realizing that he'd found his target.

Another burst of automatic fire knocked him back. A moment later he was on his feet again. Ignoring the chaos around him as people continued to stream out the exits, he walked toward the room that held his target. He tossed the now-empty Stigler to the floor and readied the 12-gauge autoloader. He stepped over the men he had killed.

Expecting it to come off its hinges, he kicked the center of the door. Instead, Twitchell was surprised when his foot and a good part of his leg broke through the wood and jammed into the room, ridiculously suspended. The door exploded in a shower of splintered wood and lead. "Goddamn!" he gasped in surprise, turning away from the volley as the door was shredded by gunfire.

Jerking his leg back, he rolled to one side as the door continued to disintegrate. He could tell that he'd been struck several times, but other than something akin to pressure, he *felt* nothing. When the firing stopped, he touched his face. He knew he had been struck by at least one bullet there, but there wasn't a drop of blood.

Regaining his feet, Twitchell burst down what remained of the door. It flew into the room like pieces of kindling. Several shots erupted, and Twitchell pulled back until the firing subsided. Then he walked into the room, holding the autoloader at arm's length.

Behind an overturned dresser, a young, well-dressed man rose, firing a long-barreled automatic into Twitchell's shoulder. Twitchell staggered slightly and watched his reciprocating blast tear off the top of the man's skull. The body toppled backward, arms spread wide, thudding dully on the carpet.

Twitchell heard a metallic rattle and turned. Another man rose from beside a king-size bed, fumbled with a malfunctioning short-barreled machine gun. Twitchell squeezed off two quick rounds. Driven backward, the man crashed into a nightstand, shattering a lamp. His lifeless form flopped against the blood-spattered wall like a broken doll.

Twitchell scanned the room for the senator. Where was he? Twitchell went to a set of sliding glass doors that led to a balcony overlooking the vast city. Opening one of the doors, he leaned out into the smog-filled air and glanced around. Clearly there was no way off the small patio other than through the room. Twitchell returned inside, focusing on the door to the bathroom.

Without hesitating, he walked to the door and kicked it open. He was momentarily blinded by a muzzle-flash and explosion. He felt a great pressure on his chin, and his head snapped back violently. Staggering back, he heard the weapon explode twice more and felt the autoloader fly out of his hand.

Twitchell's sight returned as quickly as it had vanished. A uniformed cop, holding a service revolver, was watching him with a look of fear and dread. Out of the corner of one eye, Twitchell picked up his target. The senator was crouched in the spacious bathroom near the shower.

"You should be dead," the cop blurted, his hands shaking so badly that the end of the pistol bounced crazily.

"Yeah, but I'm not." Twitchell's voice echoed in the tiled room as he moved toward the cop, took his weapon, and reversed it on the cop and fired.

Twitchell felt so exhilarated that he was almost giddy. He had such an acute sense of power that he was mildly concerned his senses would overload.

"Not so fast," Twitchell said, grabbing the senator by the shoulder as he tried to slip past.

"You son of a bitch," the senator said, turning toward Twitchell and throwing a wild punch that glanced off the side of his head.

Twitchell laughed and grabbed the senator's gray head, twisting him around in a sloppy half nelson. Groaning in pain, the man tried to twist around to compensate for the extreme position in which his head was moving, but it apparently brought little relief. Twitchell felt on the verge of fulfilling something more than a simple mission; he felt on the verge of fulfilling his destiny. As he was about to execute the whipping motion that would snap the man's neck like a twig, something caused him to hesitate. Something from a dead spot in his brain was telling him what he was doing, what he was *about* to do, was wrong, dead wrong.

The pain in his head returned so suddenly that Twitchell nearly released the senator. "No!" he screamed, long and loud like the howl of a beast. He immediately lifted the senator, then lowered him violently.

Having turned his victim's head sideways, Twitchell watched as his eyelids fluttered uncontrollably for several seconds before rolling into a death stare. He released his grip and let the senator's body drop. A sort of physical satisfaction coursed through Twitchell's body. He stared down at his hands, flexing them slowly. The power he felt was *unreal,* and Twitchell didn't want to lose it. The pain in the back of his head was gone. That was his reward.

Smiling, Twitchell left the bathroom, understanding instinctively that it was time to return to base—and get another assignment, he hoped.

A cluster of lights flashed wildly in the doorway of the ballroom. Knocked backward, Twitchell spun sideways and rolled across the bed. Three men in the doorway followed him with their weapons.

Twitchell rose, faced his attackers. Stumbling, he turned and hunkered down, moving toward the doorway. Suddenly a series of louder explosions burst from the doorway as someone fired an autoloading 12-gauge straight at his upper body. The ugly black weapon bucked as great balls of light spit from its barrel. Almost kicked off his feet as the buckshot hammered into him, Twitchell was driven back through the sliding doors of the balcony. He felt his back hit the steel railing. Shattered glass blew through the air like a crazy snowstorm. Instinctively he covered his face. Conscious of a lull in the firing, he looked up—directly into the barrel of the autoloader a bulldog-looking cop wearing a flak jacket had trained on him.

"You're mine now, you son of a bitch," the cop said, grinning sardonically.

"I'm indestructible, asshole," Twitchell replied, stepping toward the cop.

Exploding, the 12-gauge punched a round into Twitchell's chest at close range, propelling him backward as though he'd been hit by a rocket. His back struck the railing again, only this time his legs came up and Twitchell realized that he was going over. He felt something strange: fear. Twitchell, free-falling as the balcony above him moved away, dreamlike, remembered he was sixty-six floors above the dirty streets of Manhattan.

Another thought came to Twitchell at the same instant. It was his identity. I'm Number 23, Twitchell thought as the side of the building turned into a blur. And I'm indestructible. Twitchell held the thought right up to the instant his hardened skull bounced off the concrete like a hammer striking an anvil, and his vision whited out in a soft cloud of something that looked like tiny sparks.

CHAPTER ONE

HORN STOOD in the center of the ballroom and surveyed the damage. The once-swanky gathering place of the well-heeled had been turned into a slaughterhouse. Evidence technicians from Horn's precinct moved among the bodies taking video and recording their own observations by speaking into tiny microphones that curved from headsets to the front of their mouths. He had seen worse, but not by much.

"Come to see the devil's handiwork, Detective Horn?"

Horn turned toward the gravelly voice of Sergeant Jim Raece, who had been a cop longer than anyone he'd known. He focused on the big bluesuiter's face, which was built around a nose that looked like a doorknob.

"Is that who did this?" Horn asked. "The devil?" His voice was humorless.

"Ah, no, sir," Raece answered, shifting his weight nervously. "The guy that did this . . ."

"*One* guy did this?" Horn interrupted, holding up a gloved hand.

"Believe it or not, Detective." Raece cleared his throat, pulled a wadded handkerchief from his pocket and wiped it across his wide brow. "From what we can tell by talking to the survivors, one guy with a small arsenal strolled in here and started firing. He was obviously after the senator."

"Senator?" Horn turned toward his partner, Stu Winger, who had just walked up. "Sergeant Raece here tells me this was done by one guy going after a senator."

"Yeah, Senator Merrifield." Winger rubbed the stubble on his chin and pointed to a door across the ballroom. "You need to check this out, partner. Whoever did this didn't just use firearms."

"What do you mean?" Horn asked as he followed Winger across the bloodstained floor. He could hear Raece's heavy footsteps plodding along behind them.

"It's easier for me to show you," Winger answered over his shoulder, leading the two cops into the bedroom. "In here," he said, motioning toward the bathroom.

"That's Officer Trumbell," Raece said, pointing at a corpse draped across the sink. He turned toward two rubber-gloved techs and motioned for them to leave.

"I recognize him," Horn said. "But what the hell did he do, shoot himself?" The barrel of the cop's weapon was lodged between his lips, and one hand still gripped the handle, a mangled forefinger twisted through the trigger guard.

"No," Winger replied. "That's what I was talking about when I said whoever did this used more than the weapons he was carrying."

Horn's young partner walked to the body. "See?" he said, indicating the hand gripping the revolver. "The trigger finger is broken, and a couple of the others may be crushed. And the fingers on the other hand look pretty dicked up, too. I think the wrist is broken."

"Someone helped him stick his own weapon in his mouth, then pulled the trigger?" Horn looked at Raece, who nodded.

"That's what we figure. At least that's what Detective Winger and I were discussing before you got here," the big cop answered.

Winger waved a hand over the body. "And Turnbull here isn't exactly a ninety-pound weakling. Whoever did it to him has to be a goddamn weightlifter or something."

Horn gestured toward the body on the floor. "The senator?"

"Right," Winger answered. "Senator Jack Merrifield from Florida. He's the guy who sponsored all the antidrug legislation."

Horn couldn't tell how the man had died. "Shot?"

"No, his neck's broken," Raece answered, glancing nervously at Winger.

"His attacker must have had superhuman strength," Winger said.

"You want to see him?" Raece asked.

"Huh?" Winger looked at Raece, puzzled.

"The guy who did this," Raece answered. He turned toward Horn. "That's what I tried to tell you earlier. They apparently blasted the guy off the balcony, and he's still downstairs on the sidewalk.''

Horn led the way into the bedroom and through the shattered glass doors.

Sulphur-tinged air hung over Manhattan like a funeral shroud. Horn leaned over the railing. Far below, red lights flashed and people milled about. A large area had been cordoned off in which rested a tiny white dot that Horn figured was the covered body of the perp.

''There's something funny about the guy who did this,'' Raece said as Horn headed for the door.

''What's that?'' Horn asked without stopping.

''I talked to the tactics guys who finally blew the bastard away,'' Raece said, following Horn out the door. ''They said they hit the guy with at least thirty or forty rounds and it didn't faze him.''

''Hell, he was wearing body armor,'' Winger conjectured as he sped up beside Horn.

''No,'' Raece said as they walked down a wide hall toward a bank of elevators. ''The boys I got guarding his body say he ain't got no flak jacket, he ain't got holes in his body and, after falling over sixty floors to the concrete, well, he looks the *same*.''

''The same as what?'' Horn asked, stepping into an elevator.

''The same as . . . well, they said he ain't got a goddamn scratch on him.'' Raece's voice was edged with frustration as though he were having a hard time getting his idea across. He turned to Horn. ''They say his clothes are shredded, but other than that, his body is clean.''

Horn felt a cold chill run up his spine. "Is he dead?'' he asked, looking Raece in the eye.

The older, rugged-faced cop glanced at Winger, then stared at Horn as though dumbstruck. "Sure,'' he answered, nodding slowly. "Of course he's dead. He fell sixty-some goddamn floors.''

"Have you seen him?''

"No,'' Raece answered. He looked at Horn as the elevator slowed in its descent. "What the hell happened to your eye, Detective?''

Horn unconsciously moved a gloved hand up to the leather patch covering his right eye. He had almost gotten used to seeing with one eye.

"Me and the rest of the boys were wondering,'' Raece said when Horn didn't answer right away.

"No problem,'' Horn said as the doors opened. "I caught a piece of shrapnel. The doctors say it'll be a hundred percent in a couple of weeks.'' He left the elevator before the police sergeant could ask another question.

They walked through the main lobby of the building. "This way,'' Raece said, taking the lead and steering them toward a side door. In twenty seconds they were on the sidewalk, standing over a body covered with a white tarp.

"Jackson, get your ass over here!'' Raece yelled. Seconds later a young bluesuiter was standing in front of them. "Anybody been around to look at the stiff here?" He nodded at the lump on the sidewalk.

"No, Sarge," Jackson answered. "I suspect they've been busy hauling out the bodies from upstairs. Jacobs told me it looked like a war..."

"Shut up," Raece snapped. He turned to Horn and Winger and waved a hand over the body. "Be my guest, gentlemen."

As Jackson turned to disperse the crowd that had gathered behind the shiny yellow strips of plastic cordoning the crime scene, Horn grabbed the edge of the tarp and pulled it back from the man's face. Surprisingly the man *did* look normal. Stretched out on its back, the body was a man apparently in his midthirties, with short dark hair and blue eyes that were staring straight up. If his eyes were closed, Horn thought, he'd look as if he was taking a nice restful nap.

"Hell," Winger said, kneeling beside Horn. "He doesn't even look dead. It looks like he just sort of stopped."

Horn pulled off the glove on his left hand and placed two fingers on the man's neck. There was no pulse, but something struck him as odd. The skin had an unusual texture, like linen or Egyptian cotton. He ran his fingers down the side of the neck and slipped it under the back of the man's head, hefting the skull slightly.

"What are you doing, partner?" Winger asked. "You know you're not supposed to move a stiff around before the techs have had a chance to do their shit."

"His skull seems fine," Horn said, ignoring Winger. "I think his neck is still in one piece, too." He moved his hand down under the tarp and checked out the right shoulder and arm. Nothing felt broken.

"What are you trying to say?"

"How does he look to you?" Horn answered. "Where's the blood? You'd think someone hitting the concrete after falling sixty-six floors would be bleeding, wouldn't you?"

Winger nodded and glanced at the body.

"Feel his skin," Horn said, pulling the tarp away from the man's chest.

"Shit, Horn. You know I don't like touching a dead man." Winger's voice was a whining sort of protest.

"Look at his clothes," Horn said. "They look like they've gone through a shredder, but no blood. Now go ahead and touch his skin. Tell me if you feel the same thing I do."

Pulling off a glove, Winger reached out and laid his fingers on the side of the man's face. He half grunted and turned to Horn. "He doesn't feel dead."

"You mean he doesn't feel *human*," Horn said.

Winger nodded. "It feels like one of those synthetic body suits they use in sports."

"Let me see a knife." Horn held out his hand.

Winger produced an eight-inch, dark green combat knife from his leather coat. "Hurry the hell up," he said, handing the blade to Horn, then moving next to him in order to block the view.

Horn ran the blade across the base of the man's neck. A faint dent followed but quickly disappeared. Horn imagined that it was like trying to slice a steel-belted radial with a butter knife. He pinched a section of skin on the neck and tried to pull it out. Surprised at how tightly it adhered to the body, Horn stuck the tip of the knife into the fold. The blade refused to penetrate. Horn slapped down on the end of the handle in an attempt to pound the blade through the skin.

"Shit," Winger hissed, glancing nervously over his shoulder. "What the hell you trying to do, crucify the son of a bitch? If anyone sees you pulling this kind of crap, we'll be wearing uniforms in less than a week." He retrieved the knife from Horn and slipped it back inside his coat.

Horn examined the spot on the neck where he'd tried to pierce the skin. There wasn't so much as a mark. "We can't let them take this thing to the morgue," he said, more to himself than to Winger.

"What do you mean?" Winger said, pulling the tarp back up over the body.

"It's a machine," Horn answered. "You don't take a machine to a morgue, you take it to a…mechanic."

"Let me guess," Winger said resolutely as he got to his feet. "August."

Horn pulled his glove and nodded. "Go around and get the car. I'll fix it with Raece."

Turning his collar up, Horn walked toward Raece and noticed that the crowd had thinned considerably. It was nearly two in the morning and it was dead cold. November had ushered in consistent nighttime temperatures below freezing—made even colder by a wind that whipped down the polluted ribbon called the Hudson River and screamed through the Manhattan skyscrapers. Something in his bones was telling Horn it was going to be a hard winter.

Horn stopped thirty feet short of the group of cops. "Sergeant Raece," he said, raising his voice and motioning for the grizzled officer.

"Yes, sir," Raece said. He tossed the stub of a cigarette to the dirty sidewalk and walked quickly to Horn.

"Listen, Sergeant," Horn said, focusing on the big cop's face. "You guys are liable to be out here all night as slow as they're moving upstairs."

"Tell me about it." Raece laughed.

"We're going to make it a little easier on you. As soon as Detective Winger gets back with the car, we're going to take the perp's body to the morgue."

"You're not supposed to do that, are you?" Raece said, shaking his head.

Winger pulled up with the car and motioned for the uniforms to raise the yellow tape so he could drive under it. "I'm handling the investigation, right?" Horn said.

"Ah, yeah, but..."

"The quicker we get this guy off the sidewalk, the quicker you and your boys can take a break. Now, give me a hand."

Winger had backed the unmarked Chrysler Elint up to the body and opened the trunk. Horn grabbed the body by the shoulders and waited until Winger and Raece each had a leg. Then they hefted the body, tarp and all, into the Elint.

Winger took a booted foot from Raece and pushed it into the trunk. "Total absence of rigor mortis, Max," he said, closing the lid and walking around toward Horn.

Horn nodded, then turned to Raece. "Listen, Sergeant, isn't it about time you guys started your Thanksgiving food drive?"

"Started it last week," Raece answered. He eyed Horn suspiciously.

"You going to hit up the CSUs this year?" Horn asked, referring to the Crime Suppression Units in his precinct. "I think you missed us last time."

"I think you and Detective Winger were the only ones we did miss," Raece answered, appearing to loosen up a little. "I think you guys were tied up with that crazy bastard from Colombia."

"That's right," said Horn, suddenly conscious of a sour taste in his mouth. "Here." Horn pulled a handful of credit wafers from his pocket and slapped them in the big man's palm. "Come on, partner," Horn told Winger.

Winger groaned and fished around in his jacket. He pulled out several of the thin plastic wafers and held them out. Raece grabbed the money and smiled.

"We're probably going to take the surface route downtown," Horn said, walking around to the driver's side of the car. "So, it could take an hour or so before we get to the morgue."

"In case anybody asks," Winger added before getting into the Elint.

"Only if they ask." Raece grinned at Horn and gave him a half salute.

As Horn pulled the car into the street, Winger snorted. "What was that bullshit about taking the surface? And what's *this* bullshit?" He gestured toward Horn with both hands.

"Isn't it my turn to drive?" Horn answered, turning onto the Avenue of the Americas. He pressed the foot feed to the floor and the Elint accelerated. Winger groaned. "What's the matter, partner, don't like the idea of me driving into the Bronx?"

Winger shook his head. "I don't like the idea of you driving me anywhere."

"Is it because I've only got *one* of these?" Horn pointed toward his left eye.

"Not really," Winger answered in mock sarcasm. "That may actually help. The less you see, the less you can hit."

"Very funny," Horn said as he exited onto Fifty-second Street.

"You said something the other day about August taking a look at your eye," Winger said.

"That's right," Horn answered as his partner removed his coat. "But it's a little more involved than 'taking a look at it.' He's got a replacement for it."

"Replacement?"

"It's a type of visual sensor that August wants to interface somehow with my arm." Horn turned the Elint up Park Avenue.

"What for?" Winger asked.

"I'll tell you what," Horn answered. "I'll let August explain it. But I don't know if we'll have time right now. Tonight we're just going to have him take a look at our friend in the trunk."

Winger nodded toward the back of the car. "You know, that goddamn *thing* back there makes me uneasy as hell," he said.

"How so?" Horn asked, not mentioning his own similar feeling.

"You remember three or four weeks ago when the Chin family got slaughtered right in the middle of their own territory?"

Horn nodded, puzzled.

"Eyewitnesses said it was *one* guy." Winger held up his index finger. "*One guy* walked into the headquarters of the most powerful Chinese criminal organization in the city and took out over twenty of them and *escaped*."

"I've heard it wasn't one," Horn responded. "I've heard it was an inside job to facilitate the takeover by old man Chin's grandson. They just came up with the one-man story to dick up the investigation."

"Could be," Winger said, "but Chin's grandson could have hired out to have the clan taken down."

"That's true," Horn said.

"He could have hired one of these things." Winger nodded over his shoulder again. "Maybe the guy in the trunk is the same guy that did in Chin."

Horn was quiet. The hairs on the back of his neck bristled as he recalled the carnage in the ballroom.

"Or maybe it was his twin," Winger said, half joking.

"Let's hope not," Horn said, turning onto One Hundred and Twenty-fifth Street.

"Where you going?" Winger asked, suddenly interested in the route Horn was taking.

"I'm going to take the Third Avenue bridge," Horn answered.

"Why?" Winger asked, unclipping a machine pistol from the webgear that crossed his chest.

"August moved about six blocks from his old crib," Horn answered, turning up Third Avenue. "I think this way will get us there faster." He gunned the engine and let the machine pick up speed.

"Have you ever taken this route before?" Winger asked nervously as they passed a large sign declaring the Bronx to be an *unannexed* section of New York. Below the declaration, stenciled in red letters, was: Enter At Your Own Risk—Police Free Zone.

"Hey, that's new," Horn said, nodding at the sign as he fired the Elint across the bridge at well over eighty. "*Police free zone.* I kind of like it."

Horn felt uneasy as he left the Third Avenue bridge in a wake of trash and headed toward Clemente Plaza. The Bronx never failed to give him the creeps. Burned-out hulks of cars were scattered along bleak streets that were covered with potholes so numerous it looked like the aftermath of a mortar barrage. The place reminded him of a fire-bombed graveyard.

Long abandoned by the New York City fathers, the Bronx festered in its own devices. Gangs, renegade vigilante groups and packs of humans who had devolved to some aberrant form of life, roamed the no-man's-land, hunting their weaker counterparts or those foolish enough to cross the grim border.

"You know, Tatum is going to have our asses when he finds out we took the stiff and hauled it to the goddamn *Bronx*," Winger said. "But at least I have one consolation." The young cop grinned and pointed a finger at Horn. "He's going to have a hell of a lot more of your ass than mine, partner—as in *senior* partner."

"Pete's all right," Horn responded, referring to Pete Tatum, the new precinct captain to whom he and Winger reported. "He leaves me alone." Horn cuffed the young cop playfully on the shoulder. "And when he leaves me alone, he leaves you alone."

"The only reason he stays out of your hair is because you're tight with the Barracuda," Winger said, grinning.

"You're so full of shit your eyes are changing color," Horn answered. He thought of Christina Service, the assistant district attorney whom most New York City cops referred to as "the Barracuda," since she was known to have a disposition like one. Horn liked the woman: he could always depend on her to shoot straight with him. Sometimes he thought there might be something more: the age-old human attraction between a man and a woman. He kept those thoughts buried.

"Sorry," Winger said, chuckling again. "I didn't mean to cause you to lapse into some sort of emotional trance."

"What the hell are you talking about?" Horn asked, turning toward the young cop as they passed a stripped-down Mercedes sedan coming out of an alley. "We've got company," Horn said calmly as he floored the Elint.

A loud explosion erupted behind them, and the rear window of the Elint shattered.

Horn ducked and swung the car in a wild arc to the left, cutting across the center median and heading up Elton Avenue.

"I thought this was a little too easy," Winger said, leaning over the back of the seat. Pointing his weapon out the rear, he fired a short burst as the Mercedes whipped back and forth wildly behind them.

In the rearview mirror, Horn saw sparks fly off the
front of the pursuing machine as Winger fired a longer
burst, this time working the lead stream up and across
the windshield. The vehicle dropped back fifty feet, as
if preparing for another charge.

"Shit, that's a joke," Winger breathed as he released the expended clip from his smoking weapon.
"They got the Bronx Police spray painted on the side
of that junk heap." He jammed a fresh clip into the
butt of the machine pistol.

Horn slid the Elint sideways onto East One
Hundred and Sixty-first Street. He kicked the speed of
the car up to ninety and watched in the mirror as the
Mercedes came around the corner after them. "Maybe
they want to give us a citation," he said.

A long burst of automatic fire erupted behind them.
He jerked the Elint back and forth several times as the
sickening thud of bullets hammered across the trunk
lid.

"Goddammit," Winger yelped in a voice that was
a mixture of fear and anger. He pulled a smooth egg-
shaped object from his webgear. "Slow down. I'll get
those bastards off our ass."

"Hold on a second," Horn answered as he set the
Elint up in a tire-screaming slide and pointed its nose
up Webster Avenue. He looked at Winger, who had
pulled the pin on an old military-style concussion grenade. "Now, just wait," he said calmly, hoping Winger wouldn't drop the death egg. "I'll let them catch

up, then hit the brakes. Give it to them when they're right on our bumper.''

"You got it," Winger said excitedly. He climbed over the back of the seat, cursing as he flopped into a bed of shattered glass.

Horn watched in the mirror as the Mercedes barreled onto Webster after them, a rooster tail of trash and smoke following the speeding hulk. He eased off the accelerator, being careful not to slow the Elint to the extent that it would look like they were baiting the attackers.

"Ready, partner?" Horn glanced over his shoulder at Winger, who was crouched against the back seat as though it were the edge of a foxhole. The young cop nodded, his eyes wild with excitement. Horn rechecked the street ahead, then glanced in the mirror. A skinny, long-haired guy with some kind of machine gun hung out of one of the rear windows of the Mercedes and started firing.

"Here we go," Horn yelled. "Get ready." He slammed on the brakes and watched the Mercedes make a quantum leap up to their rear bumper through a haze of tire smoke. "Now," Horn ordered, slamming down on the foot feed.

Winger rose up from his crouched position and started to fling the grenade just as the Mercedes slammed into the back of the Elint. "Shit," he screamed as the grenade rolled out of his hand and bounced slowly across the dirty trunk lid.

The skinny man with the machine gun flew out of the Mercedes window and dropped out of sight, his scream fading in the roar of the two cars' engines.

Horn and Winger ducked as the grenade exploded between the speeding machines. The Elint spun around and landed with a thump. Its hood flipped up and bent backward over the windshield, while the Mercedes ploughed into a streetlight pole. Crumpling like an accordion, it burst into flames. A dirty column of black smoke rose into the night sky.

Horn wondered who was in the car and why they had felt obliged to come after them. It wasn't the first time he'd been attacked coming into the Bronx, but things seemed to be getting worse. Horn forced it from his mind.

Horn turned the Elint around and headed back up Webster in silence, watching the side streets and alleys carefully. He turned onto Claremont, then left at Bath Gate. Two and a half blocks up the dark street, he pulled up in front of a two-story redbrick building that stood beside the crumbling remains of burned-out tenements and the shells of long-abandoned businesses.

"What the hell is this place?" Winger asked. He took a portable spotlight from beneath the dashboard and shone it across the front of the graffiti-covered building. A large single steel door marked the entrance, carrying a sign warning that the structure was unsafe due to a toxic-waste hazard. "Is this August's new place?"

"You got it," Horn said, reaching across the seat and punching open the glove box. "Hand me that hand-held," he ordered, pointing into the compartment. "I don't want to patch a call through the net."

Winger handed Horn the telecommunicator, and Horn punched in a series of numbers, then waited while an intermittent buzzing sounded. After about a minute, a scratchy voice suddenly replaced the electronic ringing: "Who the hell is this and what the hell do you want?"

"Dr. August, this is the Bronx Police. We've come to check your license," Horn answered. He couldn't resist jerking August's chain.

After a pronounced silence, drunken laughter erupted from the earpiece. "Horn, you stupid bastard. What you doing here in the middle of the night?"

"You having a party in there or what?" Horn said, thinking that August sounded like he was well past being in his cups.

"Party? Goddamn right I'm having a party. Where the hell are you, my boy?" August sounded almost happy.

"Right in front of your door," Horn answered.

"You alone?" August asked.

"Winger's with me."

"That wet-nosed punk? Wait a minute. How does the street look?"

"It looks like shit."

"I mean is it clear?"

"Yeah."

"I'll be right down," August said, and the line went dead.

The two cops got out of the car. Seconds later they heard the sound of bolts being drawn. Then the door creaked open, revealing a bright shaft of light and the stooped form of Dr. August, who stood at the top of the short set of stairs. He was wearing a ratty flannel bathrobe and holding a nearly depleted bottle of red wine. Classical music echoed in the building; to Horn it seemed out of place.

"Come on up," August bellowed.

"You come down," Horn said, walking around to the back of the Elint. "We've got something to show you."

August shuffled down the steps. "This better be good," he said, pausing on the trash-strewn sidewalk long enough to down the rest of the wine. He tossed the bottle away, and it shattered on the stained concrete. "What've you got?" he asked, stepping off the curb and nearly falling as he lost his balance.

"Get the spotlight," Horn told Winger.

August ran a hand through his long gray hair. He grinned crazily at Horn, his eyes sparkling. "Whadda ya got that's so goddamn important you gotta come all the way up here to show me?" He fished around in the pocket of his robe and pulled out a pipe and lighter. He cupped the bowl and lit it, his cheeks caving in as he sucked on the stem.

Winger reached down to pop the trunk, but drew his hand back. "Shit," he said, "the grenade must have screwed this up."

Seeing that the digital locking mechanism was out of commission, Horn took a step back, then kicked up on the lid with his right foot. It popped open smoothly.

"Take a look," Winger said, motioning at August and shining the spotlight into the trunk.

August leaned into the trunk and scrutinized the strange cadaver. "So what?" he asked. "A dead body. Seen one and you've seen them all."

"Take another look," Horn said.

August stared at Horn several seconds before leaning back into the trunk.

Horn watched August move his hands over the body, then freeze. He remained motionless for a full minute before backing away and straightening. He turned toward Horn, his face pale and suddenly sober.

"Get the thing upstairs, right now," August ordered, his voice clear and void of emotion.

"But Horn," Winger interjected. "If we don't get this thing downtown in the next hour, we're going to be walking a beat for sure."

"Grab his legs," Horn said, reaching into the trunk and lifting the body's shoulders.

"Shit," Winger said disgustedly as August mounted the steps and disappeared through the doorway.

CHAPTER TWO

JULIUS TICKET STUDIED his face in the mirror and wondered what was happening with his life. Some days he felt everything was falling into place and he could quit worrying about the world falling down around his shoulders. He raised his glass of Scotch and took a healthy drink, then allowed the fumes of the liquor to permeate his sinuses.

He had been up all night, walking the floors of his massive Long Island estate. Once it had been the LaSalle Military Academy, but now it served as his laboratory and staging point for his Neuroids—machines that looked and acted like humans. Something had gone wrong with Number 23. The Neuroid had killed the senator, not to mention thirty or forty innocent bystanders, then toppled over a railing high above Manhattan. "I thought the goddamn thing was indestructible," Latch had said. Ticket didn't waste his energy explaining to his *assistant* that the droid probably failed as a result of the blow to the head, traumatizing the brain in spite of its being encased in a shell of titanium. The middle-aged doctor had told Latch to recover Number 23 at all costs. He had to keep the killer droid's shell out of the authorities' hands.

Ticket drained the last of the liquor and dropped the glass into the sink. He left the bathroom, walked across the polished wood floor of the room that had once served as the commander's office, and stared out at the murky, gray water of the Great South Bay. The sun was coming up, and the sky over the Atlantic was a reddish brown. A buzzer sounded from a desk, and Ticket jerked around, momentarily startled. He walked quickly to the desk and punched a button on a console that was built into the polished walnut.

"What is it?" Ticket asked as the image of a uniformed guard appeared on the flat screen.

"This is Cutter, sir. Mr. Latch has just cleared the main gate."

"Good," Ticket said, punching off the monitor. He lit a cigarette and went to the bar set against the wall opposite the row of windows. He poured a good four fingers from a square bottle of Ballantine's and downed almost half of it in one swallow. Drawing in his breath, he turned toward the door just as Jack Latch walked in.

"Did you recover the droid?" Ticket asked, walking toward Latch, who was pulling off a canvas bush-style jacket.

Latch tossed the jacket onto a chair and walked over to the bar. Seemingly oblivious to Ticket, he poured a shot of vodka and rubbed the back of his neck before downing the clear liquid. Then he turned toward Ticket.

"I said, did you recover the droid?" Ticket's voice had lost its edge, as though he knew the answer but for some reason felt obligated to ask.

"The police got him," Latch said, flopping down in the same chair that held his jacket.

Ticket slumped into a red leather executive chair behind the desk. He stared at Latch as ashes from his cigarette fell to the floor. "The cops got him," he repeated.

"By the time I got there, the cops already had his body surrounded. Something funny, though," Latch said.

"What's that?"

"They didn't remove the body by way of ambulance. Two cops put him in the trunk of their car and drove away. It was as though they knew he wasn't human."

Ticket cursed, dropping the cigarette to the floor when it scorched his fingers. Then he retrieved it and put it into the overflowing ashtray on the desk.

"These guys were plainclothes types, driving an unmarked car," Latch said.

Ticket downed the rest of the Scotch. "Did you follow them?"

"As far as I could," Latch answered. "They went into the Bronx."

"You've got to be kidding."

"They went in over the Third Avenue Bridge. That's where I turned around."

Ticket opened a drawer and removed a bottle of amphetamines. He didn't like to take the damn things, but he'd just lost one of his best prototypes. Shaking out two little white pills, he swallowed them, then leaned back and waited.

"Did you collect the balance of our payment from the Escabido twins?" Ticket asked, referring to the South American brothers who had hired him to take out the Florida senator.

"I pick it up tonight," Latch answered. "But don't worry. Christianson is holding it for us."

"Well, at least two things went right," Ticket said, feeling the drug begin to flow in his blood. "Number 23 did his job, and we got paid."

Latch poured another shot of vodka. "Not only that," he said, downing the liquid. "You should've seen what the droid did. I saw them wheeling bodies out of the building for over an hour, and I heard one paramedic telling another that it looked like a meat market upstairs. The point is that it makes a pretty good demo for your friend Kindu."

"But he had a failure," Ticket said, lighting another cigarette. "Kindu isn't going to like the fact that a Neuroid is indestructible as long as it doesn't get banged too hard on the head."

"Why does he have to know 23 failed at all? If I guess right, you're not going to read in the papers about a droid doing this. I'm pretty sure the cops are going to cover up that they've got their hands on one of the most sophisticated human replicas of the twenty-first century. At least they'll keep it a secret until they figure out who built it.''

"Good point," Ticket said, feeling encouraged. "I'm going to call Kindu. I want you in on this."

Latch groaned. "You know I can't stand that son of a bitch."

"Yes, I'm well aware of that. But try to put up with him for a short while. I program the droids, in case you've forgotten. Kindu wants his own personal army of killing machines? I can just as easily program him in as a target—on a delayed basis, of course."

"After he's paid us," Latch said, smiling. "But what are you going to tell that fat son of a bitch?" Latch held out his hands, palms up, as if to say, *We can't deliver and boy is he gonna be pissed*.

Feeling the full effect of the amphetamines, Ticket grinned. He took a long drag of his cigarette and blew the smoke toward the beamed ceiling. "Mr. Kindu wanted at least forty Neuroids with an option for sixty more, right?" Latch nodded. "Well, what have we got downstairs in the way of shells?"

"We've got eleven serviceable shells, not counting the ones in the junk pile," Latch said.

"Then we tell Kindu that he can have nine functioning units as soon as the neural systems are gathered, prepped and checked out in the carriers."

"Nine?"

"Of course," Ticket said. "One of the shells has your name on it, so to speak, and I will retain one as my valet."

Latch stared dumbly for several seconds before an enlightened look dropped across his face. "Right," he said, breaking into a grin. In the next instant, his expression grew suddenly sober. "But what's Kindu going to say? He's not going to like the fact that he put a deposit down for forty droids and is going to end up with nine."

"I told him up front that there was a high probability we would experience a level of scrap," Ticket said.

"Yeah, but not seventy-five percent," Latch said.

Ticket shrugged. "What's he going to do, sue us? The way I look at it, he gave us the job sole source. Now he's going to have to live with our terms."

"That bastard makes my skin crawl," said Latch. "Let's get it over with." He slid his chair around so that it was next to Ticket's.

Ticket punched a button on the inlaid console. He pulled up the screen so that it faced them. Working a small keyboard in front of the screen, he brought up a menu that consisted of a coded list of names. He selected Customer 12, then punched in a password that served as his key to the satellite net. Fifteen seconds later the image of Michael Toftoy, Kindu's personal secretary and bodyguard, appeared.

"You're late," Toftoy said.

Ticket felt the hair on the back of his neck stand up. He imagined he felt the same way about Toftoy as Latch did about Kindu. There was something about the big, athletic man that stuck in Ticket's throat and made him want to spit. As he looked at the confident, stupid expression on Toftoy's face, he figured it out. The green orbs that served as Toftoy's eyes may as well have been chunks of dead metal. They were totally void of feeling and humanity. For a moment Ticket felt a mild wave of shock as he recognized that Toftoy might be a droid. He dismissed the notion, blaming it on the amphetamines.

Ticket glanced at his watch. "So we are," he said curtly, smiling at Toftoy. "Now, be a good chap and put Kindu on."

Toftoy stared at Ticket for a long time before the screen dropped the image and displayed a Please Stand By.

"You ever wonder why Kindu would have a Westerner for his right-hand man?" Ticket asked.

"Probably because his own people can't stomach him," Latch answered. "What do you want to bet he's wearing that stupid fez and those dark glasses?"

"Do they bother you?"

"Everything about that asshole bothers me. He looks like something out of a cheap movie from the middle of the last century. And the goddamn clothes he wears look like something they'd bury you—"

Latch cut his discourse short as Kindu appeared on the screen. A black double-breasted suit was stretched over his massive body. He was sitting on a chair that resembled a camel saddle, smoking a cigarette in an ivory holder. Just as Latch had predicted, Kindu's smooth, fat face was partially hidden behind a pair of black sunglasses and a short, tassel-less fez topped his round head.

"Have you a report for me?" Kindu asked, his voice a gargle. Ticket often wondered if the man were faking his appearance. The accent, the fez, the dark glasses, the cigarette holder—everything was so outrageous that it had to be phony. But the man's money was real enough: gold or blue slip. As far as Ticket was concerned, Kindu could dress up like the Pope as long as he came across with the money.

"I'm afraid I am the bearer of the proverbial good news and bad news," Ticket said, glancing at Latch, who was staring at the screen as though mesmerized.

"Go on, Dr. Ticket," Kindu said, cocking his head slightly to one side. "I request you relay the good news first. The latter is something I do not receive well."

"We've tested the prototype on three occasions. It has performed flawlessly on each mission." Out of the corner of one eye, Ticket saw Latch flinch. "All three trials involved heavily armed resistance in large numbers."

"I am aware of two of your so-called trials, Dr. Ticket, and yes, they were quite impressive." Kindu took a slow drag on the ivory holder. "Tell me about the third test. Of that I'm not aware."

"It took place last night," Ticket answered. "With your permission, I'd like Mr. Latch here to brief you, since he shadowed the entire mission."

Latch shot Ticket an icy glance, turned toward the screen and cleared his throat.

"Go on, Mr. Latch," Kindu said. "Your report is critical to my decision regarding the purchase of your product." The huge man laughed, but it came out as more of a snort.

Latch flared at Ticket again before addressing Kindu. "One of our clients wanted a certain senator taken care of. We used the same prototype we'd used twice previously, and it went flawlessly."

"One of your clients wanted a U.S. senator killed?"

Ticket placed a hand on Latch's arm, then checked to ensure the encryption module had been activated. "That's correct, Mr. Kindu," Ticket said. "We had to hire out the Neuroids to raise enough operating capital to finance this little operation."

"But what about my deposit?" Kindu asked. "I would think six million credits would be enough that you wouldn't have to—"

"Six million credits is little more than a drop in the bucket," Ticket told the Libyan. "Don't get me wrong. It's been a help, but the results haven't lived up to my original expectations."

"Go on," Kindu ordered.

"I didn't get the yield I had expected. Your funding just wasn't enough to cover a full run." Ticket took a deep breath and watched Kindu for a reaction.

The Libyan stared at Ticket silently, nodding his head. "I see," he said. "My deposit wasn't enough to cover the forty Neuroids I ordered. Correct?"

"Correct. But I assure you, there's nothing wrong with the performance of the droid. As Mr. Latch mentioned, the last exercise was really the best showing to date. The droid single-handedly took out—what was it, Jack?" Ticket turned toward Latch.

"Almost forty armed men," Latch spoke to the screen. "Twenty others were wounded."

Ticket knew Latch was lying, but had no qualms about him doing so. He knew he'd have to make up for the lack of quantity by an increase in performance.

"Very impressive," Kindu said, replacing the butt in his holder with a fresh cigarette. He lit it with a gold lighter and inhaled deeply. "Let's cut to the chase, Dr. Ticket. What are you trying to tell me?"

"The first production run only netted nine shells," Ticket answered. "We still have to install the neural systems and run a check on them. And the price per copy has gone up."

"But we had an agreement. It was six million credits down and another fourteen when you delivered the droids. That comes to half a million a copy. If nine are all you can deliver, I should have money coming back."

Ticket noted that Kindu's accent was all but gone. The man could have been from Chicago.

"I'm sorry," Ticket said, figuring he may as well see how far Kindu could be pushed. "The price has gone up. Not only my costs, but the performance of the Neuroid warrants it. If you like, I'll refund your six million. I've got plenty of others waiting in line."

Ticket was lying. He hoped to hell Kindu wouldn't take him up on his offer. He had no idea where he could get his hands on six million. He felt sweat trickle down his back.

"How much are you talking about?" Kindu asked.

"Two-point-five a copy," Ticket answered, coming up with the figure on the spot.

The huge Libyan stared at the screen as if he'd gone into some sort of trance. After a full minute, he abruptly spoke: "Your unilateral change in our agreement disturbs me greatly, Dr. Ticket. Please stand by." He waved a hand, and the screen immediately defaulted to the alpha display of the last three words that Kindu spoke.

"Shit, you've done it now," Latch said, turning toward Ticket. "That son of a bitch is pissed, and there's no telling what he's going to do."

Ticket laughed. "I'll be damned if I ever figure out why Kindu strikes such a chord of fear in your psyche, Jack," he said. "One look from the man, and you act like a whipped dog."

Latch looked annoyed.

"Relax. I'll admit, he is an obnoxious and frightening bastard. Are you all set for your trip to L.A.?" Ticket had received nearly one million dollars for nailing the senator, and Latch was going to take it to Los Angeles to pay their suppliers for the neural systems needed to bring the droids to life.

But before Latch could answer, Toftoy's image flickered onto the screen.

"Where's Kindu?" Ticket asked, wondering what the fat man was trying to pull. He had the feeling that the Libyan knew he couldn't stomach his assistant and used him just for his ability to irritate.

"I don't really know," Toftoy drawled, then half chuckled. "Whatever you told him must have been pretty damn unsettling. He stormed out of here a moment ago, and I think he was quite annoyed."

"Well, have him call me if he wishes to discuss the matter further," Ticket said, reaching out to discontinue the link.

"Wait." Toftoy raised his voice and held up a hand. "He told me to tell you that he wants a face-to-face."

"When?"

"He'll let you know in the next couple of days."

Without responding, Ticket punched off the screen. He stared at the flat panel, wondering what Kindu's idea of a face-to-face was. It suddenly struck him that he really had nothing to worry about if he could bring another Neuroid on-line before the meeting.

Ticket turned to Latch. "Listen. Before you leave for L.A., I need you to get me one good system, a local."

"When?"

"Now. Tonight at the latest. Can you handle it?"

"Sure," Latch answered. "That's not a big problem. You'll be taking a chance from a quality standpoint, but I can get you a system, probably this afternoon."

"Good," Ticket said. "I'll get a shell prepped."

"Why the rush?"

Ticket leaned back and stared at the ceiling, blowing a long stream of smoke upward. "Just get me a system, Jack," he said.

Latch shrugged and walked toward the door.

CHAPTER THREE

"YOU KNOW, AUGUST," Horn said, watching the shrunken doctor bend over a sink half-filled with dirty dishes and splash water on his face. "This place isn't that much different than your old crib on the other side of the expressway."

"The difference is," August answered, wiping his face on his bathrobe, "that I don't have a pack of two-legged wolves howling at my door every damn night."

"You're not that far away from your old rat hole, are you, August?" Winger asked, helping himself to coffee from a pot on the cluttered counter. He inspected the inky liquid carefully, then set the chipped mug on the Formica without raising it to his lips.

"No, not that far away," August answered. "But far enough that my former neighbors don't bother me anymore."

August's living quarters were sparsely and messily decorated with a few mismatched pieces of furniture. The large, high-ceilinged room was arranged to facilitate his craft as one of the few underground mod doctors in the world who had earned a reputation for being able to successfully meld flesh with a machine. A large stainless-steel operating table sat in the center of the room, around which was scattered an array of life-support equipment, tool dollies, electronic test equipment, compressors, hydraulic mules, surgical saws and several old boxlike sterilizers. The area looked like a cross between an operating theater, an electronics test bench and the crash site of a fighter jet.

August stooped over the body on the couch. Turning the humanlike form over on its stomach, he peeled off the jacket, causing its arms to flop wildly.

"Tell me where you came upon our friend here," he said. "I've never seen anything like it." He glanced at Horn, who was leaning against the kitchen counter.

"He just finished killing a U.S. senator and thirty or so members of his entourage," Horn answered as August ripped the shirt from the form on the couch, placing one foot on the buttocks to gain leverage.

"Is that right?" he said. He sounded as though he were catching up on old times as opposed to discussing the brutal slaughter of several dozen people. "Where did this take place, downtown?"

"Manhattan. Down on the south end."

"I see." August ran his hand down the back of the body. "And how were you two able to put it out of commission so handily?"

"We didn't," Winger interjected. "He took a sixty-story dive and made a one-point landing on the sidewalk."

August scowled. "It figures," he said, grabbing the body's head and moving it from side to side. "Trauma. I'm sure this bastard couldn't have been taken out with any kind of small arms." He studied the back of the neck intensely. "Look at this," he said, motioning to Horn.

Horn approached the couch and leaned over. He sensed Winger behind him and knew the young cop was peering over his shoulder.

"See this?" August traced a finger along a barely perceptible ridge that ran down the fleshy-looking material from the base of the skull to the lower back. "This seam provides an access to the droid's nervous system." He straightened up and stretched his back. "If I'm right, this machine has an actual piece of living flesh inside this—" he slapped the droid's rib cage "—goddamn near-perfect replica of a human body."

"What the hell are you talking about?" Winger said.

"This is a machine, son," August answered. His face was almost beaming. He felt like an astronomer who had just discovered a new star cluster. "I've heard rumors that someone had finally developed a working prototype of what we in this dubious business refer to as the *ultimate inverse.*"

"The what?"

August picked up his pipe from the counter. "I know. I think it's a dumb term myself. But let me explain what it means." Lighting the pipe, he blew a stream of smoke toward the ceiling. "Thus far, most of the world's mod doctors have concentrated on modifying bodies with machine components. While the few of us who are any good at it have made great strides in integrating metal and flesh, we've never really made the crossover."

"Crossover?" Winger asked, taking a seat in an old folding chair at the end of the couch.

"I mod bodies with machines," August answered. "There are one or two techno-physicians who work on modifying machines with the parts from a human."

Horn felt a slight chill run up his spine. He gestured at the body on the couch. "You think this is one of theirs?"

"It's one of the most sophisticated droid bodies I've ever seen," August replied. "Tell me how it functioned."

"We didn't see it while it was ... *alive*," Winger answered. "But we saw what it did before it went off the balcony."

"Any reports on how it moved? Were its motor functions natural?"

"A couple of the tactics guys said they thought it had to be someone wired on string, wearing body armor," Horn said. "As far as I could tell, no one suspected it was anything other than your normal everyday mass murderer."

"Except for Raece," Winger said.

"Raece?" August said, pulling the pipe out of his mouth.

"Sergeant Raece," Horn answered. "One of the bluesuiters from our precinct. He told us there was something funny about the assassin's body."

August nodded. "This is either Ibsen's or Ticket's work," he muttered.

"Who?"

"Peter Ibsen or Julius Ticket. Both are brilliant, complex, troubled men with screws loose in their brains." He tapped the side of his head with the stem of his pipe. "I've seen bits and pieces of their work, but this—" he nodded toward the couch "—is a masterpiece. And it's probably the work of Julius Ticket."

"How do you know?" Horn asked.

"This may sound a little crazy, but the word circulating among the community is that Ticket has advertised an army-for-hire."

"An army of killer droids?" Horn added.

"Right, and for hire to the highest bidder," August said. "I also heard that he has indicated he would prefer to hire them out to Third World countries that don't have the bomb but are looking for the next best thing."

"That sounds dangerous," Winger commented.

August held up his hands. "The guy obviously has delusions."

"You ever meet this Ticket?" Horn asked.

"Yeah, about a year and a half ago. He went by the name of Spofford. I sold him a design for an electro-mechanical shoulder—similar to yours." He nodded at Horn, dumped the ashes from his pipe in the sink and took a pouch of tobacco from the countertop. "Probably the design used in the shoulder construction of our boy on the couch, which reminds me—you are going to leave it here, aren't you?''

"Sorry," Horn said. "We're already stretching it by bringing it here for this long."

"What he's really trying to say is that we've already got our shit in a sling by bringing the goddamn thing here at all," Winger said, getting up from the chair. "We're going to be explaining this little detour to the Barracuda, you can bet your ass on that."

"What else can you tell me about Ticket?" Horn asked, ignoring the young cop.

"Not much," August answered. "I think he's still around the city somewhere. I'll put out some feelers and let you know."

"I'd appreciate it."

"Let's go," Winger said, cracking his knuckles nervously. "Let's get this son of a bitch down to the morgue."

"Not so fast," August said, turning toward Horn. He pulled a pair of wire-frame glasses from the pocket of his robe and put them on. "Pull that patch off your eye and come over here." He grabbed Horn by the arm and led him to the stainless-steel table.

"Horn, goddamn it," Winger half whined, his tone reflecting the uselessness of his protest.

"Tell your partner to make some fresh coffee and relax," August said soothingly, motioning for Horn to get on the table. "This should take less than an hour," August said as Horn lay down on the table. August pressed a button on the side, and a surgical lamp blinked on, illuminating the area in a bright, blue-white light. "Winder," August barked. "Front and center, boy!"

A door near the back of the room slammed, and moments later August's obedient, dwarfish assistant was standing beside the table. Horn had the strangest feeling that the muscular, fireplug-shaped man had been waiting with his ear to the door. August tore open a foil packet and extracted a small towel. He wiped his hands as Winder opened a package of sterile latex gloves and held them out.

"That droid on the couch," August said. "I want you to take some pictures of it and take a sample of its skin...take it from some unobvious area, like the sole of one of its feet."

"Pictures, you mean X-rays, right, boss?" Winder responded enthusiastically.

August sighed. "Hell, yes, I mean X-rays. Shit," he said, pulling on the gloves. August looked at Horn and smiled. "It's hard getting good help nowadays."

He turned to Horn. "Take that patch off," August said.

Horn removed the patch and watched as August held some sort of aerosol can over his face. "Why don't you tell me what the hell you're doing so I won't get nervous?" he asked.

August chuckled. "You got me so excited over the droid that I damn near forgot about your eye. I finished it last night, and this is as good a time as any to try it out. This is going to feel as cold as hell," he said, spraying a vaporous stream directly onto Horn's face. "This will anesthetize, as well as sterilize, the socket."

Horn felt his mods flinch as the chemical painted the area where his right eye used to be. He could swear his skin was freezing as a burning sensation stabbed his face momentarily before giving way to a numbness.

August probed the area around the socket with his fingertips. "You never did tell me how you lost the eye," he said. "I pulled one fiberglass splinter out of it that had to be fifteen or twenty centimeters long." He held up a gloved hand and indicated the approximate length with his thumb and index finger. "There were several others, but that was the one that took it out for good. What the hell happened?"

"Fiberglass bullet," Horn answered. "It hit my shoulder and splintered."

"Do you feel this?" August asked, pressing firmly around the socket.

"No," Horn answered.

"I'm going to remove the glass orb we inserted to fill the space," August said, moving the thumb and forefinger of his right hand on either side of the temporary eyeball. "This may feel a little weird, so brace yourself."

Horn felt pressure on opposite sides of his socket, then suddenly something gave and a sharp pain drove into the back of his head like a dagger. His right knee kicked up involuntarily, and he sucked in his breath in order to keep from yelling. He heard as much as felt the fake eye being plucked from his skull. It sounded like a raw oyster being ripped from its shell.

"There, I've got it." August held an opaque glass sphere over Horn's left eye so he could see it.

"That didn't feel weird," Horn said, exhaling. "It hurt like a bastard."

Horn heard August fiddling with the lid on one of the old sterilizers, and moments later stared at what looked like a real eyeball that was being held in the techno-doc's fingertips. A couple of thin wires, or what looked like wires, dangled from the nerve end of the eye.

"I told you a little bit about this when I removed the damaged eye, if you remember," August said. He peered intently at Horn's face. "You're going to have some scars to go along with that big one across your cheek," August said.

"I remember you telling me you were going to design the thing to tie in with the movement of my arm," Horn said.

"That's right. I had to make the actual targeting function dependent on the laser sight of that ancient weapon you insist on carrying."

"My 9 mm?" Horn asked.

"Yeah, that piece of pot metal you drag around like a worn-out security blanket."

Horn thought about what August had just said. *A worn-out security blanket.* He figured the statement held some truth. By current standards, his old laser-sighted 9 mm automatic was slow in its action and it was heavy. Its stainless-steel chassis far outweighed the newer composite-constructed hand-held weapons, and its longer barrel, combined with the higher-charged loads Horn always used, made the automatic a sort of elephant gun, more reliant on firepower than finesse. Horn refused to *upgrade,* as Winger constantly nagged him to. The old, scarred-up weapon was dependable and had seen him through many trips along the edge. He wasn't about to get rid of one of the few friends he had.

August sprayed more of the anesthetic into Horn's eye socket. "This should greatly improve the accuracy of your weapon."

"How's that?" Winger interjected.

August grunted slightly. "This may be casting pearls before swine, but let me explain it to you." He placed the modified eye on the tray and lifted a stainless-steel device that looked like a small pair of tweezers with some type of clamping apparatus for a handle. Taking a long breath, August fished around in the eye socket momentarily before pulling out a thin, whitish-looking piece of flesh resembling a dead worm. The end August held between the jaws of the tiny clamp had been fitted with a two-sided microconnector.

"This is Mr. Horn's optic nerve," August said, glancing at Winger. "I installed the connector when I took out his damaged eye." He pointed to the end of the nerve that held the dull green interface.

Horn felt a dull tugging in the back of his eye socket that seemed to be connected directly to a part of his brain. The sensation was bizarre enough to cause him to break out in a cold sweat. He could see Winger standing next to him staring at what August held in his hand. The expression on his face said he wasn't overly enjoying the lecture. Horn thought the young cop looked a little seasick.

"Briefly," August said, retrieving the modified eye, "this piece of art will allow Mr. Horn to operate as an actual weapon system."

"How's that?" Winger said, taking a step back. He wiped his forehead with the back of one hand.

August smiled, obviously enjoying the young cop's discomfort. "Mr. Horn's new eye is a parallel digital signal processor-based infrared and video-optic module that will not only allow him to *see* out of this side of his head—" he gestured at the right side of Horn's face "—but will allow him to acquire and lock on to a target in less time than it takes to blink."

"You mean his eye is going to control the aiming of his weapon?"

"Exactly," August said enthusiastically. He held the eye up and turned its lens toward the young cop. "The lens focuses the light onto a splitter that splits it equally onto two separate mirrors. One mirror reflects the image onto an infrared detector, which provides the heat images used to fine-aim the 9 mm by baselining where the weapon's laser sight is hitting the target. You follow?"

Horn could see Winger nodding dubiously. He'd heard part of the same lecture before, but wondered how the eye would really work once implanted.

"Sure you do," August chuckled. "I'll try to make it simpler. The other mirror focuses the image through a TFT liquid crystal display onto the video gun..."

"TFT?" Winger interrupted.

"Thin film transistor," August answered, barely skipping a beat. "This acts as a sort of heads-up display and allows Horn to actually see. I've also added some overlays, menus and even cross hairs when the system is in the weapons mode."

"It sounds complicated as hell," Winger said, shaking his head.

"Actually it's quite simple from an operational standpoint. When the weapons mode is selected, the processors bring up the cross hairs and Horn's modified arm automatically and instantaneously. It will aim the 9 mm to where the eye has tracked the cross hairs. The infrared detector then coordinates the 9 mm's aiming laser with the video gun's cross hairs and centers the target in less than five microseconds. Aiming is done subconsciously, but Horn still has to pull the trigger to fire the weapon."

Horn shivered slightly as August's last statement brought back the grim memory of when he killed the assassin, Harry Trower, on the subway. He wasn't conscious of pulling the trigger in that particular instance. Trower's mention of the man who had killed his wife and daughter had caused his modified hand to seemingly act of its own volition. Horn hadn't *intended* to pull the trigger, but the result was the same. Trower's brains were splattered across a graffiti-covered wall. He wondered what surprises a modified eye would bring to a body that already sported an electromechanical knee, shoulder, arm and hand.

"How does Horn get this thing into a weapons mode?" Winger asked.

"Simple," August answered as he placed the eyeball on Horn's cheek and began mating the connectors to the ones on the optic nerve. "Shit, excuse me a second," he said, releasing the fragile-looking connector. "Winder!" August shouted.

"Yes, boss," Winder said, appearing next to the mod doctor.

"Electron glasses, please."

Within seconds Winder had replaced the wire frames on his boss's head with a set of uncomfortable-looking goggles that gave him a goofy, alien sort of appearance.

"As I was saying," August continued, turning back toward Horn and proceeding with the mating process, "he selects the mode by blinking—once to change the menu choice and twice, fast, to fix it."

"What else can he choose besides a weapons mode?" Winger asked. He was leaning across the table gazing intently at August's handiwork.

"He can go to strictly IR and, in effect, see at night," August said.

"Infrared?" Winger clarified.

August nodded. "Pretty shit-hot, huh?" He looked up at Winger and grinned crazily. "This little number is going to make your partner one hell of a . . ."

"Goddammit," Horn growled. "Will you cut the chatter? I think your anesthetic is wearing off."

"Sorry," August said, grabbing the can. He sprayed the area in and around Horn's socket. "I'm rather proud of this little hummer, as I'm sure you can tell."

"No shit," Horn mumbled.

August worked quickly. After completing the connection of the optic nerve, he bonded Horn's muscles to serrated areas around the circumference of the eyeball's high-impact case.

"Hold on," August said, spraying the socket with a mineral-based lubricant. "This may feel a little odd."

Horn thought that *odd* wasn't the word for it as August placed his left hand across his forehead and began screwing the eyeball into his skull with his right. It felt like a baseball was being forced into the socket as August applied more pressure and twisted the modified eye back and forth.

"Damn," August breathed. "This is a hell of a tight fit." He chuckled slightly, leaning over, putting some weight behind the twisting motion.

Suddenly Horn felt the bulk of the eye clear the socket and seat itself. A blinding pain flared across the front of his head as though he'd been struck with an ax handle. He closed both eyes and saw crazy phosphorescent patterns unfolding out of the darkness.

Horn was a little shocked when he realized that he was picking up the multicolored visions with his right eye as well as his left. Opening his eyes, he caught a strange, blurred glimpse of August's distorted face just before the sight filtering through the modified side of his visionary system went dark. Horn was momentarily confused, then realized that August had cupped his hand over his right eye.

"Not so fast, buckaroo," August chortled as he pulled a clean towel from the tray. He quickly lifted his hand and pressed it firmly over the modified eye. "I want you to get used to it physically before you actually look through it. I'm afraid it'll overload your senses if you bring it on-line too quickly."

August turned to the counter and poured some of the coffee that Winger had made. He tilted the mug back as though it were beer. He immediately choked and turned his head to one side, spewing the brown liquid across the floor. "Goddamn," August gasped, spitting several times before wiping his mouth with the sleeve of his bathrobe. "What the hell did you do? Piss in the goddamn coffee?"

Winger shrugged. "Is it that bad?"

"It's worse," August answered as Horn rose to a sitting position. "Hold that towel over your eye, son," he said, turning slightly. "It's a cinch I can't help you since your partner just poisoned me. What the hell did you put in there, anyway?" he asked, facing Winger.

"Hell, it looked like coffee," Winger said, his face red.

"You didn't use the stuff in that green canister, did you?" August asked, wiping his tongue on his sleeve.

"Yeah, that's coffee, isn't it?" Winger's voice was weakly defensive.

"Shit," August bellowed, then broke into laughter, shaking his head. He turned to Horn. "Your partner just made a pot of coffee out of gunpowder!" August lapsed into another fit of laughter. Winger held up his hands in a what-can-I-say gesture as Horn swung his legs off the table.

"Here," August said, grabbing the patch. He helped Horn slip it over his head and in place before taking the towel out of his hand and tossing it over his shoulder. "How does it feel?"

"It feels like a bald tire about to blow out," Horn answered, sliding off the table.

"It'll get better in a day or so," August said, smiling from ear to ear. He smoothed the black leather patch down over the modified eye. "I want you to keep this on and come back in two days. By then, your muscles should be used to being reconnected to an eyeball."

"We'll probably be in jail, so you better plan on visiting him instead," Winger said, walking toward the couch. "We've had your superdroid AWOL for nearly four hours now. I don't think the captain, let alone the DA, is going to be too pleased with us."

Horn glanced at his watch. "He's right," he said, slapping August on the shoulder. "We'd better haul ass."

August grabbed him by the sleeve. "I wasn't joking when I said keep the eye covered," he said, pointing at the patch. "Your arm is tied in with the eye, and you need to let them . . . get *used* to one another before testing their operation."

Horn looked down at August with his *good* eye and nodded. "See if you can get a line on this Ticket guy for me."

"I'll see what I can do," August answered.

Horn turned toward the door just as Winger and Winder were carrying the droid body across the threshold.

CHAPTER FOUR

THE CITY OF LOS ANGELES lay sprawled across the southern California hills, its multitude of lights dim beneath a thick blanket of gray-brown pollution, its freeways crisscrossing the overpopulated landscape like trails cut through a junkyard.

As the transatmospheric shuttle broke through the ten-thousand-foot ceiling on its downward approach to LAX, Jack Latch looked out across the back of the huge dying reptile and felt something akin to going home. He loved his trips to L.A. They got him away from the cold concrete of New York City and seemed to rejuvenate him, at least enough to last the thirty-or-so-day stretches he spent with Ticket, locked in a fog of booze and dead bodies. Here, in L.A., there would be bodies, but it was different. Ticket wouldn't be breathing down his neck. After this trip, Latch would wear the body of a machine: Ticket had promised. And although Ticket suffered from excursions along the rim of sanity, Latch knew he was anything but a liar. Ticket would keep his word, or Latch would kill him.

Latch was greeted at the concourse by Marvin Hipp, a squat, bent-over man in his early forties who weighed nearly two hundred pounds. Hipp had long, greasy black hair that he kept tied back in a ponytail, and wore mirror-finished aviators that never left the bridge of his pug nose, day or night. Hipp's stooped, ugly shape had earned him the name "Toad," but that was the only near-humorous aspect of the man. He served Latch as the head of his West Coast gathering operation and was dead serious about the job. He was cold, calculating and often brutal in his execution of whatever tasks he might be assigned.

The two men walked out of the terminal and stopped at the curb reserved for limos, taxis and airport shuttles.

"Ed musta had to make a round," Toad said in a voice that was so hoarse it resembled a loud whisper. He peered up the asphalt in the direction of the traffic and pulled a pack of cigarettes from the inside pocket of his loose and rumpled sport coat. "He should be here any minute." Toad held out the pack of smokes, and Latch shook his head.

There was a distinct chill in the air and a metallic-like smell as a damp wind blew in from the Pacific. Latch felt gooseflesh cover his scalp, then creep down his neck. It wasn't from the temperature, either; the breeze and the smell reminded him of the wind that blew in off the Hudson River. Latch was glad when a battered midnight blue Lincoln pulled up in front of them and Toad opened a passenger door.

"It smells like piss in here," Latch said, settling into a worn leather seat. He watched Toad pull the door closed and flop into the seat opposite.

"Get some air circulating back here," Toad barked over his shoulder and rapped the Plexiglas behind his head with his knuckles. "Want something to drink?" he said, turning back toward Latch.

"Give me a beer," Latch answered, figuring he'd lay off the hard stuff until he got back to New York.

Toad popped open a compartment built into the base of the seat. He pulled out a bottle of beer, twisted off the cap and handed it to Latch before opening one for himself.

The driver pulled the limo onto the San Diego freeway. "Have you lined up some help?" Latch asked.

Toad nodded. "I hired two guys. They're a little crude, but I checked out their references and they're good."

"Two?" Latch drew his head back questioningly. "I told you we have to fill nine shells. That means we're going to need at least eighteen units. Nine primaries and nine backups."

Toad pointed a thumb toward the front of the car. "Ed will drive the van, and the Sthil brothers seem competent enough...things should go smoothly." He lit a fresh cigarette from the butt of his old one.

"The Sthil brothers?" Latch asked, watching the reflection of the freeway lights in Toad's mirrored glasses.

"Yeah, they're new in the city, bounty hunters by trade." Toad opened a window slightly and blew his smoke out the crack. "They were up on that gambling resort that orbits the moon. I guess things got a little lean up there. Anyway, I picked them up cheap."

"What about donors?" Latch asked. "Do you have any targeted?"

"Yeah," Toad said, "and they all fit the profile— weak-willed, atheists, the whole bit."

"Good," Latch said, looking out the window as Ed exited the San Diego and made the twisting transition onto the Ventura Freeway. "Why didn't we take Santa Monica Boulevard?" he asked, turning his head toward Toad. "We're still camping in that dump on Sunset, aren't we?"

"Yeah," Toad answered somewhat sarcastically. He downed the rest of his beer and stuck the empty in a pocket on the door. "Your favorite place." He stifled a belch and lit another cigarette. "The reason we didn't take Santa Monica Boulevard is because part of it got closed down after that last earthquake a month or so ago. There's all kinds of detours and shit . . . and all kinds of loonies hanging around waiting to dick with anyone dumb enough to drive up one of their dead ends, especially around this time of night."

"That reminds me," Latch said. "Did you pick up a weapon for me?"

"Of course," Toad answered. He popped open another compartment at the base of the seat and pulled out a package wrapped in brown paper.

"That looks like something from a butcher shop," Latch said jokingly.

Toad placed the package on his lap and unwrapped it. "Here you go," he said, handing the massive automatic to Latch. "It's one of the new S&W .44 Mags. Total composite design with a machine-loaded lateral feed so the goddamn barrel doesn't have to jack off when you fire the son of a bitch."

"You ought to clean up your language, Toad," Latch said casually as he examined the weapon. He hefted it in one hand and was amazed at how light it was, given its size. A black cylindrical silencer was screwed into the end of the eight-inch barrel, making it look like a miniature exotic assault rifle. "I like it, Toad. Thanks."

Toad grunted and produced a wadded-up Gore-Tex shoulder holster. "Here," he said, tossing it to Latch. "The clip in the weapon holds seventeen rounds. I've got a couple of spares for you at the hotel."

Latch stripped off his jacket and strapped on the shoulder holster. He adjusted the weapon beneath his left arm before donning the jacket. "It's a big bastard," he said, practicing pulling it out of the holster.

"You were pissed off about the weapon I got you last trip," Toad said. "I thought I'd make up for it."

"Yeah," Latch chuckled. "What the hell was that thing anyway, some kind of dart pistol?"

Toad shrugged. "They can be effective."

Latch looked out the window as the limo left the Ventura and cut back onto Sunset Boulevard. "This place gets seedier every time I come here," he said, staring at the flashing lights and cheap facades that lined the street. Porno shops, topless and bottomless bars and gloomy-looking clubs with names like El Sid, Twenty-Two Split and The Green Frog were jammed together, fronting the crowded sidewalk, flashing hazy neon patterns in the West Hollywood night.

"That's why you like it," Toad said as the limo pulled into the trash-covered parking lot of the Gold Dust Inn. Its faded marquee advertised hourly rates, twenty-four-hour XXX-rated movies and free champagne.

"Right," Latch said, knowing there was a degree of truth to Toad's statement. He felt a sense of adventure—the beginning of the hunt from an outpost on the fringe of humanity. "Listen, you got us adjoining rooms, right?"

"The same ones as last time," Toad answered.

"I need to call Ticket, then I'd like to take your two new boys out and gather at least two donors. Just to see if they can handle it." Latch grabbed his bag from the seat next to Toad.

"Whatever you say." Toad popped open a door and waited while Latch exited. "I went ahead and hooked up a scrambler to the telemonitor in your room," he said, following his boss.

"Where's the van?" Latch asked, stretching. He took a card key that Toad was holding out to him.

"The Sthil brothers have it. I told them one guy has to stay with it all the time." Toad tapped the driver's window with his knuckles and looked back at Latch. "Is fifteen minutes enough for your call?"

"Yeah," Latch answered, walking toward a set of steps. He heard Toad telling Ed to park the limo and have the Sthil brothers in his room in ten minutes. Toad was efficient, Latch had to admit, but he often wondered if he was worth the ten thousand credits per unit that Ticket was paying him.

Latch stuck the card key into a slot on the dirty wooden door and popped it open. He locked the door behind him and tossed his bag on a king-size bed that was covered with a gaudy, cigarette-burned bedspread. The door to Toad's room was open, and Latch could see empty bottles and overflowing ashtrays covering the dresser and nightstand. He closed the door before walking to an old telemonitor that was hanging over a cheap plastic desk in the corner of the room. The place stank of stale cigarette smoke and spilled booze.

Making sure the tiny encryptographic module had been clamped onto the monitor's feed, Latch punched it on and entered Ticket's code on a worn keyboard next to the flickering CRT. He jumped as Ticket's image instantaneously appeared on the screen. He knew it was almost three in the morning in New York, but Ticket looked wide awake. Latch figured it was due to more white pills. He watched his boss take a sip of Scotch, then light a cigarette, the smoke curling up around his face.

"Have a nice trip, Jack?" Ticket smiled, his watery eyes squinting slightly from the smoke.

Except for his alertness, Latch thought his boss looked like the aftermath of a three-day poker game. "It was uneventful," he answered, wishing he had a drink as he watched Ticket tip his glass once again.

"Well, let's get to it," Ticket said, his voice upbeat. "Were you able to get me a donor before you left?"

Latch nodded. "Yes, as a matter of fact, I got three. They're in the safehouse down in the Village. I didn't have time to transport them to the island. They were still cold-soaking. I hope you don't mind."

Ticket waved a hand. "I don't mind," he said. "I'll take the shell I want and do the mod down there. It'll give me a pleasant change of scenery."

"I tagged the three systems," Latch said. "You'll be able to tell which one has priority. The other two may be a little marginal, but they were the only ones available on such short notice. I hope the first one goes for you, it should be a little more stable."

"No worry," Ticket said. "I've done the last three without having to use a spare."

"Have you talked to Kindu?" Latch asked.

"No," Ticket answered, "but that idiot Toftoy left a message on the record. They're going to be here on the twenty-eighth of November."

Latch exhaled slowly. "Shit," he said. "That doesn't give us a hell of a lot of time."

"I don't necessarily have to have the droids ready then, but it probably wouldn't hurt. How long is your little safari going to take?"

"I don't know. Two weeks, maybe. Toad hired a couple of new guys."

"I think Kindu probably has something worthwhile inside his ugly carcass," Ticket interrupted, his voice soft and introspective. "In one of our earlier meetings, Kindu indicated he intended to use the Neuroids to help the rebels in the lower provinces."

"Kindu interested in helping the oppressed? That's hard to believe," said Latch. He heard a door slam and voices coming from Toad's room. "Listen," he said. "Toad's here with the new guys. We're getting ready to try them out, so if you—"

"Okay. You take care of your end of business. I'll talk to you in a couple of days. Let me know how it's going."

Latch punched off the telemonitor. He went into the bathroom and washed his face and hands. Running his fingers through his hair, he stared at himself in the mirror and wondered what he'd be like once he got the new body Ticket had promised. He felt the old twisting sensation in his gut. The cancer was still there, churning away, consuming his body while he jockeyed for a new one. "Don't worry, old horse," he said. "In less than a month you'll be unbeatable."

When Latch entered the room, Toad rose and began the introductions. "This is Luther Sthil," he said, gesturing toward a big, wire-haired man sitting on the edge of the unmade bed. He was wearing a black leather bomber jacket that was worn and faded, giving it a bizarre camouflage pattern. The big man sported a goatee that looked more like animal fur than hair. He smiled and nodded at Latch, his fluorescent green eyes glowing like neon. Latch returned the nod.

"And this is Kringa Sthil," Toad said, pointing at a tall, slender man who was sitting on the edge of the dresser holding a half-full bottle of whiskey.

Latch looked at Kringa, who was in his late forties or early fifties, and wondered if the two men were really brothers. Kringa looked nothing like his alleged sibling. He had a burr haircut that made his head look almost bald and lent him a skull-like, skeletal appearance.

Kringa grinned, his jaw dropping down crookedly as he tilted his head to one side. "Pleased to meet you, Mr. Latch," he said.

Latch had never heard such a godawful hillbilly sound as Kringa Sthil's voice. He thought for a moment that Kringa was trying to pull some sort of joke. "Where are you from?" Latch asked.

"Well, I was born in Arkansas," Kringa answered, grinning from ear to ear.

"How about you?" Latch asked, turning toward Luther.

"Detroit," the big-shouldered man answered. "We were separated at birth. We didn't know either one existed until about ten years ago." Luther's voice was deep and sounded as though it were being filtered through a stone crusher.

"Well, obviously Toad didn't brief you two on your terms of employment," Latch said. He figured he better make sure the two understood whom they were working for before they got into a situation that might cause them second thoughts.

The grin fell away from Kringa's face. He glanced at Toad, who was pulling an aluminum case from under the bed. "I don't know what you're talking about, sir," he said to Latch.

Latch took the bottle from Kringa. "First, there's no drinking before or on a job." He tossed the bottle toward an already overflowing wastebasket.

"Second," Latch continued, rubbing the stubble on his jaw, "we're going to be taking some people out. Either of you got any problems with that?"

Luther shook his head. "No sir, we don't," Kringa said. "We do that all the time. And about the whiskey, well, your man never said nothin' about not sippin'. If he would have said 'no whiskey,' well, I sure as hell wouldn't a been suckin' on a bottle. To tell you the truth, we're damn glad to have this job, Mr. Latch, it can't get too dirty for us. Right, Luther?" He turned toward his brother.

"Right," Luther grunted.

Latch was impressed by Kringa's speech. He looked at Toad, who was fishing around in the case that lay open on the bed. Several surgical instruments were scattered on the rumpled sheets. Toad looked up and shrugged.

"No matter how dirty, huh?" Latch said, grinning and turning toward Kringa. "We'll see about that."

"Let's go." Latch headed toward the door, leading the odd, hard-looking crew downstairs to a dirty gray stretch van. The thin form of Ed was hunched over the wheel, and the engine was running.

"Are you in a hurry?" Toad asked, taking a seat next to Latch. He tossed the aluminum case onto the floor next to four metal boxes. A stainless-steel bottle marked Danger: Liquid Nitrogen was strapped to the top of each case, and an insulated tube ran from the valve of each bottle to a fitting on the side of each case. Each chest was fitted with digital thermometer and padded handles.

"I've been looking forward to this," Latch said as Kringa and Luther climbed into the van. Toad slammed the door.

"Yeah, right," Toad laughed. "Head out toward Silver Lake," he told the driver.

Toad pulled a worn notebook from his pocket. "What have you got?" Latch asked.

"A thirty-two-year-old plumber's helper who lives at the end of a dirt road by the lake. He hurt his foot about six weeks ago and just started collecting disability." Toad flipped through his notebook until apparently finding the page he was looking for. He ripped it out and handed it to Ed. "Here," he said. "These are the directions. Drive right up to the place.

If anyone else is there, we'll tell them we're lost. Now, where was I?'' He raised his eyebrows above the aviators and smiled.

"Oh, yeah. The guy isn't expected back to work for eight weeks or so. He's pretty much a loner.''

"Just what are we gonna do with this boy?'' Kringa asked.

Toad lit a cigarette. "We're going to start—'' he held the notebook up to the yellow dome light "—Mr. Douglas on the road to recovery. In a month or so he'll be a new man.'' Toad chuckled. Kringa smiled, nodding.

Ed pulled the van off Sunset and onto Hyperion. Ten minutes later he turned off the asphalt onto a dirt road filled with ruts and bordered by tall, dust-covered weeds. "Want me to turn off the lights?''

"Hell, no,'' Toad said calmly. "If he hears a vehicle driving up to his house with no lights to go along with it, I'm sure he'll just lock the door and go to bed. Just drive up to his front door and park. I'll take care of the rest.''

A tiny trailer house appeared in the headlights. Latch figured it had to be their donor's place. The road simply ended at the tailgate of a battered pickup parked in front of the old mobile home whose roof was covered with worn tires and cement blocks. Junk, trash and stacks of rusting pipe were scattered around the place, which was literally overgrown with weeds.

"Now, turn out the lights,'' Toad ordered. He pulled up one of his pants' legs, removed a little snubnose from an ankle holster, and pointed it toward one of the metal cases. "One of you bring the cold box, the other bring my case," he told Kringa and Luther. "Wait until you see me enter the house. And you." He turned and spoke over his shoulder to Ed. "Bring the box of devil charms."

"Let me do the honors," Latch said as Toad slid the side door open. He pulled the .44 out of its holster, aware that his adrenaline was starting to flow.

"Sure," Toad said, although disappointed. "Go ahead."

Latch walked straight to the scarred metal door of the trailer. He peered into a small diamond-shaped window cut into the center of the door. The inside was as much a mess as the outside. Latch could see the back of a man lying on a sagging couch. The tiny room was illuminated by an ancient console television that was covered with a stack of newspapers and magazines. Soda cans and fast-food wrappers littered the floor.

Latch knocked three times and was surprised when the door popped open. Without hesitating, he walked into the trailer, pointing the long-barrelled .44 at the man on the couch.

"What the hell..." The man rolled over and slipped off the couch. He looked up at Latch, blinking. He managed a sitting position before seeing the automatic.

"Just take it easy, and we'll make this as painless as possible," said Latch, aiming the weapon toward the right side of the chest. If he had to shoot, he didn't want to injure the spinal cord.

"Mr. Douglas?" Toad said.

"Who the hell are you?"

Toad had his right hand behind his back and was holding a hypodermic that looked like it was made for injecting elephants. The sight of the two-inch needle gave Latch the creeps. "Take it easy, Toad," he said without thinking.

Toad turned toward Latch. At that moment the doomed man dived toward a door near the back of the room, dragging his right foot, which was wrapped in a bandage.

"No, you don't!" Toad yelled. He leapt onto Douglas's back, and raised the hypo over his head like a dagger. "You son of a bitch," he grunted as Douglas twisted violently, nearly throwing him.

Kringa walked calmly to the two struggling men. He placed a booted foot on Douglas's neck and shoved his face into the floor. A whimpering squeal erupted from the pinned man.

"Not so goddamn hard!" Toad said, struggling to his feet. He grabbed Kringa's leg, tried to pull it off Douglas's neck. "Don't damage his spine!"

"I'm not!" Kringa yelled without moving. "I eased off, now go ahead and stick him!"

Toad looked down at the squirming hostage, then up at Kringa. There was a mad grin across his flat face. "Watch this," he said, bending over. "I hope this hurts!'' Toad jammed the big needle squarely into Douglas's kidneys.

The man's scream filled the tiny trailer as fifteen cubic centimeters of ice-cold sodium pentothal spread through his body, immobilizing him in less than ten seconds.

"There you are," Toad said, pulling out the needle. "Another dead fish." He turned toward Luther, who was standing near the door with the aluminum brief-case. "Bring that over here," he ordered. Luther handed the case to Toad, who made a sweeping motion with one hand. "Clear some of the shit out of the way. I need room to work," he said, turning Douglas over on his back. "Help him, Kringa. We've got less than five minutes to get this son of a bitch into the can."

Latch watched in morbid fascination as Toad dragged Douglas to the center of the floor. Stripping the body to the waist, Toad opened the briefcase and removed a pair of protective rubber gloves. They were bright yellow and extended well past his elbows when he pulled them on.

"I want you two to watch closely," Toad said, opening a bottle of clear liquid. He splashed it over Douglas's neck and along his back to his buttocks. "This is going to be your job, so pay attention."

Toad withdrew a stainless-steel scalpel from the case. It looked more like something with which one would skin a large animal than a surgical instrument. He pulled his victim's head back and in one swift motion cut a complete circle around the man's neck. Blood flooded the floor in a spreading crimson stain.

Kringa grunted in disgust. He staggered toward the door, gagging in the darkness.

"Are you also a wimp like your brother?" Toad asked Luther, who was staring intently at the crude operation.

"Not hardly," Luther answered. "Is there something I can do?"

"Just watch for now."

Toad made deep cuts along either side of the spine. Then he took what looked like an old pair of vise grips and clamped them onto the skin at the base of the skull. Grunting, he pulled the skin away from the body, revealing the blood-smeared spine. "The trick is to do this fast," he told Luther as though teaching him how to change a flat tire. "Hand me that cordless bone saw, will you?"

Luther pulled the flat-bladed, oscillating saw out of the case and handed it to Toad. Smoke rose and the stench of burned flesh filled the room as Toad sawed the ribs away from the spinal cord. The smell made Latch gag slightly.

"Now, here's the real trick," Toad said, handing the saw to Luther. Positioning himself so that he was looking toward Douglas's feet, he placed a shoe on either one of his shoulders, then grabbed Douglas's head tightly. "Ready?" he asked. Luther nodded in dumb fascination. Grunting like a weight lifter, Toad straightened up, ripping the head and spine completely free of the body. He held it up. The bloody cord dangled beneath the neck like the tail of a reptile.

"Quick," Toad ordered, "bring the cold box."

Luther quickly brought the chest.

"Open it," Toad said. "There should be a bottle of antibiotics and saline solution in there along with a plastic bag and tape."

"Got them," Luther said, removing the objects from the chest.

"Pour the bottle into the bag then slip it over the spinal cord. Pull the bag up over the neck. I'll hold it while you tape it."

Luther did as he was told, wrapping the top of the bag with the entire roll of tape. "How's that?" he asked, tossing the empty spool to one side.

"Good, Luther." Toad grinned and stepped over the remains of Douglas's body. He gently placed the neural system into the chest and shut the lid. "Turn on the nitrogen," he said, nodding at the valve. Luther complied. Almost immediately the chest was covered with a thin layer of frost.

"Good job, Luther," Toad said, peeling off the gloves. "Ed! Bring your toys in. It's almost time to leave. He closed the briefcase. Ed entered carrying a cardboard box. He put it on the floor and pulled out several small animal skulls, which he placed round the body.

"This is a nice touch," Latch said as he watched Ed dip a rag in Douglas's blood and paint a pentagram on the screen of the television. "Was this your idea, Toad?"

"Yeah. You like it?" Toad answered. He pulled a Bible from the box, tore out several pages and placed them in the pool of blood where Douglas's head should have been. "That's enough," he said, straightening up. "Let's get the hell out of here."

Stepping out of the door Latch nearly ran into Kringa, who was lighting a cigarette. He grabbed him by the neck and shoved him toward the van. "Get in the truck, son," he said, mimicking Kringa's voice. "At the next stop we're gonna let you do it all."

"What the hell are you talkin' about?" Kringa snapped halfheartedly.

"No job's too dirty, right?" Latch tilted his head back and laughed crazily. God, how he loved L.A.

CHAPTER FIVE

THE GOLDEN BULL had evolved over the years into a meeting stop for those doing business in and around Greenwich Village. And the business, for the most part, wasn't the type that ultimately resulted in figures on tax returns; it was more oriented toward the ill-gotten gains of criminals of one type or another. Located on Mercer Street near Chinatown, the bar catered to a wide range of drug brokers, flesh dealers, con artists and other seedy types.

Gus Cota, the owner and person normally found behind the scarred walnut bar, didn't really care that most of his clientele had bottomed out—as long as they were drinking. No one got by with nursing their beer in the Golden Bull. Cota's byword was, "Order another round or shoot the shit in the street, boys."

Horn walked through the double wooden doors of the bar and stopped to allow his eye to adjust to the dim light. As usual, the place was crowded, and Horn noticed that few of the patrons looked up when he entered. He figured they considered him just another face in the crowd, and wondered if their dispositions would change if they knew he was a cop.

Horn felt a little uneasy treading in the Golden Bull; it was territory considered out-of-bounds for New York's finest. He'd been in the bar once before and had been told by Cota that cops weren't welcome. "Get out, stay out and don't bother leavin' a god-damn tip," the withered little Irishman had said. Horn wondered if the cocksure barkeep would recognize him, given that their previous encounter was five years earlier and that now he wore a patch over one eye and a scar across his cheek.

"Horn!"

Horn turned toward the sound of Winger's voice and saw the young cop wave from a small round table near the end of the bar. He walked through a maze of tables and slapped his partner on the shoulder before sitting down. Two frosted mugs of beer were on the table in front of Winger—one full and one nearly empty.

"One of those mine," Horn asked, "or are you bulking up on alcohol?"

Winger ignored the question. "Dartt should be here any time," he said, glancing at his watch. "I think he's got something for us."

"What're ya drinkin', mac?"

Horn turned toward a rough-looking woman in her fifties who was carrying a serving tray and had a dirty towel slung over one shoulder. Her bleached hair was teased up into a mushroom shape that reminded Horn of an atomic weapons test, and a pair of plastic reading glasses was perched on her pointed nose. Her foot was tapping impatiently.

"Give me a beer," Horn answered, seeing beyond her to Cota bobbing behind the bar.

"How's Dartt doing?" Horn asked as the waitress left. He was interested in the man Winger had hired to do a little free-lance snooping. On previous occasions Dartt had come through in some really tight spots, even to the extent that Horn believed they owed the stocky reddish-haired man their lives. When Dartt showed up in New York, Horn and Winger had eagerly put him to work at what he did best: driving and finding things. Winger suggested Dartt investigate Julius Ticket, and Horn had encouraged it.

Horn started to pull a credit wafer from his pocket as the waitress set a foaming mug of beer in front of him, but Winger raised his hand. "No, this is on me," he said, sliding a stack of odd-denomination wafers toward the tired woman.

"Thanks," Horn said, sipping the beer. He surveyed the crowd, looking for recognizable faces. Seeing none, he turned back toward Winger. "You said Dartt may have something interesting for us?"

"Better than that, I hope," Winger answered quietly. "He said he was going to show us something that would blow our minds."

"Did he elaborate?"

"No, but we'll find out soon enough." Winger looked at his watch.

It seemed to Horn, as he glanced toward the bar, that Cota's beady green eyes had locked onto him. He turned slightly so that the man would be looking at the patch side of his face.

"I never did ask you, partner," Winger said, lapsing into his characteristic lopsided grin. "How did your meeting with the Barracuda go?"

"It went," Horn replied sarcastically. "No thanks to you."

"I appreciate you getting me out of that meeting," Winger said. "But how did it go, no shit?"

Horn chuckled. Christina Service, the Barracuda, had a well-established reputation for stripping the flesh from cops' bones using nothing more than words and the razor-sharp tone of her voice. While Horn shared his fellow cops' view that the assistant district attorney was as tough on cops as she was on crooks, he also greatly respected the woman who had a propensity for getting straight to the point, no matter how insensitive the route might be. There was something about the woman that Horn was *attracted* to, but he couldn't quite put his finger on it.

"Come on, Horn." Winger snapped his fingers. "I mention the Barracuda, and you start swooning. Sometimes I think you've got the hots for her."

"Screw you," Horn answered, and realized he was, for some crazy reason, blushing.

"Yeah, you'd like to," Winger said, downing the rest of his first mug of beer. "Now, how did it go, *really?* You're still on the job, so I assume she wasn't that hard on you. What did you tell her?''

"*We're* still on the job," Horn corrected. "Your name was as much a part of the conversation as mine.''

"Great," Winger answered, shaking his head at the waitress who had floated over to their table and was asking *Another round?* with her eyes. "Go on," he said, directing his attention back to Horn.

"I told her we made a little detour to the Bronx and that it didn't matter since we weren't transporting a *real* body." Horn half shrugged his shoulders and took a small swallow of beer. "She basically wants us to find out as much as we can about the droid—where it was manufactured, what drives it and so on.''

"What are they doing with it? The one we brought in?''

"They're going to have some biomechanical expert from Canada come down and look at it. They want to keep it under wraps until they can nail the source.''

"They must be pretty worried about something like that running loose in the city," Winger said.

"You should be, too," Horn said, glancing again at Cota, who was stacking glasses on a row of shelves with his back to them. "You saw the damage the thing did. Think about what a dozen of them could do.''

"Yeah," Winger said. "I guess we'd have a hard time getting them all to fall out of sixty-story windows.''

Horn wished he could adopt, at least sometimes, Winger's almost perpetually casual outlook on life. It would certainly make things a lot simpler. "Why worry about things until they happen? It's a waste of energy." That was the young cop's philosophy.

"Here comes Dartt," Winger said.

Horn watched Les Dartt move through the crowd. He was wearing a rumpled trench coat, open in the front, black parachute pants that were bloused over a pair of old-style jump boots, and a maroon beret cocked so far to one side of his head that it looked about to slide off.

"Hello, Maxwell," Dartt said, pulling over a vacant chair from a nearby table. He turned the back of the chair toward the table and straddled the seat, resting his arms on the back.

"What are you drinking?" Horn asked as the waitress appeared.

"Shot of Jack and a beer," Dartt told the woman. "And bring another round for my friends here." He looked at Horn and smiled, his unkempt Fu Manchu dangling on either side of his mouth.

"You know one of your friends is a cop?"

Horn didn't have to turn around to know that the voice coming from behind him was Gus Cota's. The Irish-Bostonian accent grated on Horn's nerves like the sound of a dentist's drill. He watched Dartt look up over his shoulder, an expression of mock amazement spreading across his face. "Who?" Dartt asked incredulously. "Him?" he pointed at Winger, who

looked as though he were enjoying Dartt's performance. Horn noticed, however, that the young cop
had his hand in his jacket pocket, and remembered
that he had blasted holes through coat linings in order to allow him unhindered access to the arsenal
hanging from his chest.

"No, this one," Cota said.

"Well, how the hell do you know I'm *not* a cop,
too," Winger said, smiling crazily.

Irritated, Horn turned toward Cota, who was
sneering. A huge bald man the size of a water buffalo
stood behind the bartender, slapping a sawed-off
baseball bat in the palm of one hand.

"Look," Horn said, rising, "we're drinking." He
gestured to the beer on the table. "I thought that was
the only requirement for staying in this place."

Cota stepped to one side, giving his goon a clear
path to Horn. "I told you the last time you were here
that I don't want cops stinkin' up the place." He
smiled and gestured at the other tables. "It makes my
other customers nervous."

"Hell, I can see why it would make them nervous," Winger chuckled, "most of them look like they
just got out of the joint."

Several rough-looking faces from the surrounding
tables turned in their direction.

Cota's goon stepped closer to Winger, but Horn
blocked his path.

"Listen, cop," Cota said, "don't piss Warren off.
I'd hate to see you wearin' a patch over both eyes."

Ignoring the bartender, Horn waited for Warren to make a move. He didn't have to wait long. The huge bouncer's eyes bulged as he swung the bat around in a blurring half circle and aimed it straight for Horn's head.

Horn raised his right forearm. The hardwood splintered as it smashed into the titanium-covered mod. Warren, looking surprised and angry, stepped back, pulled a leather-covered blackjack from the waistband of his trousers and swung. Horn blocked the blow by allowing Warren's wrist to slam into his forearm. The big bouncer screamed in agony as the sap flew from his hand, glancing off Horn's shoulder.

Horn grabbed Warren's face. In the heat of the moment, he had to keep his hand from exercising its full power and crushing the man's skull as though it were an eggshell. Horn shoved the bouncer backward across a table surrounded by bikers, who scrambled out of the way as their drinks went flying.

"You son of a bitch," Cota hissed. He pointed a small-caliber, chrome-plated revolver at Horn's stomach.

Winger spoke. "Drop it, asshole, or I'll shred you like a piece of cabbage."

Winger's machine pistol was protruding from beneath his jacket. It was aimed at Cota. Likewise, Dartt had pulled out a long-barreled Magnum and was covering the crowd.

Cota dropped the little revolver. Winger prodded him backward with the barrel of the ugly-looking machine pistol, grabbed the weapon on the floor and flung it across the room. Someone, apparently the victim of Winger's errant throw, cursed in pain.

"Let's get the hell out of Dodge," Winger said, backing toward the door.

Horn considered showing the crowd his badge, but figured it might do more harm than good. Instead, he pulled out his 9 mm and followed Winger and Dartt, scanning the crowd with the red beam of the laser sight.

As soon as the trio cleared the door, Winger broke into a run, leading them around the corner onto Grand where the Elint was parked.

"Listen to your partner," Dartt said as the three piled into the car and Winger smoked the tires, shooting the unmarked car across Wooster, running a red light. "He's laughing like a kid stealing his first watermelon."

"My first *what?*" Winger chuckled.

"Never mind," Dartt said, pulling a long thin cigar from his coat. He lit it and opened the window, blowing a stream of smoke into the cold evening air. "Pull over here," he said as Winger turned north on Thompson Street. "We're not far from where I need to take you guys."

Winger pulled the Elint into a loading zone, but left the engine running. "What have you got?"

Dartt took a long drag on the cigar, smoke curling up around his face. The pungent odor of the tobacco filled the car.

"I've got a line on this cat who supposedly works for this guy you were telling me about," Dartt said. He pulled a thin electronic notebook from his pocket and punched a couple of its plastic keys. "Ticket, Julius Ticket." Dartt smiled and glanced at Horn. "This guy I got a line on is Jack Latch and he supposedly works for Ticket." He took another drag on the cigar. "One of my contacts down here in the Village heard from a friend of a friend of a friend that this cat Latch has some sort of safehouse or holding tank down here, just off Eldridge, where some pretty weird shit goes on."

"What do you mean, *weird shit?*" Winger asked.

"Well," Dartt said, hesitating momentarily. "I checked the place òut, and it's like a morgue or an operating room, something like that."

"You broke into the place?" Winger asked.

Dartt looked at Horn and shrugged.

"What was in the place?" Horn asked knowingly.

"Like I said, medical-type equipment," Dartt answered. "It was clean and seemed pretty much out of place, seeing it was part of a dumpy warehouse."

"Anything like a body or body parts in the place?" Horn asked.

"You mean like a corpse?"

"Sort of," Horn answered. "Maybe more like a robot." He wondered if they had gotten lucky and stumbled onto Ticket's mod facility.

"No," Dartt said, shaking his head. "No bodies, no parts, and no goddamn robots. What the hell kind of a case are you guys onto anyway? You're giving me the creeps."

"Didn't you look around?" Winger asked, rolling his window down as the smoke from Dartt's cigar thickened.

"Not a whole hell of a lot," Dartt answered. "I spent most of my time fixing the skylight I'd come through so no one would know they'd had a visitor. But let's go there now. You can look for goddamn body parts to your heart's content. I'll wait in the car."

Winger looked at Horn. "Want to check it out?"

Horn nodded.

As Winger put the Elint in gear and proceeded to cut a U-turn, he looked at Dartt. "How sure are you that this place is connected to Ticket?"

"Not that sure," Dartt answered. "Hell, I haven't been in the city long enough to cultivate any real dependable contacts. I think the quality of their information is directly proportional to the number of these I pass across their palms." He produced a stack of one-hundred-credit wafers.

"Where to?" Winger asked, pulling onto Eldridge.

Dartt directed Winger to a graffiti-covered three-story brick building at the back of a trash-covered parking lot near Canal Street.

"It looks like a goddamned training ground for rats," Winger said.

"It is," Dartt said, laughing. "But wait until you see what's inside."

Winger parked the Elint by an abandoned gas station across the street. A faded Gulf sign hung crookedly over the front of the boarded-up building, and rusting pipes stuck out of the concrete islands that once held the station's pumps. They got out of the car. Horn looked around cautiously. There was a van parked a half a block farther down, next to the Canal Street entrance. "That machine look familiar?" he asked, pointing toward the vehicle.

Dartt shrugged his shoulders. "No, but there's always cars parked around here." He took a final drag on the dwindling cigar, then tossed it in the street. "This is a place where a lot of couples come to park. You know, a lover's lane."

Feeling uneasy, Horn followed Dartt and Winger across the street and into the warehouse through a mangled door that hung sideways from one hinge. The place smelled like a backed-up sewer, and rats could be heard scurrying in the dark. Winger shone a penlight onto the trash-covered floor. Several dozen red eyes glinted from the shadows. Winger had pegged the place right as a training ground for the long-tailed rodents, Horn thought.

"Which way?" Winger whispered. Dartt took the light from the young cop and moved toward the far corner. His partners followed.

"See this?" Dartt said, indicating a thick steel door at the back of the huge room. "I think this is the entrance to the lab." He pointed the light to the floor, illuminating a fan-shaped swath in the dirt and garbage that suggested that the massive door had been opened recently.

"This bastard looks more like tank armor than a door," Winger commented, rapping his knuckles on the scarred steel. "How the hell do you open it?"

"Probably radio controlled," Dartt answered. "Now, follow me." He turned and stepped through a hole that looked like it had been chewed into the brick.

The opening led to a room the size of an elevator shaft. The sewer smell was stronger. A feeling of claustrophobia and revulsion swept over Horn as he looked about the cryptlike room.

"Give me a boost," Dartt said, pointing the light up at a small opening over their heads.

Winger cupped his hands and helped Dartt go up through the manhole-sized opening. "You ready?" he asked, turning toward Horn.

"No, partner," Horn said, cupping his hands. "You forget I already have some help, built-in."

"Yeah, that's right." Winger grinned sheepishly as he stepped in Horn's hands and was literally shot through the hole in the ceiling.

Now it was Horn's turn. Shifting his weight to his right leg, he crouched and leapt upward, flexing his modified knee as though he were releasing a spring. His upper body easily cleared the edge of the opening, and he allowed Dartt and Winger to pull him the rest of the way through. Horn discovered they were outside on a small ledge that ran along one side of the building.

A set of steel rungs led to the warehouse roof. Dartt took them two at a time, disappearing over the edge in less than ten seconds. He immediately reappeared and waved. Winger went up next. Horn waited until his partner cleared the last rung before starting up.

On the roof Horn found Dartt and Winger bent over an old, hinged skylight, peering down through its dirty glass panes. He moved next to Dartt.

"There's a light on," Dartt whispered.

The room below them contained a number of covered stainless-steel tanks. One wall of the immaculate room was lined with silver canisters bearing some sort of warning stickers. Insulated tubes ran from the canisters to the tanks; wisps of vapor rose from the edges of their lids like fog. As well, light was streaming into the room through a door that was slightly ajar.

"That light wasn't on two nights ago," Dartt whispered.

"Seen any movement?" Horn asked.

Dartt shook his head. "But just because nobody's moving doesn't mean there ain't nobody down there."

"There's only one way to find out," said Winger.

"Let's check it out," Horn said simply.

Dartt grabbed the rusted padlock that was hooked through the skylight's hasp. With one swift twist he ripped it from the metal frame.

Dartt lifted the skylight until an arm on its side unfolded and locked it open with a loud snapping sound. Horn cringed and watched the light coming through the door below for signs of movement. He saw none.

"Here goes nothing," Dartt said, peeling off his trenchcoat. Climbing through the opening, he lowered himself to the top of one of the tanks.

Horn watched Winger do the same, then followed, lowering himself to the tank, then sliding to the floor.

Winger drew his machine pistol and peered through the partially opened door. Horn followed. They peered down a long empty hallway containing four other doors, two on either side, with light coming from under two of them. The hallway was silent.

"Holy shit!" Dartt gasped.

Horn turned and saw that Dartt had raised the lid on one of the tanks. Vapor was floating upward, rolling around his head and partially obscuring his face.

"What is it?" Winger asked, speaking over his shoulder.

"Just keep watch," Horn said. He walked over to Dartt. "What is it?"

"Get a load of this," Dartt said, fanning the vapor away with one hand.

The inside of the tank was extremely cold, Horn noticed, as he peered down through the fog. A shock wave ran up his spine and caused his mods to involuntarily flinch. Two dead and frozen eyes stared up at him from a milk white face that looked like it had died of fright.

"Damn," was all he said.

"What the hell is it?" Winger hissed from the doorway.

Horn turned toward the young cop just as the door came off its hinges and blew into the room. He saw Winger do a somersault. Then the lights in the hall blinked out, plunging the room into darkness.

Dartt screamed as the tank's lid slammed closed. Horn pulled his 9 mm and activated the laser, scanning the darkness for *something, anything*. Winger's machine pistol erupted somewhere across the room. The strobelike muzzle-flashes lit up the room as bullets ricocheted off the tanks.

"Winger!" Horn yelled as something that felt like a wrecking ball slammed into his chest. He was propelled backward like a rag doll and upended over one of the tanks, knocking the breath from his lungs.

The room was a den of chaotic screaming and firing weapons. Dartt's big Mag roared, sounding like an elephant gun fired inside a garbage can. Horn tried to yell, but could barely choke down enough air to keep from passing out.

A sharp, clipped voice cut through the darkness. It seemed to come from the hallway. It registered in Horn's mind as being distinctly British. He forced himself from the floor when he realized what the voice had ordered: *Kill them all.*

Horn continued fanning the laser sight about the room, but couldn't distinguish a clear target. He wished he had a set of Night Eyes and felt helpless in the ink black darkness. Across the room he heard a series of low grunts and a scream and knew his partner was taking a hell of a beating.

Feeling his way across the room, Horn suddenly remembered his *eye* was a built-in IR sensor. He ripped the patch off his face and blinked several times, waiting for the thing to come on or whatever it was supposed to do. Suddenly light flared in front of his face like a sunspot. For a moment Horn thought he was hallucinating. The light was so intense that he could swear it was burning a hole somewhere in the back of his head. Instinctively he raised his forearm across his face and clamped his eyelids shut. Another scream, this one from Dartt, caused Horn to force his arm down and his eyes open. He concentrated on forcing his sight through the right side of his head and realized he was *seeing*. Everything was bathed in a green alien luminescence, as though he were viewing the scene through emerald water.

Another shock ran up Horn's spine as he saw a naked man tear the lid from one of the tanks and try to slam it down on Winger, who managed to evade the stainless-steel slab which smashed into the tiled floor. Horn felt his heart jump into his throat when he realized the man was a mirror image of the droid body he and Winger had been carrying around just days earlier. He started to aim the 9 mm at the *thing,* but discovered that it was already trained on the side of its head. Remembering what August had said about the weapon automatically following his line of sight, he squeezed off three quick rounds and watched as the naked attacker staggered sideways a couple of steps before turning toward him.

It's definitely a goddamn droid, Horn thought, firing twice into its chest. The thing came at Horn, lunging with both fists jammed together like the business end of a pile driver. Horn took a half step sideways and cocked his right arm, consciously flexing his E-mod. Just as the droid's head came into range, he drove his right forearm against the right temple, knocking the body off its feet and into a wall.

"Horn! Where the hell are you?"

Winger was across the room. Horn glanced toward the doorway. A curly-headed, lab-coated figure wearing night-vision goggles leaned into the room, barking out something that sounded like "Twenty-four follow." Almost instantly the droid turned and slipped out the door.

Cautiously Horn crept toward the doorway and peered down the hall. The man in the lab coat was bending over a puddle of liquid that filled half the hallway. The man looked up at him, the goggles making him look like some sort of strange insect. He struck a flame with a cigarette lighter and touched it to the puddle, which immediately ignited.

Horn backed into the room as the heat from the flames threatened to scorch his face. His right eye had blinked out—at least the IR function had—and Horn figured the light from the fire had overloaded the sensor. Turning, he could see Dartt helping Winger to his feet. The flames illuminated the room in yellow-orange light. Horn figured it was time to get the hell out.

"What happened?" he asked, grabbing Winger by the arms.

The young cop winced. "I think I dislocated my shoulder," he said. "Whatever the hell that thing was managed to nail me with his foot or knee or something."

"Come on," Horn said, nodding to Dartt, then toward the tank under the skylight. "Get him up there. We've got to get out of this place. I don't want to be here when those canisters start cooking off."

With some effort they managed to boost the young cop through the skylight. As Horn cleared the metal frame and rolled onto the roof, he heard tires squealing in the street and figured it was the van he'd seen parked a half a block down. Starting to run, he realized that the IR sensor in his eye was on again. Looking toward the Manhattan skyline, he was amazed at the sensitivity of his visual mod. The sky seemed to be awash in a light that hung across the darkness like a fiery curtain.

"Let's go, Horn," Dartt urged. "This place is going down fast."

"Right," Horn answered. He turned and watched Winger crawl over the edge of the building, his left arm hanging uselessly at his side. Dartt went next. Horn took one more look at the skyline before following suit.

CHAPTER SIX

"YOU KNOW I told you not to use the goddamn thing until I trained you," August said angrily as he stared through a pair of electron glasses into Horn's modified eye. "I'll be surprised if you didn't dick something up."

"You told me I had to get used to it," Horn responded, trying not to move his head, but feeling obligated to defend himself. "I don't remember you saying anything about getting trained."

"You probably weren't listening," August said. "Now, hold still before I damage this baby and really screw you up."

Horn was aware that some sort of device was being fitted over his modified eye and figured he'd better do as August said.

"Now, this is going to seem funny to your senses," August said. He fiddled with a piece of electronic equipment on a table next to where Horn was sitting. Several thin wires and a tiny fiber-optic cable ran from a connector on the machine to the cup-shaped apparatus that was suctioned over Horn's right eye. "Now just relax."

Horn had been seeing darkness through the modified eye. Suddenly it changed to a bright, kaleidoscope pattern. The sensation was like star shells exploding in his head. He thought it was going to make him sick.

"Just relax," August said. "I'm calibrating the IR sensor. Are the images still blurred?"

"They're coming into focus now," Horn said as the pattern in his head resolved itself into the ordinary objects in the room. The light show subsided in intensity, but he still felt dizzy.

August sucked on the stem of his pipe and exhaled slowly. "It's obviously too sensitive, but how much, I don't know. The first time you look through it will naturally seem like too much." August chuckled. "Probably like watching a nuclear explosion."

"I'm worried about the focusing," Horn said. "Things just didn't seem too clear."

"I'll be able to correct that to a certain degree," August said, "but remember, you're seeing through a sensor that picks up *heat*. The clarity you're looking for should be provided by the TFT and the video, which I see is nonfunctional." August fiddled with some dials and Horn could hear him muttering under his breath. "You may feel a mild shock here," he said, and put a hand on Horn's shoulder.

"Damn!" Horn yelled as a surge of electricity spiked into the front of his brain and caused his mods to buck violently. "Mild shock, my ass!" he exclaimed, and started to pull off the patch that August had taped over his left eye.

"There, there," August said soothingly, grabbing Horn's wrist and pulling his hand away from his face. "I didn't know you were allergic to a little electricity," he chuckled.

"That sure as hell wasn't a *little*," Horn said, feeling some aftershocks course through his mods.

"Well, it got your video on-line," August said. "Don't be a wimp."

The mod doctor slapped Horn's shoulder and resumed adjusting the fixture next to the chair. The patterns dancing in Horn's head began to fade, and he felt August's fingers gripping the cup.

"When I pull this off," August said, unhooking the wires and cable, "you're going to be looking through video for the first time. Now, don't worry." He began to pull the cup away from Horn's eye. "You're not going to be able to see jack-shit until I uncover your natural eye. That'll give the mod a reference, and it should come into focus almost instantly." August grunted as the cup finally came free, sounding like a champagne cork leaving its bottle.

Through his right eye, Horn saw only a blur. "You're right," he said, trying to focus. "I can't see a damn thing."

"Stand by," August said, pulling the folded gauze from Horn's real eye. "Now," he said. "Tell me what you see."

As soon as his left eye was uncovered, Horn's modified eye came into focus as though a quantum switch had been thrown. He could *see*, but there was something different about it. His left eye was taking in a view that seemed normal; however, the scene through his right eye was similar to high-definition television. The difference between the two eyes gave Horn an odd sensation that made him even more conscious of his modified shoulder, arm and knee.

"So this is what a machine sees," Horn said, looking at August.

August walked over to a cabinet next to a bench covered with miscellaneous electronic and hydraulic components, and pulled out a bottle half-full of an amber liquid. August unscrewed the cap and tilted the bottle back, swallowing for a good three seconds before setting the booze down.

"Can I have a shot of that?" Horn asked, getting up from the chair.

August held the bottle out to Horn. "Nature's dead, Max," he said. "Technology is all Man has left."

Horn was raising the bottle to his lips but stopped cold as an image flashed in his mind. He could see his wife and daughter lying dead on the floor, their bodies twisted and broken, blood smeared on the hardwood. Horn felt his mods glitch and heard the bottle shatter in his hand as the image of his murdered family burned into his brain as if he were seeing it for the first time. For a moment Horn thought he was going to black out and was prepared to welcome the loss of consciousness, but something was drawing him back. He was aware of something striking him on the face, and forced open his eyes as August's hand swung across his cheek. The mod doctor raised his hand and brought it down again, but Horn caught him by the wrist before he could strike another blow.

"I'm okay now," Horn said, releasing August's wrist.

"Ready to test it?" August asked tentatively.

"Sure," Horn answered. "You don't think I'd come down to the Bronx just to turn around and head back, do you?"

"Good." August glanced at the shattered glass on the floor. "It's probably good that you didn't have a shot of whiskey, anyway," he said. "It can screw up the functioning of the mod."

"How do you want to do this?" Horn asked, slipping on his shoulder holster, which was hanging from the back of the chair.

"Let's try it outside," August said, leading the way toward the door. "Where's that snot-nosed partner of yours, anyway? Usually he's like your shadow."

"Hurt his shoulder," Horn answered. "They gave him a steroid treatment and told him to take it easy tonight. Otherwise, he would've been here." Horn smiled. "I think he likes you."

August grunted. He opened a closet by the front door and pulled out a faded leather bomber jacket. "Your partner is so green that he looks permanently seasick."

Horn laughed. "You ready to tell me what you learned about Ticket?" he asked as he followed August into the cold night air.

"Sure," August answered, lighting his pipe. "But first tell me what happened when you and your shadow checked out the place in the Village."

"I told you already," Horn answered. "There was a droid, similar to the one we brought over here, that pretty much shortened our visit."

"You said this place belonged to a guy named Latch?" August narrowed his eyes. The yellow light over the doorway made his skin look jaundiced.

"I don't know if *belonged* is the right word," Horn answered, "but he supposedly controlled the place. My contact also said he works for Ticket."

"He does," August said, rubbing the gray stubble on his chin. "He's his chief gatherer."

"Gatherer?"

"Yeah," August said, walking down the short flight of steps and motioning for Horn to follow. "I got hold of an old colleague who had been involved with Ticket and Latch. He said Ticket had been able to implant a neural system into a droid shell and have it function just like a human." August stopped and turned toward Horn. "And it's true. The X-rays Winder took of the body you brought over here last week showed a complete human brain and spinal cord encased in the droid's shell. The brain also had some sort of microchip embedded in its cerebellum. It's my guess that's how he controls the thing."

"That explains the head in the tank," Horn said.

"What head?"

"There was a head, at least that's all I could see, in a tank of some sort of chemical. At the place in the Village."

"Why didn't you tell me before? That place must have been one of Latch's holding tanks."

"I don't get it," Horn said.

"It's where Latch kept his supply of parts," August said. "I told you Latch was Ticket's gatherer. His job is to gather what Ticket needs to get his droids operational. In this case, it looks like neural systems." August seemed to drift off, lost in thought. "If he were able to multiplex all the motor functions into the spine, then he wouldn't need any kind of central processing unit...."

"What the hell are you talking about?" Horn grabbed the mod doctor by the shoulder and shook him gently.

"What?" August seemed startled. "Oh, I'm sorry," he said, apparently recovering from his momentary lapse. He pointed the stem of his pipe at Horn's nose. "Ticket's a genius, Max. And Latch is his errand boy. My friend told me Latch is in Los Angeles, as we speak, picking up a fresh set of neural systems for his boss. If you find Latch, I'm sure you'll find Ticket."

"Where's Ticket?"

August shrugged. "I heard he's in New York. If I were you, I'd concentrate on finding Latch. I would guess he's the key to Ticket's whereabouts."

"Where would I find Latch? L.A.'s a big place."

"Shit." August laughed. "I'm surprised you didn't get lost driving down here without the man-boy you call a partner. All right," he said, pulling a scrap of paper from his pants pocket and unfolding it. He turned toward the lamp over the door and held the paper down so he could read it. "Latch always stays at a place called the Gold Dust." The paper flew from August's fingers into the stiff breeze that was blowing in from the east. "It's on the Sunset Strip."

"Does that place still exist?" Horn asked.

"You bet," August answered. "In all its decadent glory. Now, pull out that hog leg you call a weapon and move into the center of the street."

Horn took the 9 mm out of its holster. "You want live fire?" he asked, looking at August questioningly.

"No, I want blanks," August replied sarcastically. "I'm making a goddamn movie here, in case you hadn't noticed . . . Hell, yes, I want you to shoot, live. You need to know how the whole system works."

"Don't get indignant," Horn said, suppressing a laugh. "By the way, what's this Ticket character look like?"

August held a hand six inches over his head. "He's this tall, blondish gray hair, bloodshot eyes. And the son of a bitch drinks like a fish."

Horn hadn't told August about the man with the night-vision goggles. "Is his hair curly?" he asked.

August turned and stared at Horn before nodding slowly. "You've seen him?"

"He was in the place in the Village. Torched it after I managed to get the upper hand."

"You better watch your ass," August warned. "I think you were nothing but lucky."

"Okay, what now?" Horn pulled back the slide on the automatic and made sure a shell was in the chamber.

August set up a row of empty bottles along the curb. "I want you to turn your back to the bottles," he said, moving behind Horn. "At your leisure turn around and pick out a target with your eye."

"Weapons mode, right?" Horn asked, blinking his eye and moving the prompt down the menu.

"Right," August answered. "Remember, your arm should already have gotten a bead on the target. You simply fine-aim it by centering the cross hairs on the part of the target you want to hit. Then *will* the trigger to pull. Watch what happens, it'll blow your mind."

"Sure we're not going to disturb your neighbors?" Horn asked, turning his back to the bottles.

"All my neighbors walk on four legs." August laughed. "They don't mind a little shooting as long as it's not at them."

"I'm ready."

August stuck his index fingers in his ears and half yelled, "Just let it happen naturally. See how it works with the bottle on your left."

Yeah, let it happen *naturally,* Horn thought as he spun around and watched the bottle appear in the cross hairs as if by magic. This is too easy, he thought, aligning the cross hairs on the neck of the bottle. As he started to pull the trigger, the big automatic bucked violently in his hand, startling Horn. It had seemed to fire on its own. "Damn," he whispered. Shifting to the next bottle, he took the neck off without flinching, then did the same with the remaining three, firing so fast that he half expected the weapon to jam.

"Goddammit!" August said, his face red and his eyes wild with anger. "What the hell are you doing? I told you to try one goddamn bottle, and look what you did, hotshot, you didn't hit a freaking one." He waved a hand toward the curb.

"Take a closer look," Horn said. He popped the old clip out of the butt of the weapon and inserted a new one while August inspected the glass targets.

"Well, I'll be damned." August walked back to Horn. "You did that intentionally?"

Horn nodded. "If you mean just taking off the necks, that's correct, but I really didn't have to do much." He looked at August. "The mods do all the work, I just have to sort of *think* about it."

Horn brought his eye to bear on the bottle farthest to the right. This time he relaxed and let the mods take the lead, his hand a jerking sort of blur as it followed the designated targets, taking them out so quickly that he thought something had gone wrong.

"Holy shit!" August exclaimed, his hands still cupped over his ears. "Are you all right?"

Horn could see that August was amazed. "I'm all right," he answered, blinking out of the weapons mode.

"Damn," August said. "That was fantastic."

"Thanks to you," Horn said, lowering the hammer on the automatic. He flipped on the safety before sticking it in the holster.

Horn felt something cold invade his spirit as he followed August back to the crib. The combination of his enhanced mods with the eye gave him a new dimension. He felt he'd been *upgraded* and laughed sadly to himself. It made him think of fighter aircraft when they went through product-improvement programs, typically changing their model designators. Horn wondered if he were now a *B-model*.

He wondered how he would react when it came time to kill. He wondered how much of his body had to become a machine before he crossed over and killed because that's what he'd been built to do.

"You coming in, or are you just going to stand there and stare?"

August's question snapped Horn out of his contemplative state. "Let me get my jacket. Then I'm out of here."

"Stay and have a beer," August said. "It's early. It's not even nine o'clock."

Horn grabbed his bush jacket off the back of the couch. "Thanks, anyway," he said.

August walked over to a telemonitor next to the kitchen, responding to a red light flashing on the console.

"Stand by," August said, turning his head slightly as he punched in a code on the keyboard. "It's for you," he said as Winger's image flashed onto the screen. "He wants you to call him ASAP...very shit-hot important." August spoke mockingly, then went to a chipped and fading refrigerator and pulled out a bottle of beer, holding it up. "Sure you don't want one?"

Horn shook his head and walked to the telemonitor. He punched in the code for Winger's apartment and waited. Five seconds later the young cop's image flashed onto the screen.

"Where the hell have you been?" Winger asked.

"What's up?" Horn asked. He noticed Winger had several weapons laid out on a table behind him and appeared to be in the process of cleaning them. Several empty beer bottles were scattered among the hardware, solvents and lubricants.

"Your girlfriend called," Winger answered, grinning.

"My girlfriend?" Horn's mind did a double take. He wondered if Winger was talking about Sarah Weed, a woman he sometimes saw who lived in the Village.

"The Barracuda," Winger said. "She called about a half hour ago. She said she tried to get you through the dispatcher, but your radio was dead. She wants you to call her at home, right away." Winger looked down and appeared to be reading something. "Her number is..."

"I know what it is," Horn said, reaching up and punching off the monitor. He watched the surprised face of Winger fade from the screen, then punched in Christina Service's private code. Horn glanced over at August, who was fixing a sandwich, folding a piece of Swiss cheese onto a stack of corned beef. He turned back to the screen just as Christina Service appeared on the monitor, her ice blue eyes locked onto Horn's.

"Hello, Max," she said.

"I got a message to call," Horn answered. "Winger said it was urgent."

There was the hint of a sneer visible in Service's smile. "Detective Winger has a tendency to infer what he reports," she said. "I have some important information regarding the, ah, *body* you picked up the other night."

Horn noticed out of the corner of his eye that August had stopped spreading mustard on his rye bread and had cocked his head in the direction of the monitor. August doesn't miss a beat, he thought, directing his attention back to Service.

"I've got some information you should probably be made aware of, too," Horn said. "I think Winger and I need to make a little trip."

Service raised her eyebrows. "Where are you?"

"I'm in the Bronx," Horn answered, "but I'm getting ready to head back to the island."

"Why don't you come by my apartment?" Service asked. "You've got my address, right?"

"No," Horn answered, puzzled. He figured Service knew he didn't have her address.

"I'm on the southwest corner of First Avenue and Fifty-fourth. Apartment 320."

"I'll be there soon," Horn said, punching off the monitor.

When the telemonitor faded to black, August asked, "You'll let me know what she tells you about the droid, won't you?"

"You bet," Horn answered, heading across the room. "And thanks, Doc," he said, tapping a finger next to his right eye. "It's good to have two of these again."

"Wait until you get my bill," August growled. "You might change your mind."

Half an hour after leaving August's crib, Horn parked the Elint in front of Christina Service's apartment building. He'd made the transition out of the Bronx with relative ease, suffering only a minor crack in the upper passenger side of the windshield from a bottle thrown by one of three street dwellers near the Third Avenue bridge. Horn chuckled, knowing Winger would have a fit, since the unmarked car was signed out in his name.

Horn IDed himself to the uniformed security guard in the lobby of the relatively plush apartment building and was told to take the elevator up—he was expected. After punching the button for the third floor, he leaned back against the wall and stared at himself in the mirrored doors. Horn's eye was in its video-only mode, and he closed his left eye, gazing at his image through the high-resolution medium. The picture struck him as odd, as though he were watching himself from inside a camera.

The doors on the elevator opened, and Horn walked into the wide, carpeted hall. It suddenly struck him that it was a little out of character that the woman would invite him to her apartment for an exchange of information that could certainly wait until the next day. At least it *seemed* a little unusual.

An odd feeling came over Horn as he walked down the hallway. While he couldn't quite mentally peg *what* he was feeling, he knew it had something to do with the woman. Over the past two years, he'd developed a respect for her toughness and an undeniable attraction to her that confused him. He considered her physically attractive, possessing an energy that he found refreshing. Everything about her said that she stood on her own, and maybe, Horn figured, that's why he felt comfortable in her company; she didn't *need* him. At least it seemed that way. Still, as he rang the buzzer on the door of her apartment, he realized the odd sensation he'd been experiencing was a subtle sort of excitement in anticipation of seeing her. The feeling had been absent for so long that he'd failed to recognize it.

Christina Service swung the door open and motioned Horn inside. "I'm glad you were able to stop by," she said, closing the door behind him. "Why don't you have a seat? Give me your coat first, and I'll hang it for you."

"Thanks," Horn said, pulling off the jacket. He handed it to Service before taking a seat on an L-shaped sofa that bordered the living-room area of the apartment. She walked over to a coatrack in a corner of the room and hung the jacket.

Horn was mildly surprised by the assistant DA's demeanor. She was wearing heels and a red silk dress that was cut just above her knees. Her lean athletic body and long legs seemed to be highlighted by the dress, and Horn noticed that her blond hair, usually pinned in some conservative manner, flowed down over her shoulders like spun gold.

"Were you wearing that outfit when I talked to you a while ago?" Horn asked as Service took a seat on the short leg of the L and turned to face him.

"Yes," she said, laughing lightly, "I got stuck with covering for the DA at a fund-raiser. Is something wrong with it?"

"As a matter of fact, there is," Horn heard himself say, surprising himself. "I can't seem to take my eyes off it."

Service looked at Horn without reacting. He thought she was about to tell him to bug off. Instead, and much to Horn's relief, she let it pass.

"Speaking of eyes," she said, crossing her shapely legs. "I see you got rid of the patch. Was that your doctor you were seeing in the Bronx?"

Horn didn't answer right away. He hoped she wouldn't start asking him questions that could lead from his eye to his arm and even to his knee, whose modifications were considered felonies, even if you were a cop. And here he was, sitting across from one of the people whose job was filing charges against *any* lawbreaker, regardless of who they were. Horn figured the safe thing to do was change the subject, even though he suspected Service knew more about his artificial appendages than she revealed.

"Winger and I need to go to Los Angeles," he said, shifting uncomfortably and turning slightly so his right eye was out of her direct line of sight.

"Oh?" she responded, her expression changing to the business-oriented seriousness Horn was used to. He relaxed a bit and leaned back against the over-stuffed cushions.

"You remember I briefed you on Latch and the place in the Village?" Horn paused and Service nodded. "Well, I've got word that he's in L.A., picking up neural systems for Ticket's droids."

"Picking up what?" Service drew her head back slightly.

"Neural systems," Horn answered. "The brain and spinal cord. I've found out that's what Ticket uses to power his droids."

"How do you know that?" Service asked. "I'm still waiting for a profile from the morgue."

"What happened to the expert you were bringing in?" Horn asked.

Service shrugged. "Who knows? He's probably charging the city by the hour. But really, how do you know about this *neural* thing?"

"Let's just say I've got my own sources of information."

"What's the story on your eye, Max?" she asked. She was staring intently at him.

Horn took it from the manner in which she spoke that he shouldn't try to bullshit her. And, for whatever reason, he didn't feel like trying. "Does it look different to you?"

"Yes," she answered. "It looks different than your left eye. It's sort of hard to describe, but it's not exactly the same color, and the size of the pupil seems a little off."

"It's a mod," Horn said simply.

"So that is why you were in the Bronx."

Horn laughed. "I don't go there for the nightlife." Service returned his smile.

"The guy that did the eye, is he a friend of yours?"

"Yes. He's also one of my sources of information on Ticket and his pal, Jack Latch."

Horn was caught off guard as Service got up and moved beside him on the couch. She grabbed his right arm in both hands and asked, "Is he the same *mechanic* who did this?"

Horn started to pull his arm away, but she tightened her grip and locked onto his eyes with her own, making him feel like he was being targeted by a strange new radar. He could smell her perfume, and it sent an odd chill up his spine, given the anxiety her questions had created.

"I don't know what you're talking about," he said. The video image of Service translated through Horn's right eye gave the scene an ethereal quality. It reminded him strongly of his experience with Virtual Reality and was not unpleasant, albeit somewhat unsettling.

Service laughed, her eyes flashing like blue lasers. "Come on, Max," she said somewhat cynically. "It's common knowledge that you traded your state modifications in on something a little more *durable*. What did they do with your eye, hard-wire it into your arm so they could work in sync?" She moved one hand up to his shoulder and probed the seam where the mod joined his flesh.

Her speculation about his eye surprised him. "People like to speculate..." he said, trying to get her off the subject. "I didn't know you were into gossip." It didn't work.

"This is a felony, Max," she said, rapping her knuckles on his upper arm. A muffled metallic sound echoed briefly. "I've done some research on E-mods, and from the way they move, well, I know these aren't the ones the state gave you."

Horn turned slightly so he directly faced the woman and started to deny her conjecture, but hesitated. Instead, he kissed her full on the mouth, moving his right hand around to the small of her back. Horn felt the softness of her lips, but they were still, as though she were too surprised to react. He squeezed her firmly, flexing his mod enough that her body was drawn to his.

Horn could taste her lipstick. The smell of her body ran straight to his brain. His heart was beating like it had been pumped with adrenaline. He moved his hand up her back and pressed her against him, feeling the firmness of her breasts.

Horn felt himself momentarily suspended in a soft, warm zone that he'd almost forgotten. He was conscious of his lips touching hers, a moist point of contact with her senses through which his own senses danced, electric and crazy. For a moment Horn saw the two of them on a windswept beach, dancing madly beneath a starry sky while the surf pounded. Horn was aware of a prickling sensation sweeping across the back of his head, making him mildly giddy. Christina, returning his kiss, was touching the back of his neck.

Then she pulled away. For the first time since he'd known her, she avoided his eyes. It seemed like a long time before either one of them spoke. It was Service who broke the silence, clearing her throat slightly and moving farther away from Horn on the couch.

"Listen," she said, "I asked you over her to talk about your case, not . . ."

"Talk about my body," Horn said, leaning back and resting his arm across the back of the couch.

"Ah, right," Christina said, a trace of nervousness in her voice. She looked at Horn and half smiled. "I guess this gives us both a way out."

"If you want out," Horn said, suddenly feeling relaxed and comfortable.

Service got up from the couch. "You want something to drink?" She was walking toward an archway that opened into a spacious kitchen area.

"Coffee, if it's ready," he answered, glancing at his watch. It was past ten.

She returned in a moment with a tray holding two cups, a small ceramic pot and a sugar and cream service. She poured two cups and gestured toward the sugar and cream.

"No, thanks," Horn said, picking up the steaming cup.

Sipping the hot liquid, he could taste Service's lipstick along with the coffee.

"I told you I had some information that would interest you," she said, sitting with her knees together. "This thing with Ticket and the body you brought in has taken a new turn."

"In what way?"

"Someone has claimed responsibility for the death of Senator Merrifield," she said. "He says it's a demonstration of things to come."

"Demonstration? I don't get it. I assumed Merrifield was killed because of the damage he was doing to the drug business."

"True," Service said. "But that doesn't necessarily conflict with what I'm telling you. You ever hear of a Libyan named Kindu?"

"Libyan?" Horn shook his head. "No."

"At least, he says he's a Libyan. He calls himself the head of the Resurrection Committee and says he wants the country admitted to the United Nations—under his rule, of course."

"I thought Libya was under some sort of joint international control," Horn said. "Anyway, if this is some sort of international problem, why don't we let the State Department handle it?"

"I'd like to," Service answered, "but Kindu seems inclined to use New York as his theater, if you will, for what he calls his demonstrations of Third World power. That's why you're still on the case instead of cooling your heels at a desk, especially after you pulled that trick with the body."

Horn gave her a what-can-I-say look. "So what's next?" he asked. "Since I'm still on the case."

"Don't be an ass, Max. Kindu and his rebels say they're going to perform one more demo, then take their country back by force, if they have to."

"And the 'one more demo' is going to be in New York?"

"Correct. At least, according to the message received by the State Department."

"Using more of the same type of droids that did in Merrifield?"

"Kindu says he can mount an army of the things." Service rose and walked behind the couch. "What do you think?"

"I don't know," Horn answered. "If Ticket is building the droids for this Kindu, I doubt he can put together an army." He looked at Service, who had her arms crossed over her chest. "Still, from what I saw, it wouldn't take too many to create some major problems."

Service walked back around the couch and took her earlier seat. "I'm worried about this upcoming demonstration," she said, pouring more coffee.

"Just out of curiosity," Horn asked, "how do your State Department friends know this Kindu isn't just using the Merrifield thing as a vehicle to raise hell? I mean, what makes them so sure there really is a connection between Kindu and the droid?"

"The message Kindu sent to the UN described the droid almost perfectly," Service replied. "Even the human neural system you mentioned a while ago."

"Wait a minute," Horn said, straightening up. "Why did you play dumb a few minutes ago when I mentioned the droid's neural system?" He felt angry and wondered what kind of game the assistant DA was playing.

"I had to see how much you knew," she answered sheepishly. "They told me not to tell you everything unless you already understood the droid's capabilities."

Horn laughed. "That's funny." He stood and walked to the coatrack.

"Wait a minute, Max," Service said, getting up from the couch. She intercepted him at the door. "I would have told you everything up front, but the Feds have classified it. Besides, you haven't been exactly up front with me."

"What are you talking about?"

She lowered her penetrating blue eyes to Horn's right arm, then raised them again to his face. Horn felt his irritation dissolve almost instantly.

"You've got a point," he said.

They stared into each other's eyes for what seemed like too long a time. "When are you going to L.A.?" she asked as Horn walked into the hallway.

"In the morning," he answered. "Which reminds me. Can you do me a favor?"

"What?"

"Clear it with Captain Tatum. We shouldn't be gone more than a week."

"I'll call him first thing in the morning," Service said.

As Horn started down the hall, she called to him. "Max?"

"Yeah?" Standing by the elevator, he looked back at her. She was leaning against her doorway.

"Maybe next time you come over, we won't have to talk business."

"Maybe," he answered. Then he stepped into the elevator and pushed the lobby button, conscious that his heart was pounding like a jungle drum.

CHAPTER SEVEN

WINGER WAS STILL complaining when the transatmospheric shuttle touched down in Los Angeles. Horn had roused him from bed at one in the morning, and they had spent two hours tracking down Dartt, finally dragging him out of a bar in the Village called the End. Horn noticed that Dartt had spent most of the hour-long trip in one of the private telemonitor booths on the aircraft, and figured he was making arrangements for their stay in L.A. His suspicions were confirmed when a short, slick-haired man wearing a wrinkled double-breasted suit met them at the terminal.

"Terrence here got us a car," Dartt explained to Horn and Winger. "We're supposed to meet my main connection at a joint in West Hollywood." He looked at his watch. "It's five a.m.," he said. "I can postpone it if you want to get some rest. Otherwise, Terrence says we're supposed to meet Skinny Jack in an hour and a half."

"Skinny Jack?" Winger asked.

"Yeah," Dartt answered. "He's an asshole, but we go back a ways. You'll probably like him."

"I don't want to wait," Horn said, ignoring the discourse between Dartt and his partner. "I assume Terrence here is going to drive us?"

Dartt laughed. "I wouldn't let this little beggar drive a nail into a piece of wood. I'm driving."

"You know your way around L.A.?" Winger asked, raising his eyebrows.

"Sure," Dartt answered, shoving Terrence toward the escalators and motioning the two cops to follow. "I was practically raised in this maze of concrete."

Horn took up the rear of the mismatched entourage. He remembered the first time he'd met Dartt. Although he'd been skeptical about the man's self-professed abilities behind the wheel of anything, he was soon converted. Dartt's skill when they'd run the ditches on the Outland Strip had made Horn a believer. The longer Horn knew Dartt, the more he liked the stocky, slow-talking man who, if he were on a ball team, would best be deployed as a utility player. Dartt was an arranger *extraordinaire* whose connections in obscure as well as well-traveled places constantly amazed Horn. Even when the man was new to an area, as had been the case in Lower Manhattan, he seemed to come up with multiple contacts almost overnight. The thing that impressed Horn the most about Dartt was that he could trust him. Lately he'd become like another partner.

Terrence led them out of the main terminal and across the looping airport streets to a short-term parking lot. "Here she is," he said, stopping in front of a twelve-year-old Chrysler Windtrace sedan. It had been painted flat black and looked like it had spent years parked in the exhaust of a running jet.

Dartt walked slowly around the machine, one hand sliding along its worn surface, as though examining a work of art.

"What the hell is this piece of shit?" Winger exclaimed sarcastically.

"You puntz," Terrence said, lighting a cigarette. "It's obvious you don't recognize a classic highway machine when you see one." He patted a scarred-up fender lovingly.

Dartt, crouched down next to one of the tires, was running a hand across the tread. "Let's get the hell out of here, Les," Winger said. "If we're supposed to meet this buddy of yours, we better get rolling."

"Right." Dartt reached in his jacket and pulled out a fifty-credit wafer. "Here, go have some breakfast." He held the piece of plastic out to Terrence.

"I'm going with you, right?" Terrence asked, grabbing the wafer and stuffing it in the pocket of his dirty trousers.

"Sorry," Dartt said. "What's the code."

A distressed look crossed Terrence's face. "Ah, come on, Les," he said. "You ain't going to leave me here."

"What's the code, Terrence?" Dartt put his hand on the little man's shoulder, then slid it around and grabbed his neck. "Stu here is right. We gotta hit the road, boy."

"Ah, sure, Les, but can't you at least drop me off at Sherman Oaks?"

"The code, Terrence." Dartt raised his voice and shook the man's head. "You're trying my patience, I hope you know that."

"All right," Terrence said, holding up his hands. "It's thirty-four, fifty-one, thirty-six."

"Thanks," Dartt said releasing Terrence. "And yeah, we'll drop you off at Sherman Oaks."

Dartt punched the code into a small keypad over the door handle and opened the door. Reaching into the car, he popped open the trunk. Then he walked to the back of the Windtrace and tossed his bag in the trunk. Horn and Winger followed suit.

Dartt walked back to the driver's door, pressed a button on the armrest and unlocked the other doors. He let Terrence into the back before climbing in behind the wheel.

Horn sat next to Dartt, Winger in the back.

In less than ten minutes they were on the 405 heading north. Dartt had kicked the Windtrace up to ninety, and they barreled along in the fast lane, the machine's big engine roaring. Horn watched the lights of Santa Monica slide by as Dartt changed lanes, maneuvering in the traffic, which was relatively heavy in spite of the early-morning hour.

"Listen," Dartt said, turning his head momentarily in Terrence's direction. "Where the hell was it I'm supposed to meet Skinny Jack? Pier Nine?"

"Shit," Terrence said. "You're lucky I'm here. I never said a damn thing about Pier Nine. That rat hole isn't even in Hollywood."

"Don't give me a lecture," Dartt said. "Just tell me where the hell I'm supposed to meet the guy."

"He said he'd be at the AWOL Lounge."

"Right," Dartt said, jockeying the car onto the Sherman Oaks exit. At Terrence's request, Dartt let him off at a Denny's twenty-four hour restaurant on Ventura Boulevard. Terrence scrambled out of the Windtrace and slammed the door, waving as the trio pulled away.

As Dartt cut back toward the freeway, Horn recalled an earlier trip to Hollywood several years prior and remembered it to be a seedy, cheap conglomeration of run-down buildings and street hustlers who promised anything and everything from weird sex to weird drugs. It was still dark as Dartt drove down La Brea Avenue, but the place cast its own decadent kind of light. Neon and colored strobes lit up the street, reminding Horn a little of Atlantic City. All manner of the human animal cruised the sidewalks: male and female hookers, down-and-outers dressed in rags, slick-dressed dudes flashing gold rings on every finger and other two-legged bottom feeders who didn't seem to care that it was nearly dawn. The place hadn't changed. Horn figured it just looked dirtier.

"I haven't seen one cop since we left the airport," Horn said as Dartt pulled into a potholed and garbage-strewn parking lot.

Dartt parked beneath a dim neon sign hanging from the graffiti-covered wall of a cinder block building that looked like a warehouse for chemical weapons. The sign declared the place to be the AWOL Lounge, but the A had shorted out, leaving WOL.

"It's too early for the hypos to be on the freeway," Dartt said, getting out of the car. He waited until Horn had exited before he finished his explanation across the hood of the Windtrace. "And I doubt if you'll see too many city cops here in Hollywood. It isn't exactly comparable to the Bronx, but it's getting there."

Horn noticed two guys standing next to the entrance to the AWOL as they approached the double metal doors. He figured they were going to get hassled and wasn't disappointed when one of them, a tall, leather-clad man with a red bandanna stretched over his head like a skull cap, stepped in front of the doorway, blocking their path.

"Shit," Winger said tiredly. He looked at Horn as if to say, *This is all I need*.

"What's a matter you guys?" the man asked. His long, stringy hair hung down over his shoulders, and his eyes looked like the pupils had all but disappeared. He gestured to the other man who was similarly dressed. "Hey! Listen to me, goddammit!" He reached out and slapped Winger across the shoulder. "Jimbo and me—we're talkin' to you."

Dartt took a few steps back as Winger turned toward the man. Horn moved slightly toward the one called Jimbo in preparation for Winger's move. The young cop looked pissed.

"If you two assholes want to keep from eating the rest of your meals through a straw, I suggest you get the hell out of the way." Winger rubbed his chin and stared at the man who had slapped him.

"Well, get a load of you, dipshit," the man said, suddenly shaking down his right arm and bringing up a curve-bladed knife. He held it in front of Winger's face. "No one gets into the AWOL without payin' us a cover charge."

Winger seemed about to sneeze but instead of covering his mouth and nose, he brought up a knee and buried it in the man's groin.

"Sheee...it!" the man screeched at the top of his lungs. Winger grabbed the knife hand by the wrist and bent it backward over his shoulder.

Horn took a step toward Jimbo, who had pulled a small bat from somewhere and was raising it over his head. Horn brought his right arm around in a slapping motion just as Jimbo swung the bat down toward Winger's head. He felt his mod flex involuntarily and watched the wooden weapon break across his forearm like a matchstick running into a buzz saw. His hand caught Jimbo square in the mouth, causing several of the man's teeth to break loose as his head snapped violently backward. Grabbing his hair, Horn rammed his head into the side of the building. He watched the man's pinpoint eyes roll back into his head as his body went limp.

Releasing Jimbo, Horn turned toward Winger and was shocked. His partner had twisted the man's arm around and, using a foot for leverage, had pulled the arm out until it was almost straight. Dartt, meanwhile, had climbed onto the fender of the Windtrace. Dartt then dived off the car and brought an elbow straight down across the stretched-out arm. The man howled in pain, and Horn knew that bones had fractured. Winger had gone too far in the heat of the fight.

The knife had fallen to the asphalt. Horn grabbed it and flung it on top of the building before realizing it probably wasn't necessary. Neither of the men was in any shape to use it.

Winger released the man's arm, which flopped next to his side like a limp rag. He fell to his knees and began whimpering. Winger walked behind him and placed one of his boots in the middle of the man's back, then shoved him facedown in the parking lot.

"That's enough, partner," Horn said, grabbing Winger by the arm and pulling him toward the door. "Let's go inside. I'll buy you a beer."

"Yeah, right," Winger answered, turning around. He had a strange, faraway look in his eyes, and Horn wondered what the young cop might have done next if he had have let him go on.

Dartt opened the door to the AWOL. "You're going to love this place," he said, waving them inside.

The AWOL Lounge looked like a bombed-out garbage dump. It also smelled like one. Mismatched tables and chairs, some overturned, were scattered around a small dance floor that looked like a helipad cut out of a jungle war zone. Even though it was almost six in the morning, several couples graced the trash-covered tile, doing a tired sort of slam dance to music that blared from loudspeakers. Smoke, along with the stench of stale booze and puke, hung thick in the club, whose walls were covered with peeling rock posters and graffiti.

Dartt led them across the room to the bar, which was tended by a rough-hewn woman wearing an olive drab T-shirt tucked into a pair of camouflage fatigue pants. A black leather vest hung from her broad shoulders, an unfiltered cigarette from her painted lips. She had her hair pulled back severely, making her eyes look slanted. This effect was highlighted by the green glitter mascara smeared in wedges above her brown orbs.

"Three beers," Dartt yelled over the din of the music. He tossed a credit wafer onto the bar and turned around, surveying the crowd. As the barmaid set the foaming glasses on the bar, Dartt asked her, "You seen Skinny Jack?"

"Who the hell wants to know?" she replied.

"The name's Dartt. I'm supposed to meet him here."

"If you're talking about Jack 'the Chump' Bennett, he's over there with his usual bevy of gutter hags." She nodded toward a far corner of the bar.

"Thanks, babe," Dartt said, tossing another wafer onto the bar, then motioning for Horn and Winger to follow.

The man they were set up to meet was sitting at a table with his back in a corner, surrounded by three women who looked like prostitutes. Their faces were thick with makeup, and each wore a revealing, low-cut outfit that barely contained the business parts of their bodies.

"Well, well, look what crawled in from the freeway," Jack said as the three men approached the table.

As he rose to greet them, Horn knew where he'd gotten the name Skinny. Except for his face, he looked like a junkie.

After Dartt made the introductions, Jack invited them to sit down and motioned for the women to leave. He smiled graciously, revealing a perfect set of teeth set beneath a neatly trimmed moustache. His closely cropped hair was combed straight back, and his sideburns were trimmed even with the top of his ears. If it weren't for his slick-boy suit and emaciated body, Jack could have been taken for an investment banker or corporate lawyer.

"Good news, Mr. Dartt," Jack said. "We got a line on your boy."

"What have you got?" Dartt asked.

The skinny man held up his hands. "Not so fast, Les. I believe there was a finder's fee, right?" Jack flashed a smile.

"Shit." Dartt produced a stack of wafers and tossed three hundred-credit units on the table.

"You better make that two more, Les," Jack said, his smile fading. "The deal was five C's."

"You're real good with numbers, Jack," Dartt said quietly. "But you're not going to be able to count shit when I stick your head up your ass." He abruptly leaned back in his chair, appearing to relax. "Three hundred now, the balance when your information checks out."

Horn had to admire Skinny Jack. He didn't cave in, even with Dartt, who could be pretty intimidating. "The deal was five hundred," Jack reiterated somewhat nervously. "What's this bullshit about checkin' out my information? I never stiffed you before."

Dartt laughed. "All right, Jack," he said, pulling two more hundred-credit wafers out of his pocket. "This makes five." He picked up the three from the table and stuffed all five wafers into the breast pocket of Jack's suit. "Now, start talking."

Jack picked up a glass of clear liquid from the table and chugged it unceremoniously. He slammed the glass down and tapped his chest with his fist, appearing to be attempting a belch. "I don't know why the hell you're tracking this Latch character," he finally said, shifting his eyes from Horn to Winger to Dartt. "I checked him out like you wanted and found out he's hooked up with a puke called Toad."

"Toad?" Dartt shook his head. "Never heard of him."

"He's one grim son of a bitch," Jack said. "The word on the street is they got some deal going where they're kidnapping people and freezin' them, cuttin' their heads off or some kind of weird shit. I know it sounds fucking crazy, but from what I've heard about Toad, I wouldn't put it past him. The bastard is like Dracula."

"You know where they're supposed to be doing this freezing?" Dartt asked.

"The old Burbank Studios, Lot C. I followed them there myself and watched them unload a bunch of silver tanks from a van."

"Them?"

"Latch and this Toad guy," Jack explained, "and two other assholes I've never seen before."

Dartt looked at Horn and shrugged.

"Listen," Jack said, tapping Dartt on the arm with the back of his hand, "for another half a hundred, I'll tell you where the whole freak show is staying."

"I'd bet they're staying at the Gold Dust," Horn couldn't resist interjecting.

Jack turned and stared at him, his mouth hanging slightly open. "Yeah, the Gold Dust over on the Strip," he said slowly.

"Well, give him fifty credits!" Dartt said loudly, slapping Jack on the shoulder so hard that it almost knocked the little man onto the table.

"Go to hell," Jack wheezed as Dartt rose from his chair. "Better yet," he said, "I hope the Toad freezes your ass."

CHAPTER EIGHT

CURSING LOUDLY, Ticket removed the electron glasses and hurled them across the room. He peeled off the rubber gloves and flung them in the same direction, then leaned against the table and rubbed his eyes. "What the hell is wrong with me?" he asked aloud before turning and walking to a counter along one side of the spacious operating room. He picked up a pack of cigarettes and lit one.

Ticket punched the intercom button on a telemonitor over the stainless-steel counter, and a uniformed guard's image appeared. "Tell Mr. Dineen I need his assistance in the OR immediately," Ticket ordered.

"Yes, sir," the guard answered, flashing a nervous salute.

Across the room, Number 24 lay splayed out, face-down on the marble slab that functioned as Ticket's operating table. Most of the droid was covered with a sheet; its arms protruded over the edge of the table. The back of Number 24 was exposed, and several tubes, wires and fiber-optic cables ran from a bank of support and test equipment into the body cavity, from which emanated a gurgling, suctionlike sound.

Ticket took a deep drag on his cigarette as Mark Dineen entered, wearing a worried smile and a white lab coat smeared with dried blood. "What is it?" he asked, peering through his round horn-rimmed glasses. His expression said he didn't want to hear the answer.

Ticket grabbed a clean lab coat from the counter and tossed it to Dineen. "Put this on," he said. "I need your assistance."

Dineen removed his dirty lab coat and tossed it into a plastic drum. Donning the clean one, he asked, "Do you still have traffic coming out of both sides of the brain, or is it an interface problem with the droid itself?"

"I can't figure out what the hell is wrong with the droid," Ticket said, nodding toward the table. "It was working okay in the Village and then, all of a sudden, it went into convulsions." Ticket looked across the room at the bottle of Scotch on a table.

"I told you that we might have problems with the neural system, didn't I?" Dineen said. "I think Latch warned you about it, too. Didn't he say the donor may have been a string addict?"

"Did he?" Ticket asked, stomping his cigarette on the floor.

"Sounds like Latch may have been right," Dineen said, pulling on a pair of rubber gloves. "If the donor was a string addict, the droid could have some strange reactions, especially when the drug started wearing off."

"That's got to be it," Ticket said, lighting another cigarette. "It's a chemical problem with the donor brain."

Dineen held up a hand, the same tentative smile creasing his face. "That *may* be the problem. Don't discount the fact that it could be a problem with the droid. You know we've had—"

"It's not a problem with the droid!" Ticket yelled, and slammed a fist down on the counter.

Dineen cringed, his face turning red. "I don't mean a *design* problem," he said, obviously regretting the direction the conversation had taken.

"Well, what the hell do you mean?" Ticket stubbed out his cigarette and went to where Dineen was standing, suddenly dropping the hostile edge to his voice. "You've always implied that there has been a problem with the design of the droid," he said, his face within inches of Dineen's. "I'm giving you a chance to speak your mind, and believe me, I won't hold it against you."

"No, really," Dineen said, backing away. "I don't think there's a design problem, Julius."

I'm sure you don't, you spineless asshole, Ticket thought as he walked back to the counter and grabbed a fresh pair of gloves. He pulled them on as he walked to the table, nodding at Dineen to follow.

Ticket scanned the data flashing across a monitor. "What I want to do," he said, "is run a probe into the motor convolution and temporarily deaden it."

"What's that going to accomplish?" Dineen asked.

"When the motor function thaws out, I'm betting whatever caused the malfunction won't be present," Ticket said. "It'll be like hitting the system's reset button." He picked up a strange-looking device that resembled a small flashlight with a rubber-cupped eyepiece on one end and a long, hair-thin wire protruding from the other.

Dineen shrugged. "I guess it's worth a try," he admitted. "How are you going to access the cerebellum?"

"Through the first hinge. I need you to give me enough room to run the probe in."

"You want me to pry the goddamn flap open?" Dineen raised his eyebrows. "I mean, if you or I slip, we could really fuck the...*guy* up."

"Well, what the hell shape do you think *he's* in now?" Ticket asked, waving the probe over the droid. "The son of a bitch isn't exactly dancing in the street, right?"

"You got a point," Dineen said, picking through a pile of instruments on the tray.

I've got a couple of other points, too, Ticket thought as he bent over the droid. One of them was to get rid of Dineen as soon as Latch got back from Los Angeles. Ticket wanted Latch to kill the motor-mouthed Irishman. Ticket chuckled aloud at the thought of using Dineen's neural system in a droid.

Ticket looked into the opening that ran down the middle of Number 24's back. The spine had been encased in a polished titanium tube that was hinged in sections resembling a sort of bizarre ectoskeleton or alien insect. The spine fed straight into the base of the droid's titanium skull. Ticket could see a good portion of the smooth metal where the skin had been rolled up from the seam that ran around the neck.

"I'm going to reduce the blood flow before you access the sheath," Ticket said, pressing a latching device on the side of the radioactive module. The top of the device popped open, and he adjusted a potentiometer before closing the lid and turning back toward Dineen. "Go ahead, but take it slow and easy."

"You're not dealing with some rookie," Dineen said as he inserted the fine-tipped edges of the prying device into the seam.

Ticket consulted a digital readout on one of the pieces of test gear. "I don't want to leave the blood flow down any longer than I have to," he said.

"If this doesn't work," Dineen argued, "it isn't going to matter a whole hell of a lot if the brain gets oxygen starved."

Ticket had to admit that Dineen was right as he watched a tiny drop of bluish-colored synthetic blood appear on the seam.

"That's all you're going to get," Dineen said as a trickle of sweat ran down the side of his face. "Get your probe in there. I can't guarantee how long it'll hold."

Without hesitating, Ticket bent over the eyepiece and slipped the tiny probe into the seam. Almost immediately the droid bucked violently as though it had been hit with high voltage.

"Goddamn!" Dineen yelled. He placed one hand on the back of Number 24's head and tried to keep it from bouncing like a pinball. "Pull it out! Now!"

Ticket literally jerked the probe out of the droid's spine, and the body went limp. "Son of a bitch," he hissed, setting the probe down and walking to the counter. He opened a small cabinet and pulled out a syringe and a small vial of clear liquid. "I'll fix the bastard," he said, filling the hypo. He walked back to the table and once again opened the module that controlled the blood flow. "This will calm him down."

Ticket stuck the needle into a receptacle that was built into the module and pressed the plunger. He tossed the spent hypo to the floor and turned up the potentiometer momentarily in order to speed the drug into the droid's neural system.

"I don't think you need to—"

"Shut up," Ticket snapped, detuning the control. He picked up the probe and once again inserted it into the seam. This time the droid didn't move.

"All I was going to say was I didn't think you needed to up the flow—"

"Like I said," Ticket repeated, "shut up." He stuck his eye into the rubber cup and gingerly adjusted a small knob on the side of the device. "Sometimes you can be a royal pain in the ass, Mark," he said without looking up.

Ticket's attention was suddenly diverted as a beeping erupted from the telemonitor. "Will you get that, please? And tell those idiots I don't want to be disturbed for at least thirty minutes."

Dineen took the call while Ticket resumed his work. Seconds later the assistant returned. "It's Toftoy."

Ticket's expression turned sour. "What the hell does that son of a bitch want?" He tossed the probe on the tray and peeled off his gloves. "Close him up, will you, please?" he said, tossing the gloves toward the plastic drum. "The anesthetic should wear off in fifteen minutes or so. Make sure you up the gain on the pump, too."

"I know what to do," Dineen answered. "But do you really think this *reset* business is going to work?"

Ticket didn't answer. He filled a glass to the brim with Scotch and downed it in three swallows before filling it again. Lighting a cigarette, he stared at his reflection in the dead screen of the telemonitor and wondered what the hell Toftoy wanted other than to make his skin crawl. He took a large mouthful of Scotch and let it slowly trickle down his throat. Taking a long drag on his cigarette, he punched the telemonitor off its hold mode, and Toftoy's image flickered to life on the flat panel.

"Hello, Dr. Ticket," Toftoy said, adjusting his tie as though he were looking into a mirror.

"What do you want?" he asked. "Is my meeting with Kindu on the twenty-eighth still on?"

"Of course," Toftoy answered in a dry monotone. "But Mr. Kindu wants to have the Neuroids available for—have you got your crypto on?"

Ticket examined the encryption module on the control panel. Its red LED was flashing, indicating that it was operating. "Yeah, my *crypto* is *on*," he answered, trying to emulate Toftoy's drawling voice. He wondered if there was anything about the man that didn't irritate him.

"Good," Toftoy said, apparently oblivious to the fact that Ticket was mocking him. "What we want is for the droids to be operational on the twenty-eight."

"Hell, I can't guarantee that," Ticket said, his irritation running toward full-blown anger. "I haven't even received the goddamn neural systems." He pointed at the screen. "You can tell Kindu that I'm not running a goddamn take-out service."

Toftoy chuckled and held up his hand as if to keep Ticket at bay. "Slow down, hoss," he said. "Don't shoot the messenger. Mr. Kindu realizes it may be a strain, but he's willing to make financial compensation for your inconvenience."

Ticket's anger subsided almost instantly, but the scowl didn't drop from his face. *Money* was the magic word. He'd been thinking about coming up with another reason to up his price, but now he didn't have to; the fools were doing it for him.

"I can't really expedite the implants until I get the systems," Ticket said nonchalantly.

"Then I suggest you expedite the acquisition of the neural systems," Toftoy said.

"Huh?"

"Speed up the delivery of the neural systems," Toftoy repeated. "You know, *expedite* them. I'm sure a little blue script will motivate your suppliers."

Ticket felt the hair on the back of his neck rise. It was just like Toftoy to think he hadn't understood the meaning of the word *expedite*. "I know what the hell you said." He rubbed his chin and took a drag on his cigarette. "We might be able to have maybe half of the droids operational by then."

"Sorry," Toftoy said. "We need them all. Mr. Kindu was disappointed enough when you told him you couldn't deliver all we'd originally contracted for. You might say that this is his way of letting you off the hook." Toftoy smiled. "But he wants all nine. We're willing to pay you three million a copy if you have them ready on the twenty-eighth."

"Why so soon?" Ticket asked.

"Mr. Kindu needs them—how should I say it?—to press home a point. But that's none of your concern."

"Where is Kindu?" Ticket wondered how Latch was doing. The offer of three million was more than he expected, and he resisted accepting it on the spot. "Maybe I should discuss this with him personally."

"That isn't necessary," Toftoy answered. "I have full authorization to make this offer. Besides, Mr. Kindu is incommunicado."

Ticket didn't like negotiating with Kindu's errand boy, especially one as obnoxious as Toftoy. He butted the stub of his cigarette in an ashtray on the table. "I'll accept your offer," he said, "but I'll need half the money in advance."

Toftoy looked confused. "Listen," he said. "You've got six million, right?"

"Yes, but that's not enough. If you want all nine droids operational by the twenty-eighth, I need another seven and a half."

Toftoy wore a blank expression. "Wait a second," he said, and the screen went to a flashing Stand By.

Ticket lit another cigarette and downed the Scotch in his glass. He was considering getting a refill when Toftoy returned—looking, Ticket noticed, a little less confused.

"Sorry," Toftoy said, "I had to check my notes."

Ticket almost laughed. He imagined Kindu standing to one side of the monitor holding up cue cards.

"I think we can give you another four million," Toftoy said. "You'll get the balance after the Neuroids have proven they're all you've advertised them to be."

What sort of demonstration did Kindu have up his sleeve? Ticket wondered as he subconsciously raised the empty glass to his lips. Lowering the glass with some embarrassment, he said, "It's a deal. Route the money to the same accounts as last time."

ULTIMATE WEAPON   151

"It's already being taken care of," Toftoy said, looking almost relieved. "You can expect us on the twenty-eighth, sometime in the morning."

"What kind of operation is Kindu planning?" Ticket asked.

"He's going to put on a little show of force," Toftoy answered. "Rattle a saber, if you will."

"Where?"

"New York, of course. He's going to stage a song and dance at the UN. But enough chatter. I've got another call I need to take. See you on the twenty-eighth."

The screen went blank. Ticket figured Toftoy was probably getting his ass chewed out for disclosing where Kindu planned to utilize the droids. The plan made his skin crawl, but his main interest was in getting the balance of the payment.

Ticket returned to the OR to find that Dineen had finished the surgical procedure. The droid was on its back, and the sheet had been removed. Ticket walked to the table as Dineen peeled off his gloves. "How did it look?" he asked.

"How did it look?" Dineen repeated, drawing his head back. "I don't know what you mean. If you're asking if I think the little trick you came up with is going to work, I'll have to honestly say that I doubt it."

"You've always thought I never really had my shit together, isn't that correct, Mr. Dineen?" Ticket asked, smiling.

Dineen gazed warily at Ticket. "I didn't say that," he said.

"You didn't have to *say* it. You sort of wore it around on your shoulder like a chip." Ticket slapped Dineen on the neck hard enough for it to echo loudly in the room.

"Hey! What the hell are you doing?"

"Just knocking that goddamn chip off, Mark old boy," Ticket said, smiling. He slapped Dineen hard across the cheek.

"Jesus!" Dineen squealed in pain. "You son of a bitch. You've been pushing me around long enough." He pushed into Ticket, grabbed his wrists, driving him to his knees. "Yeah, that's it. Get on your knees, you asshole, it's your turn to grovel."

"Take it easy," Ticket said. "You're hurting my wrists."

Dineen laughed. "I can't believe you actually slapped me. You know, I've spent damn near the last two years kissing your ass, listening to your biomechanical trips and watching you screw up even the most elementary shit." He applied more pressure to Ticket's wrists.

"Take it easy," Ticket said. "You're hurting me."

"I've been dying to tell you something for over a year," Dineen said. "You're really not as good as you think you are."

Ticket broke out in a maniacal laugh that caused Dineen to cringe.

"What the hell are you laughing about?"

"I think I'm pretty damn good," he said, nodding his head at something over Dineen's shoulder. "See if this makes you change your mind."

Dineen screamed in terror as Number 24 grabbed him around the neck and jerked him away from Ticket. The droid had risen to a sitting position on the operating table and had Dineen in a headlock.

"Insomuch as I value your opinion," Ticket said, rising to his feet and rubbing his wrists, "I'm certain that Number 24 here can help sway you to join my following, so to speak." He looked at the droid. "Bring him over here, please."

The droid slipped off the table and literally dragged Dineen after Ticket, who walked to the table by the door and filled a fresh glass with Scotch.

"Stand him up against the door," Ticket said, turning toward the naked droid and Dineen, whose head was locked in the monster's arms.

"What the hell are you doing?" Dineen asked as the droid clamped a hand around his neck and backed him up against the door.

"Shut up," Ticket said before taking a long drink. He felt himself getting a little tipsy. "You know, you're not that bad around the OR," Ticket said, tipping his glass toward Dineen, who was whining and squirming beneath the droid's grip. "If I could just get you to shut your mouth, we'd get along just fine."

"Don't worry," Dineen said, his eyes reflecting a begging sort of fear, "I'll keep my mouth shut from now on, I swear."

"I know you will," Ticket said, figuring he'd jerk a couple of Dineen's mental strings before letting him off the hook. "What I think I'll do is cut your tongue out."

Dineen stared at Ticket in horror. "You don't have to do that, Dr. Ticket," he pleaded. "I promise you won't have another problem with me."

"Or maybe I'll just have Number 24 here crush your larynx. It'll be a lot less of a—" Ticket stopped, feeling a chill run up his spine as a crunching sound erupted from Dineen's neck.

"Holy shit!" Ticket yelled, dropping his glass. He realized that Number 24, taking his speech as an order, had closed his grip on Dineen's throat. "Let him go! Let him go!" Ticket grabbed the droid's arm and tried to pull it away, but the action was useless. Dineen's eyes bulged, and his tongue protruded from between his lips as though it had been squeezed out.

"Number 24," Ticket said calmly, "release the man."

The droid slowly relaxed his grip. Dineen crumpled in a heap on the floor, a gurgling sound coming out of his throat.

"Shit!" Ticket bent to the floor and rolled Dineen over. He considered doing a tracheotomy, but abandoned that notion when he examined Dineen's neck. Ticket was almost certain that the man's spine had been crushed along with his windpipe. "Damn, I can't even use the bastard's neural system," he said aloud. The droid was standing like a store mannequin, its arm still extended, its hand in the same position in which it had gripped Dineen's throat.

"I think he's dead, mate," Ticket heard himself say. The droid stared at him, its face expressionless, its eyes gazing out from a neural zone somewhere in its captive brain.

Ticket suddenly broke out in an insane laughter that bounced around the room like the pealing of a high-pitched bell. He managed to pull himself up and stagger to the table. He grabbed the nearly empty bottle of Scotch and tilted it back, draining it in a single swallow. He looked at the droid, which was still standing over Dineen's body as though guarding it. "Number 24," he said drunkenly. The droid turned. "Toftoy," Ticket said, waving his hand. "Remember that name."

CHAPTER NINE

DARTT PULLED the Chrysler into the parking lot of a liquor store across the street from the Gold Dust Inn, and killed the engine. "Nice place, huh?" he said, taking his .44 Magnum from his jacket and checking the chamber.

"It's a nice place if you just came out of hell," Winger replied. He turned toward Horn in the backseat. "What's the plan?"

"Let's find out what room they're in," he answered. "Unless you want to stake the place out all day."

Dartt was already out of the car, lighting one of his thin cigars. It was midmorning, and the Strip seemed to have taken on a lull. The sidewalks were relatively empty, save for a couple of alley dwellers pushing grocery carts filled with their meager belongings. Steam was rising from the street as the sun heated up the pitted asphalt, giving the place an eerie appearance in the dead, fall morning.

"I've got a feeling they're not here," Horn said, turning up the collar of his jacket. The wind started to pick up, blowing the steam and pieces of trash down the street.

"You cops are always getting these *feelings*." Dartt chuckled. "Don't you ever come up with anything tangible?"

Horn laughed. "Let's go," he said motioning for Dartt and Winger to follow.

"Let me handle this," Dartt said as Horn opened the door to the inn's office.

Horn shrugged and allowed Dartt to enter first. "Wait out here," he told Winger, who sauntered down the sidewalk toward the rooms.

The office was a mess of crumpled magazines, empty beer cans and overflowing ashtrays dumped around a sway-backed couch and a dead television. Behind a small counter, an ancient row of key slots, credit machine and telemonitor stations served as the Gold Dust's registration, checkout and general-business area.

"What do you want?"

A huge unshaven man in a dirty undershirt appeared from a darkened hallway behind the counter. To Horn, the man looked like he'd just crawled out of a sewer. His bare arms were covered with tattoos, and his long greasy hair hung down from the sides of his balding head like the strings of a worn-out mop. He scowled at the two men and leaned against the counter, scratching his neck.

"What? No 'Good morning, may I help you, please?'" Dartt mocked. "This is a service establishment, isn't it?"

"No, it's a hotel," the man answered.

Dartt reached in his pocket and pulled out a ten-credit wafer. "We're looking for somebody," he said, tossing the piece of plastic on the counter.

The man looked down at the wafer in silence. Dartt tossed another. "Tell me," he said. "Which *suite* is Jack Latch in?"

"Got no Jack Latch here," the man answered, knocking the wafers to the floor in front of Dartt. "If you guys are cops," the overgrown desk clerk said, "you're in the wrong part of town."

The man whipped up a sawed-off double-barreled shotgun and pointed it at Dartt. Slowly and instinctively Horn moved aside to spread the man's target.

"Move another inch, and I'll aerate your ass." The man swung the weapon toward Horn.

Dartt's hand was a blur. He ripped the shotgun out of the man's hands so quickly that the fat man and Horn seemed equally surprised.

"What the goddamn hell?" the fat man gasped.

Horn drew his 9 mm and focused his right eye on the center of the desk clerk's forehead. The red beam of the laser was instantly dead-on, surprising Horn in that the entire targeting process seemed to occur outside his consciousness. He couldn't remember having willed his arm to pull the big automatic out of its holster and sensed that his finger had tightened the trigger to the thin edge of its tripping point.

"Take it easy, man," the man stuttered, holding up his hands. "You can have the money, take it all."

Horn's natural eye focused on the desk clerk's face, which had turned a sickly color. He felt a strange prickling sensation run up his spine as he *forced* his E-mod to relax and back off the 9 mm's trigger.

"You all right?" Dartt said, glancing at Horn. He had turned the shotgun around and had the twin barrels resting on the counter, aimed at the desk clerk's gut.

"Yeah," Horn answered. A trickle of sweat ran down his neck.

"Like I said," the man stammered, "take the money. It's in the box."

"We don't want to rob your fat ass," Dartt said. "Like I said before, we just want to know which room Jack Latch is in."

"Don't have no Jack Latch registered here," the man replied nervously.

"How about a cat that goes by the name of Toad?"

A flash of recognition shuttered in the man's eyes, and he looked from Dartt to Horn as though weighing whether to take the shotgun's load in the center of his fat belly.

"Toad?" the man said weakly. "I . . . I don't know no Toad."

Dartt sighed and heaved himself up onto the counter, then swung over and slid in front of the clerk. "Punch a T into that dinosaur and see if Toad doesn't show up," he said, pointing the shotgun at an old PC that should have been in a museum. Its ancient monochrome monitor was displaying some sort of spread-sheet.

The desk clerk glanced nervously at the PC, then lunged toward Dartt, grabbing the barrel of the shotgun. He shoved his shoulder into Dartt's midsection and slammed him backward into the counter. Horn moved toward the two men, intending to help Dartt.

"Let me take care of this," Dartt grunted.

Horn watched as Dartt released the shotgun and slapped the clerk on the ears with both hands. The man screamed and tried to club Dartt with the gun, but struck only air as Dartt sidestepped and brought a knee up into his groin.

The clerk dropped the shotgun and grabbed the front of his baggy trousers as his face turned purplish gray. Dartt rammed his balding head into the computer monitor, which popped and erupted in a shower of sparks and smoke.

Horn grabbed Dartt's jacket and pulled him away. "Don't kill the bastard, okay?"

"Sorry," Dartt answered. "The guy pissed me off."

Dartt pulled the man to his feet, and he immediately began coughing and rubbing his eyes. Several trickles of blood ran down his forehead and across his face.

"Listen, Moby Dick," Dartt said, grabbing a handful of the man's hair. "What room is this Toad guy in?" He shook the clerk's head violently.

"Room 248. It's down at the other end." The clerk held out a plastic key card that resembled a credit wafer. Taking it, Dartt released the man and turned as if to leave. Instead, he swung back and planted his right fist squarely on the clerk's jaw. The sound was like a bottle being smashed by a hammer. The clerk's eyes rolled in cartoon-style, and he dropped to the floor. Dartt turned toward Horn and smiled. "Not exactly five-star service, is it?"

Horn exited the office behind Dartt. Winger appeared from a doorway over which hung a sign that read Laundry Room.

"What's going on out here?" Dartt asked.

"Not much," Winger answered. "The place is pretty dead. I haven't seen a body, not even a maid."

Dartt lit one of his thin cigars. "What do you think?" he asked Horn.

"Let's check out the room," he answered. "I've got a feeling no one's there, but you never can tell."

"What room?" Winger asked. "I'll check out the back while you guys take the front."

"Supposedly he's in 248," Dartt said, pointing toward the far end of the motel. "I don't know if there's a back to the place or not, but go ahead and check it out."

"If it stays pretty quiet," Horn said, "come back around and cover the parking lot."

"You got it," the young cop replied before heading down the sidewalk.

"May I?" Dartt asked, nodding toward the stairs that led to the second-floor balcony.

"It's been your show so far," Horn answered, slapping Dartt on the back. "You'd make a good cop, you know that, Les?"

Room 248 was the last room on the second floor. Dartt placed an ear against the faded door and held up a hand. He shook his head and went to the window, crouching down to peer through the crack between the curtains and the sill.

"Nobody's home," Dartt said. He slipped the card key into a slot below the handle and pushed open the door.

Horn followed Dartt into the darkened room, blinking his eye into its IR mode and scanning the gloom for a heat source. He didn't have to look down to know that his 9 mm was tracking with his eye, seeking out a target in the shadows. Horn knew that he didn't consciously pull the automatic from its holster, but its appearance in his hand didn't spook him as it had previously. He wondered if he were becoming adapted to his *system mod,* as August had called it. "By allowing your mod to see with its own *eye,*" August had told him, "you'll find that it becomes more reflex-oriented, becomes more like a part of your body than a mechanical crutch."

Dartt walked to the door that led into the next room and shoved it open with the barrel of his .44. "Want to head to Burbank?" Dartt asked, looking toward Horn.

"Let's take a quick look around," Horn answered, stepping past Dartt and flipping on the overhead light in the adjoining room.

"All right," Dartt said, turning toward the cluttered dresser, "but from the looks of the place, we may as well be scrounging in a Dumpster."

Horn walked straight to a kit bag on the bed and dumped out its contents. He picked up a blue Delta folder and saw the name J. Latch printed across its top. After sifting quickly through the other items, he stuffed them back in the bag and returned to the other room.

"Look at his shit," Dartt said, glancing at Horn. "This Toad guy is some kind of strange duck."

Dartt opened several dresser drawers and rummaged through them. He held up a pair of handcuffs that had tiny spikes welded into the metal rings.

"I see what you mean," Horn said, reaching into one of the drawers. He pulled out a small plastic box. Inside were several syringes and vials of drugs whose names Horn didn't recognize. He noticed one vial was labeled Not For Human Use.

"Dig this." Dartt held up a harness attached to a large dog-collar, ringed with silver studs.

"Let's split." Horn headed for the door and motioned for Dartt to follow. Something about the scene wasn't sitting well with him, and he had the sensation that they were being watched. He looked over the balcony at Winger, who was leaning against the fender of an old Audi station wagon.

"Get the car," Horn ordered as Winger looked up.

"I've got a bad taste in my mouth about these guys we're tracking," Horn told Dartt.

"What do you mean?"

"I mean, I can't help feeling this little manhunt is going to get ugly before it's all over."

Horn climbed into the back of the Windtrace.

"You sure you don't want me to drive?" Dartt asked Winger as he got into the passenger side. "Driving in L.A. is a little different than New York."

"Shit." Winger laughed. "New York makes this place look like a church parking lot." Winger peeled out of the Gold Dust lot and headed east, following Dartt's directions. "Just past the Hollywood, take a left in Los Feliz," Dartt said, pronouncing Feliz, *Feel-Ez*. "This is a roundabout way to Burbank, but the Hollywood Freeway is all torn to shit."

Winger turned onto Los Feliz and picked up speed. "Where do you think our boys are?"

"Hopefully they're where we're going," Dartt answered.

"What about the locals?"

"*Locals?* You mean the LAPD?" Dartt shot Horn a look as though he'd just been told a joke that wasn't funny.

"Yeah," Horn responded. "Shouldn't we at least tell them we're here and let them know what we're doing?"

"Hell, that's your concern, not mine." Dartt grunted a cynical laugh.

"I think we're better off playing this low-key," Winger interjected. "We don't have a warrant, we don't have extradition papers, we don't have—"

"Jack-shit," Dartt finished the sentence. "I agree. Get on the Golden State. We want to go north."

Horn figured Dartt and Winger were right. They'd be better off keeping a low profile than bringing the Los Angeles police in on what they were doing. At the least, Horn figured, involving the LAPD would slow things down and, at worst, might result in their quick expulsion from the city. He wondered how much help Christina Service could be across the country.

As Winger pulled into the traffic flow on the Golden State Freeway, Horn noticed a beat-up Mercury station wagon on their right. A wire-haired man behind the wheel smiled insanely before laying the barrel of a shotgun across the edge of the open window.

"Down!" Horn screamed, leaning forward. He grabbed Winger's shoulder and jerked his upper body back just as the shotgun cooked off, shattering the front passenger window and spraying the interior with lead shot. The car drifted to the far left lane and slammed into a van.

"Goddamn!" Winger yelled, jerking the wheel hard and flooring the gas pedal. As the car straightened out, the vehicles around them maneuvered out of the way.

"Where'd the son of a bitch go?" Dartt said, raising up from beneath the dashboard. Tiny shards of glass covered his head and shoulders, and blood oozed from a small crease in his forehead. Magnum in hand, he craned his neck and scanned the traffic.

"He's right behind us!" Winger whipped the Chrysler across two lanes of traffic as another explosion erupted behind them. A shot slammed into the back of their car.

Tracking his sight through the rear window, Horn, 9 mm in hand, watched the station wagon sideswipe another car, forcing it into a concrete abutment.

"Can you take him out?" Dartt asked.

"It'll get pretty messy if I do," Horn answered, figuring a crash could involve twenty or thirty cars. He could see the traffic come to a standstill behind them where the car had run into the reinforced median. "See if you can lead the guy off the freeway," Horn told Winger.

Winger responded by jockeying the Chrysler into the far right lane. One eye fixed on the rearview mirror, he laid on the horn and stomped on the accelerator. "Here they come again!" he yelled.

Horn slammed forward against the front seat and realized they'd been rear-ended. He peered out the back window just as Dartt's .44 hammered out three shots, shattering the glass as the Mercury moved up and rammed them again.

"Get off the freeway!" Horn yelled as he opened fire at the station wagon's windshield.

Exiting the highway, Winger managed to take out a green-and-white sign that read Victory Blvd. It flew over their car and bounced off the hood of the wagon.

"Goddamn!" Winger screamed as the Chrysler bounced over a curb and plowed through a weed-covered flower bed.

The station wagon slid to a stop and backed up in order to make a side street that would once again put them on their tail.

"I know that son of a bitch driving the wagon," Dartt said almost casually. "He looks like one of those guys on the Outland Strip."

Horn had to admit that the guy did look like one of the two men who had man-tracked them on the gambling resort.

For a moment it seemed that they had lost the station wagon that had been in hot pursuit.

"You can slow down now. This is a residential area," Dartt told Winger.

"It looks like one of those cities in Nevada they test nukes on," Winger said as he let the machine slow to a crawl.

"Well, it's nice to know that someone in L.A. loves us," Dartt said, replacing the spent rounds in his .44 with new cartridges. Horn also resupplied his weapon.

"Think this little scenario was courtesy of your buddy, Skinny Jack?" Winger asked, glancing at Dartt.

Dartt was silent as he considered this. "Maybe they picked us up at the motel."

Winger nodded. "Sounds plausible," he said.

Dartt was advising Winger about the best route to Burbank Studios when a roaring sound bellowed be-

hind them, and the station wagon cut out from behind two run-down houses, coming straight toward the
Chrysler.

"Shit!" Winger stomped on the gas pedal and ran
two wheels over the curb.

Horn watched the Mercury correct its trajectory and
swing toward them. It bounced wildly as it cleared the
curb and slid into the street, tires smoking. Then it
swung sideways into the Chrysler. The sound of
grinding metal echoed in the street as the two cars slid
to a stop. Horn ducked as several muzzle-flashes lit up
the inside of the station wagon.

"Get the hell out of here!" Dartt screamed over the
din of the gunfire.

"I can't!" Winger yelled, revving the engine and
jerking the shift lever into reverse. "We're stuck!"

Horn raised his 9 mm and fired blindly through the
side window, shattering the glass and filling the inside
of the car with gun smoke. Automatic-weapon fire
came from the other car. Horn felt the Chrysler rock
as the slugs tore into its side.

"Damn!" Dartt yelled in pain.

"You okay?" Horn asked, chancing a quick look.
Dartt was clutching his thigh.

"He's okay," Winger answered for him. "See if you
can use this." He tossed a concussion grenade into the
back.

Horn took the little death sphere and crawled out
onto the sidewalk. Near the trunk, he rose, tracked the
9 mm to the station wagon and fired five rounds. The

gunfire that had been coming from inside the vehicle halted. With a metal ripping lurch, the station wagon broke away from the Chrysler and burned down the street, fishtailing as the driver fought for control.

Pulling the pin of the grenade, Horn waited two seconds, then threw it after the speeding car, which was already half a block away. The vintage grenade struck the rear of the station wagon and exploded in a ball of flame and white smoke. The car spun wildly out of control, bounced over a curb and rammed into a garage.

"Let's go," Horn said, climbing back into the Chrysler.

They drove slowly by the garage, inspecting the wreckage of the station wagon. "Want to see if they're hurt?" Winger asked.

"You gotta be shitting me." Dartt laughed. "Those bastards were obviously trying to kill us, and you want to see if they're okay?"

"They could probably tell us who sent them," Winger said gruffly.

"That's right, pull over," Horn ordered.

"Damn," Dartt breathed.

Winger pulled next to the curb and shoved the shifting lever into park. He left the engine running.

"You stay here," Horn told Winger. "Les, is your leg okay?"

"Yeah, the sons of bitches just nicked me," Dartt answered, getting out of the car.

Horn walked to the garage and peered through the ragged hole in the siding around the rear of the station wagon. It was dark and dusty and quiet inside. Horn and Dartt walked around to the door. "Take it easy, Max," Dartt whispered. "They could be waiting in there."

"I wouldn't worry too much about it," Horn replied. "I got a feeling they're either dead or gone. More than likely they're gone." Cautiously he entered the building, crossed the trash-covered floor and jerked open the front door of the station wagon. He didn't bother explaining to Dartt that the IR sensor in his eye had picked up the heat from the vehicle's engine and nothing more. The front seat was smeared with blood and covered with shattered glass. Horn swung the 9 mm up and swept the back end of the car with the beam from the laser sight; he noticed several dozen spent cartridges, but that was it. "They're gone," he repeated, turning toward Dartt, who was crouched next to the side door, peering across a pothole-covered yard toward the house.

"Want to check it out?" Dartt asked, pointing the barrel of his magnum toward the abandoned dwelling whose sides were covered with graffiti. The back door of the house hung sideways from one hinge, and every window was broken.

"We could be here all day," Horn answered, stepping around Dartt. He looked down the row of houses that made up part of the inner city ghost town. The slum spread out around dead trees and asphalt streets offered seemingly endless places to hide or set up an ambush.

"Let's get over to the studios," Horn said. "These guys were obviously trying to keep us from getting there."

Dartt turned toward the front of the station wagon. "Hold it a second. I don't want the bastards following us." He aimed the .44 at the grill of the Mercury and fired twice.

As they left the garage, the radiator of the station wagon gurgled and hissed as its contents spilled.

"What the hell happened?" Winger asked excitedly as they got back in the car.

"Get going," Horn said, "Les just killed their car, that's all."

Winger dropped the Chrysler into gear and headed up the street. "Killed their car, huh?" he said. "So you found no one?"

"Right," Dartt answered, lighting a cigar. "Turn up here," he said, pointing toward a sign that read Hollywood Way. "Take a left and as soon as you cross Burbank Boulevard, take another left. The studios are going to be right there."

Horn was surprised at the run-down condition of Burbank. For the most part, the city appeared to be dead. There was hardly any traffic on the streets, and most of the shops and businesses had been boarded up and left to the weather and vandals. None of the traffic lights was working, and several abandoned cars lined the streets, their stripped-down hulks looking like the carcasses of dead animals.

"I thought this was supposed to be some shit-hot place for making movies and television shows," Winger said. "It looks like *New York,* for chrissakes." He laughed and slapped the steering wheel with one hand.

"Most of the movie studios moved to Florida," Dartt said, blowing a stream of smoke through a shattered window. "There's still a couple of television studios, but they're farther down, next to the Ventura Freeway. Like the song says, Hollywood is dead."

"No shit," Winger muttered, turning onto Burbank Boulevard. "Where to?"

"Pull into that lot over there." Dartt indicated a driveway that wound past a conglomeration of broken-down wooden buildings resembling some sort of Old West fort. A big sign hung over an archway that had been spray painted with the warning Keep Out. An odd symbol had been painted beside it.

"What the hell is that supposed to mean?" Winger asked, pointing.

"I think it's some sort of gang trademark," Dartt said, reloading the spent rounds in his .44. "I think it means Keep Out." He laughed heartily.

Winger pulled the Chrysler next to a rusting semitrailer loaded with huge spools of cables and wooden crates. "I don't know if this is Lot C," he said, looking around.

"Let's look around," Horn said. He got out and scanned the area, noticing that his right arm seemed automatically to follow the movement of his eye. The weather-beaten structures were covered with dead vines, making the abandoned studios look like a strange overgrown city in the middle of the jungle.

The sky was overcast, filled with several dark clouds, casting the place in a weird, prestorm light that made the abandoned buildings look even spookier. "What is it going to do, rain?" Winger said.

"The place looks dead," Dartt said.

"We're looking for some type of operation, probably similar to the place in the Village," Horn said. "Why don't we split up? Look for a power source or tanks or something. If you find anything, make sure the others are with you before you move in." He looked from Dartt to Winger. "Let's meet back here in thirty minutes."

"I don't like it," Winger said, pulling his machine pistol from his jacket. "Let's just torch the place and wait and see what runs out into the street."

"Just pretend you're in the Bronx," Horn said.

"Yeah, right." Winger started down an alley between two old buildings resembling old storefronts. Dartt rounded a corner and disappeared. Horn walked away from his partners, toward a large domelike structure whose curved top stuck up above the surrounding buildings like the back of a giant turtle. Horn figured he'd check it out since it looked a little more capable of withstanding the weather than the other structures.

Turning his collar up against the wind, Horn picked his way through a maze of walkways and narrow streets until he reached the dome. Stacks of lumber, vehicles, props and junk were scattered around the humpbacked building. Horn heard a low-frequency humming sound, which he assumed was from a generator. He thought about going back for Dartt and Winger, but figured it wouldn't hurt to have a closer look first.

The twin steel doors of the windowless dome were locked tight. He walked around the building and found an overhead garage door, but it too was shut. There didn't appear to be any other way in or out.

Horn returned to the front. Grabbing one of the door handles, he flexed his mod and pulled. The sound of metal ripping filled the lot as the door easily tore off its hinges. Horn pulled out his 9 mm and entered the darkened interior.

The humming sound was louder inside. Horn paused just over the threshold in order to orient himself with the layout of the building. He blinked his eye into its IR mode and scanned the shadows, his 9 mm tracking his sight like a faithful dog. A curving hallway ran around the perimeter of the building, and he followed it to the left. Compared to its exterior, the interior of the dome was immaculate. The tiled floors were highly polished, and a smell permeated the place that reminded Horn of a hospital.

A hissing sound drew Horn to a set of swinging doors, and he slipped through cautiously into a large room that was pitch-black. He scanned the area and caught movement across the gym-sized floor. Crouching behind a couple of cylindrical-shaped objects, he realized they were the same type of tank he had seen at that place in the Village. He cursed himself for not going back and picking up Dartt and Winger.

"Here we go!" someone suddenly shouted in the darkness, the words echoing off the domed ceiling.

Horn watched the green-tinted image of someone run between two rectangular-shaped tanks in the center of the room, and tracked the 9 mm toward the figure. Suddenly a bright flash erupted in front of his face and everything he'd been *seeing* with his right eye washed out like an overexposed photo. Blinking off the IR, he realized someone had turned on the overhead lights. The sound of laughter caused him to turn, and he saw Skinny Jack on a walkway circling the room, ten feet above the floor.

Horn stepped from behind the containers of gas and brought his 9 mm up just as a muffled sort of shot rang out directly behind him. He swung around as a man wielding a small rifle disappeared through the swinging doors. Horn was conscious of a stinging sensation spreading out from the center of his back. He reached around with his free hand and felt something stuck through his jacket.

"Damn!" He gasped in pain as he jerked the object from his back and brought it around to his face. It was a feather-tipped tranquilizer dart, its hollow needle tip dripping a mixture of blood and some clear liquid.

Horn felt a numbing sensation sweep over his body and turned back toward Skinny Jack, who was laughing. He felt himself fall to his knees and realized the 9 mm had slipped from his fingers. He tried to will his mods to move, but got no response. He stared down at the automatic and wondered if the stuff he'd been hit with was poison.

"Feeling a little under the weather?"

Horn looked at the person who had spoken. He was surprised to see a woman standing only a few feet away. She was wearing a gray skintight jumpsuit that was unbuttoned to the middle of her chest, revealing the valley between her large breasts. Her long black hair was pulled back away from her face. Her dark brown eyes were outlined in blue mascara and highlighted with a glittering material that fanned out from the corners, making her look catlike in a whorish sort of way.

"Who the hell are you?" Horn slurred, wondering why he hadn't fallen on his face.

She laughed and turned her head. "You ready to go for a little ride, sweetheart?" she asked, reaching out and touching his hair. Horn saw the overhead garage door open across the room and watched a dirty green van back into the dome.

"Leave the poor bastard alone," Skinny Jack said, approaching.

"You," Horn managed to say, feeling an almost overpowering drowsiness.

"I know, I know," Jack said, holding his hands up, revealing a Glock automatic stuck in his waistband. "I set you up, right?"

Horn nodded, figuring it was futile to try to speak. He watched the van back up between the tanks and stop behind Skinny Jack.

"We're going to take you to a little place just up the street," Jack said, opening the van. "There's a guy there interested in knowing why you're interested in him."

A big guy in a jumpsuit similar to the woman's came around the van and grabbed Horn's arm. The man dragged him to the back of the van. Horn was conscious of the woman stepping over him and taking a seat on a bench that ran along one side.

"Don't worry," said Skinny Jack from somewhere. "Crazy Janice is going to keep you company."

Jack laughed madly as the doors closed and the van lurched forward. With great effort, Horn looked up and saw the woman's face hovering over his, framed strangely as he became enveloped in tunnel vision. Horn could swear that she was leaning down to kiss him as everything went to black.

CHAPTER TEN

HORN OPENED his eyes expecting to see the painted face of Crazy Janice. Instead, he saw a crisscrossed pattern of steel roof supports a hundred feet over his head. A ragged banner that read Zero Fod was hanging from one of the beams. Horn tried to rise, but his body felt numb. There was some sort of canvas strap stretched across his chest.

"How are you feeling, Mr. Horn, or should I say *Detective* Horn?"

A gray-haired man with a rugged, square-jawed face was thumbing through a folder. "You must be Latch," Horn said, mildly surprised that his words didn't come out slurred and incomprehensible.

"That's right," the man answered, tossing the ID folder to the floor. "Jack Latch. I guess I should be flattered that you followed me here from New York."

Horn willed his mod to move but got no response. Looking down at his arm, he discovered that his shirtsleeve had been ripped open nearly to his shoulder, exposing the titanium-covered mod, which lay beside his body like a dead fish.

"Don't worry," Latch said, moving around the table and tapping his knuckles on the mod, "it's not out of commission. At least, not like you might think it is. I gave you a mild spinal block. Everything below your neck is taking a little nap. Who did this for you?" Latch shifted his eyes to the mod, then back to Horn's face. "Whoever it was did a hell of a job."

"Where am I?"

"You're at the fabulous Burbank Airport," Latch answered, waving a hand. "More precisely, you're in one of the hangars that used to be the home of Lockheed Aerospace, but they're long gone and soon you will be, too."

"Why didn't you kill me?"

"Your brain, Detective Horn. I thought I might have use for it. Excuse me a moment," he said, turning. "Get the goddamn freezers on the plane, we've got a flight plan out of here in forty-five minutes."

Horn craned his neck and could see an old, beat-to-hell Citation II jet sitting near the huge doors of the hangar. The van was parked next to the aircraft, and Crazy Janice and the guy who had helped her load him at the studios were unloading what looked like ice chests from the back of it. They both looked over in Latch's direction. Janice waved and started to walk toward them, but Latch held up his hands.

"No! Just load the airplane." Latch turned toward Horn. "This woman's nuts. She probably thinks I'm ready to hand you over to her."

"What do you mean?" Horn asked as the woman turned back.

"I mean," Latch said, waving at someone out of Horn's field of vision, "that she made me promise to let her kill you." Latch shrugged as though he were discussing a rather boring political situation. "Since we rejected you as a donor, I saw no harm in it. She's like a spider, you know. Wants to breed first."

Latch leaned his head back and laughed, the sound echoing strangely in the cavernous hangar. Horn detected someone else's laughter and managed to twist his head enough to see a short, long-haired man wearing mirrored sunglasses approach the table. The man, bent over, slightly reminded him of a fairy-tale troll.

"Toad," Latch said. "I was just admiring Detective Horn's body modification. Ever see one like this?"

Toad ran his stubby fingers over the mod. Horn tried to flex the arm and was surprised when it did flinch slightly.

"Goddamn!" Toad screeched, and jumped backward several steps. He pulled a long-barreled revolver from beneath his leather coat and aimed it at Horn's head.

"Hold it!" Latch laid a hand on Toad's arm, forcing the gun barrel down. "Take it easy. I'm sure that was a random spike in his electrical system. Anyway—" he turned back to Horn "—I gave him enough of a local to knock out a goddamn rhino."

"Why did you reject me as a donor?" Horn asked, wanting to keep Latch's mind off the subject of his mod. He thought he *felt* some sort of sensation returning to his lower body and figured he'd better reserve whatever strength he had for whatever Crazy Janice might have in store.

"Your mods," Latch answered, waving a hand over Horn's arm, then pointing to his right eye. "I figured they probably biased your primary motor signals. Anyway, I decided that it would be too much trouble gathering another system. Toad here got us more than enough systems to satisfy Dr. Ticket."

"Ticket?" Horn figured he may as well glean as much information from Latch as he could, especially since the man seemed in a talkative mood. "You mean Julius Ticket?"

Latch seemed surprised. "You've heard of him?"

"Let's just say that the guy who did this—" Horn nodded toward his E-mod "—and your Ticket person float in the same circles."

"Of course," Latch responded. "Well, this is nothing compared to what Dr. Ticket has accomplished." He slapped the titanium forearm. "We've got a process now that utilizes a droid shell, a totally nuke-powered electromechanical *being,* with the brain and spinal cord from a living human that functions as its master processor unit."

"I assume one of your droids was responsible for the Senator Merrifield—"

"Massacre," Toad finished Horn's sentence.

Latch scowled at Toad.

"Hell, it was in the *Times* out here," Toad replied, his voice hoarse to the point that it sort of wheezed from his throat, "and it *was* a goddamn massacre."

"It wasn't exactly what a military mind would call a surgical strike," Latch said, not seeming to mind confiding in a man who would soon be dead. "Give us another couple of weeks, and you'll read about a squad of Ticket's Neuroids taking out the United Nations General Assembly. It'll make the Merrifield thing look like a tea dance." Latch looked at his watch, then toward the jet. "But I just realized," he said, looking down at Horn. "You'll be dead."

"Yeah, right," Toad chimed in, suddenly swinging the side of his pistol down across Horn's cheek.

"You bastard!" Latch yelled, pushing Toad away. "Why the hell did you do that?"

"The son of a bitch scared me," Toad answered. "You're going to let that crazy broad kill him, anyway, so what's the difference?"

Horn felt the pain from the blow run down his spine and cause his mods to glitch mildly. He hoped Latch or Toad didn't notice and counted it as a good sign. He felt a prickling sensation in his lower body and he figured the anesthetic was beginning to wear off. In spite of the pain, Horn stifled a laugh. It was pretty damn funny that Toad was referring to Janice as the "crazy broad" when both he and Latch had to be prime candidates for a set of straitjackets.

"Where the hell is Skinny Jack?" Latch asked, looking around as Toad stuffed the revolver back into its holster beneath his jacket.

"Over there." Toad nodded. "Counting the blue slip you gave him."

"Ask him to come here," Latch said. "The stupid bastard should have split when he had the chance."

Toad disappeared and Latch looked down at Horn. "You should enjoy this," he said, smiling. "The guy turned you and your two friends over in a heartbeat. Toad calls him 'Mr. Flapjack.' Unfortunately I can't risk having the little puke putting some other bastard on my trail. So—" he shrugged and held his hands palms up "—I gotta do what I gotta do."

"Here you are, Mr. Latch," Toad wheezed. Latch turned and faced Skinny Jack, who was holding a black leather briefcase.

Horn watched as Toad slipped behind the man. He knew Latch was getting ready to kill Skinny Jack, but he felt no remorse or anxiety about it. What Latch had said was true. The shrunk-down man had turned them over without blinking. Horn tried to find something, a *feeling* that said he was against what was about to come down, but all he got was a voice saying that the man knew what he was doing and now had to pay the price. *Street law* was what Winger called it: unwritten, self-enforcing and brutal as hell.

"It's all here, Mr. Latch," Skinny Jack said, patting the side of the briefcase.

Horn watched Toad pull a coiled wire with a metal ring at either end from his coat pocket and stretch it between his hands.

"It's too bad you're not going to be able to enjoy it," Latch said, nodding at Toad.

Skinny Jack spun around, but too late. Toad jumped onto his back and wrapped the wire around his neck, then jerked hard, as though reining in a wild horse. Skinny Jack's eyes bulged, and his tongue stuck out as Toad applied more pressure.

"Ease off," Latch ordered, pulling the silenced Smith & Wesson from his bush jacket.

Looking disappointed, Toad relented. Skinny Jack fell to his knees. Grabbing the briefcase, Toad backed away as Skinny Jack gagged and clasped his neck with both hands.

"Jack, Jack, Jack." Latch shook his head and aimed his weapon at Skinny Jack's forehead. "I sort of hate to have to do this, but I sure wouldn't want you hanging around waiting to tell someone about what Toad and I have been up to."

"I won't tell no one about you, honest to shit," Skinny Jack gasped.

Latch laughed. "I'm certain you're right," he said. "You probably made the same promise to Detective Horn and his pals." He casually patted Horn on the right knee. "What the hell?" Latch turned around and rapped on Horn's modified knee, then felt above and below the titanium covering as if measuring it.

"Why, you bastard," he said, looking up at Horn's face. "What others parts of you are mods?"

"That's it," Horn answered.

"Hey!" Toad yelled. "Want me to stop him?"

Skinny Jack was scurrying across the floor with Toad giving chase.

"Get away from him," Latch barked, aiming the automatic. He fired twice and Skinny Jack pitched headfirst onto the concrete floor. Blood poured from two holes in his thighs.

"Damn," Latch said, walking toward the prone figure. "See what you made me do?" He stood over Skinny Jack's body and aimed the weapon at the back of his head. "So long, chump." Horn heard the muffled report of the weapon and watched Skinny Jack's body twitch wildly before growing still.

Latch holstered the automatic and motioned for Toad to head for the plane. "He's all yours," Latch told Crazy Janice, jerking his thumb toward Horn. "Open the goddamn doors!" he yelled, then began talking with a man who had come down the short steps of the Citation holding a clipboard.

Janice wore a crazy smile as she approached. Horn was somewhat surprised when she bent over the table and kissed him full on the mouth, running her tongue down his throat to the point that he nearly gagged. A mixture of fear and a strange sort of eroticism crawled into the pit of Horn's stomach as Crazy Janice ran a hand down his chest and grabbed his crotch. She gripped him firmly and kissed him again, sucking on his lower lip so hard that it hurt.

"I'm not going to do you much good," Horn said when she finally broke her kiss. "At least not down there."

"Why not?"

"Your boss shot me up with a spinal blocker. I can't feel a damn thing you're doing," Horn lied. He could feel himself starting to respond to her touch.

"Well," she said, a throaty laugh hanging behind her words like a curtain, "he didn't shoot up your face, did he?"

Horn watched Latch climb into the jet as the man he'd been talking to opened the hangar door. Toad handed Latch the briefcase before mounting the steps and pulling up the Citation's crew door.

Shifting his gaze back to Crazy Janice, Horn watched her unzip the top of her jumpsuit and peel it down from around her shoulders, revealing her breasts. Flexing his mod slightly, he figured he had control of about half its capability.

"Don't move, and nobody gets hurt!"

Janice froze, looking toward the sound. Horn had recognized Winger's voice and hoped his partner wasn't too late to stop Latch. The whining of the Citation's turbines filled the hangar as the little jet prepared to taxi.

"Damn," Janice swore. She reached beneath the table and pulled out an old M-20 military-style automatic and sprayed bullets at a catwalk above the hangar floor.

Horn jerked his arm up as hard as he could and heard the canvas strap snap free of the table. He turned toward Janice just in time to see a small hole appear above her left breast. An explosion of blood and flesh from her back blew out across the concrete floor. Gasping as though she'd been immersed in ice water, she fell backward, the M-20 flying from her hands and clattering across the floor.

Horn rolled off the table as the man at the far end of the hangar opened up with some sort of automatic weapon. He made a dive toward the M-20, but landed facedown on the concrete, his legs and arms feeling like soft rubber. Turning, he watched the Citation taxi out of the hangar. The man with the weapon fired toward the catwalk.

"Horn!" Winger yelled from the rafters. "Can you give us some help?"

Feeling like a fish out of water, Horn crawled toward the weapon and had to maneuver around Crazy Janice's spread-eagled body in order to reach it. He picked it up and swung the muzzle toward the man who had been firing at the catwalk. Seeing him, the lone gunman turned. Horn watched flashes erupt from the weapon. Pieces of concrete flew up in front of his face as a stream of bullets stitched a line less than ten feet away.

Horn forced himself to aim the M-20 at the man, who had dropped to one knee and was in the process of changing clips. It seemed as if it took all his strength to squeeze the trigger, and when he did, the weapon kicked back and slammed into his cheek. He watched one of the man's legs go out from under him and heard him curse loudly. Horn tried to draw a bead on him again, but couldn't seem to get his finger through the trigger guard.

"You're dead meat," the man yelled, struggling to his feet. He staggered out from behind the van and aimed the rifle in Horn's direction.

A volley of gunfire erupted as the man cleared the back of the van, and Horn watched him do a strange death dance. The rifle flew out of his hands, and he stutter-stepped forward ten yards or so before falling on his face.

Horn managed to bring himself to his knees and looked out of the hangar as the Citation did its take-off rotation and disappeared into a low bank of clouds. "Damn," he muttered, standing the M-20 on its barrel and using it to pull himself shakily to his feet.

"You okay, partner?" Winger asked, walking across the blood-splattered floor.

"Where's Dartt?" Horn asked, wondering if his legs were going to give out.

"Take it easy," Winger said, moving up next to him and grabbing him under one arm. "Did you get hit?"

"Just in the face," Horn answered, feeling steadier. "On the cheek."

"Here?" Winger touched the welt that Toad's pistol had left and that had been enhanced by the recoil of the M-20. "Shit, that's nothing," Winger chuckled, relieved. "I meant, have you been *shot?* And now that I know you haven't, what the hell is wrong with you?"

"I was shot with a needle," Horn answered, seeing Dartt walk through the hangar and nudge the dead man on the floor with his toe.

"Drugs?" Winger asked as Dartt joined them.

Horn nodded. "We'd better get back to New York," he said, tossing the M-20 to the floor. He flexed his arms and shook his legs one at a time. "It probably won't do a hell of a lot of good, but you can call the precinct and have them put out an alert on the airplane."

"It had a piece of tape or something across its tail number," Dartt said, holstering his Magnum.

"Yeah, and it'll probably go into Newark or some little Podunk airport we've never heard of," Winger said. He turned and spit on the floor.

"Call it in just the same," Horn said. "What did you guys do, follow us here?"

"Sort of."

"What do you mean?"

"He means," Dartt said, reaching inside his jacket, "we damn near lost you because your partner insisted we wait until you and your little party cleared the dome so we could recover this." He held out Horn's 9 mm by the barrel.

"Damn, thanks." Horn took the weapon and inspected it to see if the chamber was charged; it was.

"Where's the car?" he asked, sliding the weapon into its holster.

"This way," Dartt said, turning and heading toward the back of the hangar.

"I don't really know how long I was out," Horn commented.

"Not that long," Winger said. "Do you realize you're the only one of us who's gotten any sleep on this trip?"

Horn chuckled, but his mind was already engaged in what Latch had said about the United Nations and what Christina Service had told him about the Libyan, Kindu, planning another demonstration of his alleged power.

They stepped through a rusting door that led out of the hangar. Horn wondered what the hell had happened to his jacket. He licked his lips and tasted Crazy Janice's lipstick. He couldn't tell if it was that or the cold wind that was making his skin chill.

CHAPTER ELEVEN

"WHAT'S HE DOING HERE?" Latch nodded toward the droid that stood in a military stance by the door.

"Number 24?" Ticket asked. "Number 24 is all right," he said, taking a long drag on a cigarette. "He's like my personal bodyguard, a manservant at arms, so to speak. Aren't you, Number 24?" Ticket looked at the droid and smiled. "He'd kill for me."

Latch glanced at the droid and grunted. "That one gives me the creeps," he said, taking a seat in front of Ticket's desk. "Does it respond?"

Ticket laughed. "Oh, yes, *he* responds all right. I have to be very precise when I give him an order. He takes things quite literally."

Latch glanced at the droid once again and felt a chill run up his spine. He wasn't kidding when he told Ticket the Neuroid gave him the creeps. "We did pretty well, even with the shortened schedule," he told Ticket, picking up his glass of vodka from the desk.

"How many did you end up with?" Ticket asked, leaning back in his chair.

"Eighteen," Latch answered before taking a sip of the liquor. "I prioritized them using the physical and psychological profiles you devised. If you get a good enough yield, there shouldn't be any problems.''

"I'll get a good yield," Ticket responded. "I developed a new technique when I was bringing up Number 24. I should get a one-hundred percent yield."

Latch glanced at Number 24 again and wondered what it was about the droid that made it look a little odd and dull-witted. The expression on its face reminded Latch of a boy he'd grown up with. The kid had eventually been committed to a mental hospital after his parents had found out he'd tortured and killed neighborhood dogs and cats. Number 24 reminded him a lot of that kid.

"Having second thoughts about getting plugged into a shell?" Ticket asked, breaking Latch out of his contemplations.

"No, not at all," he answered.

"You seem a little spooked," Ticket commented. He picked up a tall glass of Scotch from the desk and downed half of it in one long swallow. "Damn, that hits the spot. Here's to you, Jack," he said, raising the glass, "for a job well done." He downed the rest of the booze and set the glass on the table.

Latch took another sip of the vodka and enjoyed the warmth it created as it rolled down his throat and hit his stomach. Maybe he *was* getting second thoughts about becoming a Neuroid, especially if he wound up like Number 24. Latch shook the thought from his mind.

"I noticed you brought someone with you," Ticket said. "Some short, long-haired man."

"Toad. Things got a little hot just as we were leaving L.A. and he ended up on the charter. I'll bring him up here soon for you to meet him."

"I got another call from Toftoy while you were gone," Ticket said, stomping out his cigarette and lighting another. "The bastard Kindu wants all nine of his droids operational by the twenty-eighth."

Latch decided he wouldn't tell Ticket they'd already had this conversation. Instead, he asked, "Can you do it?"

"Of course. I may need you to assist, though. That bastard Dineen ran out on us."

"He did?" Latch was shocked. He knew what Ticket had been paying him and also knew that Dineen needed every bit of it to support a gambling habit that was eating him alive.

Ticket shrugged. "You've still got the touch, don't you, Jack?"

"I guess so," Latch answered, looking down at his hands.

Ticket laughed. "Don't worry about it. I probably won't need you. I called Larry Hayes, and he agreed to give me a hand."

"That screwup? He took more drugs than he ever administered to his patients."

"Don't worry," Ticket chuckled, "I'll just pump him up with metaphene 12 and he'll do all right."

"Listen," Latch said, moving up to the edge of his chair. "It may be a good idea to move this little operation once Kindu takes delivery of his droids. As a matter of fact, it's probably not a good idea to be here right now."

Ticket looked puzzled.

"Like I said," Latch continued, "things got a little hot in L.A. Apparently we've got a New York City cop on our ass."

"In L.A.?" Ticket drew his head back in surprise. "What the hell was a New York cop doing out there?"

"Apparently the bastard followed us there," Latch said. "He had two guys with him. We may have killed him, but there was a shit-load of gunfire just as we were leaving. I've got Toad checking on it now to find out what happened."

"Killed *him* . . . who the hell is *him?*" Ticket shook his head. "I don't know what the hell you're telling me. You want to slow down and explain it so I can understand it?"

"Sorry," Latch said, holding up a hand. "We managed to nail one of the cops, a guy named Horn." Latch leaned back in his chair. "This cop was *different,* Julius. He had a modified arm, from the shoulder down, and it was enhanced. A good job, too."

Ticket raised his eyebrows. "Incredible," he said.

"One of his eyes was also modified, but I don't know to what extent." Latch remembered Horn's knee, but didn't bother mentioning it.

"Go on," Ticket said, making a brushing motion with one hand.

"We left the cop with one of Toad's operatives. He should have been dead, but like I said, there was a lot of gunfire as we were leaving."

"What happened to the two guys with the cop?"

"I don't know." Latch walked around the desk. "May I?" he asked, pointing to the built-in telemonitor.

"Go ahead." Ticket nodded, and slid out of the way.

Latch punched up the main guard station. "Where's Toad?" he asked the uniformed man whose face filled the screen.

"Toad?" The guard looked confused.

"I mean Mr. Hipp," Latch corrected. "Where is he?"

The guard looked down for a couple of seconds. "He's in the guest house, sir. Want me to patch you through?"

Latch nodded and the screen blinked up the image of Toad, who had his back to the monitor and was in the process of changing shirts. Latch was a little taken back by the man's skin, which rolled in folds down his bulb-shaped body and was the color of milky oil.

"Toad."

Toad jumped around, obviously surprised. "Damn, Jack. You have to do that without warning?"

"Sorry," Latch said as Toad pulled a sweater over his head. "Did you manage to find out the status of the cop and his two friends?"

Toad's expression turned sour. He picked up his sunglasses from a dresser and put them on. "Yeah, I got a report, but it's not good news."

Latch glanced at Ticket, whose face was drawn and expressionless. "Come up to Dr. Ticket's office," he said. "You can tell both of us." He punched off the monitor and walked back around the desk.

"It sounds like we've got a problem," Ticket said calmly.

Latch grimaced. He didn't feel good about the whole scenario: Kindu, Toftoy, using the droids to mount a terrorist attack on an international peacemaking organization—and the cop, an unexpected wild card in a game that was being played much too fast. And now, after seeing Ticket's latest handiwork in the form of Number 24, Latch wondered whether he wanted his brain and spinal cord plugged into one of the droid shells. What's to keep Ticket from inserting one of his controlling implants into his brain while he was under? Latch figured he might be better off taking his payment in gold and letting the cancer take its course while he lived it up in Zurich or down in the islands. He was confused and depressed.

A knock on the door announced Toad. He walked in, combing his stringy hair back with his fingers. Latch introduced him to Dr. Ticket, and Toad made a sort of bow before sitting. "I've heard a lot about you and feel really honored to finally get to meet you," he said.

Ticket smiled and nodded at this visitor who was acting like he was with the Pope instead of talking with one of the world's most infamous mod doctors. He poured Toad a drink to set him at ease, and another for Latch and himself.

In his wheezing voice, Toad described the scene as they had been leaving the Burbank Airport. "The cop's two partners showed up just as we were leaving. Crazy Janice and that idiot, Noonen, both bought it. The cop and his two buddies are back in New York. I've heard—I just talked to Mick Jones, your old buddy in Greenwich Village, and he knows about this Horn cop. Apparently one of the guys with him is his partner. The other guy, I don't know. He's some sort of free-lance bounty hunter."

"Jones *knows* about the cop?" Latch asked.

"Well, apparently the dude has a pretty bad rep," Toad said, taking another slug of his whiskey. "He's got an RCMP reputation."

"What does that stand for?" Ticket asked.

"Sorry." Toad chuckled. "That stands for the Royal Canadian Mounted Police. You know, they always get their man."

"It sounds like this Horn and his friends could really screw things up, doesn't it, Jack?"

"I can get Jones and a couple of his best hitters to take them out before they get to be a problem," Latch suggested. He regretted that he hadn't killed Horn when he'd had the chance. It would have been so easy.

"I doubt it," Toad said, surprising Latch. "From what Jones tells me, this cop and his partner are like a recurring case of very bad news. They're no easy marks, and now Jones—"

"Shut up," Latch snapped. He turned and glared at Toad, who sunk back in his chair. He couldn't wait to get the little man out of Ticket's sight.

"Take it easy, Jack," Ticket said calmly, holding up his hands in a restraining gesture. "I may have a more interesting solution to your problem."

"Yeah, what is it?" Latch asked, noticing that Ticket referred to the problem as being his.

"You two are probably the best—" Ticket appeared to be searching for the proper word "—body snatchers in the country."

"Body snatchers?" Toad broke out in his wheezing laughter.

"Gatherers." Ticket waved a hand. "You know. Anyway, I've got an idea that at the very least will slow down your cop enough that our business with Kindu can be accomplished without any interference. Let's go downstairs and I'll show you what I have in mind." He stood and walked toward the door.

Toad started toward the door but froze when he saw Number 24. "Holy shit!" he gasped, backing up several steps and bumping into Latch. "I forgot he was there."

Ticket laughed, and walked up to the big droid, slapping it on the shoulder. "This is the end product of what you've been involved with."

Toad walked cautiously toward the droid. He started to touch it but hesitated. "May I?" he asked, looking at Ticket.

"Go ahead. He won't bite."

"Damn," Toad said, running a hand up the droid's arm.

"Let's go," Latch said, opening the door. He wasn't surprised that Toad was taken with the droid. In a lot of ways they were alike: amoral and without conscience.

"Come on," Ticket urged Toad. "I'll give you a demo later if you like."

Ticket led them through a maze of cipher-locked doors.

"Where we going?" asked Latch.

"The storage area," Ticket replied.

Toad followed obediently. Finally they reached a large vaultlike door at the end of a long hall in the basement. Ticket positioned himself so Latch and Toad couldn't see the code he punched into the electronic lock. Seconds later he pulled the heavy door open and motioned his companions to enter.

Latch flipped on the light switch. One wall of the low-ceilinged room was lined with ten droid shells, standing erect and covered with sheets of clear plastic.

"Jesus," Toad breathed as he stared down the row of droid bodies. "This looks like a vertical morgue."

Ticket turned toward Latch. "One of those is yours, Jack. They all look the same, but you can pick one now if you like."

"I think I'll wait," he answered, suddenly aware of someone behind them. He turned and felt his skin jump as Number 24's form filled the doorway. "Goddammit," he snapped, turning toward Ticket. "Does that son of a bitch follow you around?"

"That's right," Ticket answered, walking to a far corner of the room. "Just like a dog." He waved for Latch and Toad to follow.

The area contained stacks of crates and boxes of electric motors, hydraulic actuators and other by-products of Ticket's droid factory. Cylindrical bottles of various gases were situated in one corner, and various machine tools had been stacked helter-skelter against the wall opposite the droid shells.

"Here's what I wanted to show you," Ticket said, grabbing the corner of a large piece of canvas covering an odd-shaped mass. "You've never seen this, either, Jack," he said flipping the canvas off and revealing a hideous droid that was more machine than man.

"Damn," Toad gasped as though he were viewing a breathtaking piece of art. "I like it." He moved toward the thing, which was in a sitting position against the wall. "What is it?"

"One of my earlier experiments," Ticket answered, smiling as though he were talking about one of his children. "I like to call him Number 1 since he was really the first machine I ever designed specifically to kill."

Looking at the droid, Latch could see why Ticket had kept it under wraps. It was ugly. The right half of its face was a normal, human shape with synthetic skin and a synthetic eye that resembled a male in his mid-thirties. The left half, however, was a metallic grid of plates and machined screws. Instead of an eye, a short camera lens protruded from the round metal socket. The portion of the mouth that extended across the machine side of the droid's face consisted of a weird half set of stainless-steel teeth that made Number 1 appear to be constantly grinning. The plating covering the left side of the face extended up and over the skull, while the right half of the droid's head was covered with a reddish sort of hair that looked more like animal fur than something human.

"What's that?" Toad asked, pointing to the droid's left arm, which consisted of a set of metallic rods and exposed actuators that ended in an ugly set of pincers where the hand should have been.

"That's hardened steel," Ticket said. "I got it off one of those robot submarines they use to rescue trapped divers."

"I like it," Toad answered, nodding. "You must've used a weight lifter as a model for the human parts," he said, gesturing at the droid's powerful legs.

"Something like that," Ticket said, turning toward Latch. "What do you think?"

"What am I supposed to think?" Latch responded, holding his hands out, palms up, and shrugging.

"Like I was about to say upstairs," Ticket said excitedly. "You two snatch Horn's partner."

"Then what?"

"Then we mod the bastard's neural system into old Number 1 here, and we send him after Horn."

"Shit," Toad said, turning toward Latch. "That ain't a bad idea."

Latch held up a hand. "Let me think about this." He looked at Ticket, who was smiling, his watery eyes glinting like gemstones. "You want us to gather the cop's partner and you'll mod his neural system into...this?" He gestured toward Number 1.

"Exactly," Ticket answered. "I guarantee it will keep the cop off our backs long enough to finish the deal with Kindu."

Latch rubbed his chin and looked down at the strange-looking droid. He had to admit it was a better idea than any he could muster, given the circumstances.

CHAPTER TWELVE

HEARING A KNOCK, Winger opened the door and let Dartt into his apartment. Dartt walked in and saw Horn sitting on a worn couch in the living room.

Horn greeted Dartt and asked, "Have trouble finding the place?"

"No problem," he answered, walking to a folding chair beside a card table covered with gun-cleaning equipment and empty beer bottles. Winger's machine pistol lay in pieces on top of some newspapers, the handle of a cleaning brush sticking out of its short barrel. Dartt turned the chair toward Horn and was about to sit when Winger stopped him. "Not there," the young cop said. "I'm cleaning my hardware."

Dartt moved to an overstuffed armchair next to the couch.

Winger took three bottles of beer from an old refrigerator and handed one to Dartt, another to Horn and kept the third. Screwing off the cap, he tilted it back. "Good stuff," he said, wiping his mouth with the back of his hand.

Dartt took a long drink, the malty beer tasting good as it rolled down his throat.

"Yeah, partner, thanks." Horn set the bottle on a coffee table. "Any luck with your friends down in the Village?" he asked Dartt.

"Not really," he answered. "I'm supposed to meet a guy at the Golden Bull late tonight."

Winger took a seat in the folding chair and rested his arms over its metal back. "I hope Cota doesn't remember you." The young cop laughed and took another swig.

"Maybe you should go with him," Horn said.

"Yeah, right," Winger answered. "That bastard remembers my face as much as he remembers yours. Anyway, August wants us to stop by his crib later."

"When did he call?" Horn asked, picking up the bottle of beer and unscrewing its cap. He took a long swallow.

"This afternoon," Winger answered. "Said he'd been trying to get in touch with you but wasn't having much luck."

"I'm not surprised," Horn said. "I spent all afternoon giving the captain a detailed rundown on our little excursion to the West Coast."

"What did he say?" Winger asked eagerly.

"He said that my partner's lack of professionalism was starting to give me a bad name." Horn looked straight at the young cop, his face deadpan.

Winger's jaw dropped slightly, and he stared at Horn dumbfoundedly. "You shit," he finally said, realizing that Horn was jerking his chain.

Dartt laughed and leaned back. He enjoyed the two cops' company and felt at ease in their presence.

"Actually—" Horn grinned and picked up his beer "—I was told to try to locate this Ticket character. After what the droid did to Senator Merrifield's party, they're worried about what might happen at the United Nations."

"Why don't they just shut the place down for a while?" Winger asked.

"Hell, the UN gets two or three terrorist threats a month," Horn answered. "The State Department wants to play it by ear."

"I'm kind of surprised they're letting you stay on the case," Dartt said. "I'd think they'd put the FBI or somebody like that on it."

"They're involved," Horn said, shrugging slightly, "but the DA's office is insisting they keep their hands in it. That's mainly why we're still working the case."

"The Barracuda strikes again," Winger sighed.

Horn looked at his partner. "Yeah, I'm supposed to give her a rundown on what we've come up with so far." He glanced at his watch. "As a matter of fact, I've got to get out of here. You're going to have to venture into the Bronx on your own."

"Huh?"

"You're supposed to go see August, right?"

"Shit, that's right." Winger looked at his watch and rose. "I wish one of you guys would go with me," he said, looking back and forth between Dartt and Horn. "August says he's got some sort of *weapon* he's put together in case we come up against one of the droids."

"Like I said—" Horn grinned "—I've got to meet Service."

Dartt noticed Winger's expression had grown into a mixture of anxiety and melancholy. "I've got to meet this joker at the Golden Bull. If you can guarantee we won't get delayed there, I'll go with you."

"No." Winger held up his hands. "That's okay, I'll go by myself. You guys will be without a car, though."

"I'll take a cab," Horn said, obviously enjoying the young cop's discomfort over having to make a solo trek into the Bronx.

"And I'm driving a Rent-A-Wreck," Dartt said, "so that's no problem."

"No problem," Winger mumbled. He bent over and began assembling the machine pistol.

"Use the same route as last time," Horn said. "Tell August I'll see him in a week or so."

"Sure."

Horn looked at Dartt. "Don't take any chances, right?"

"I can't afford to," Dartt answered, chuckling. "You guys haven't paid me this month."

"Don't let the door hit you in the ass," Winger said as he walked to a peg next to the refrigerator and took down the webgear that supported the arsenal he normally carried. He hung it over his shoulder, then strapped it across his chest before picking up the machine pistol and jamming a clip into its composite handle.

"Later," Horn said as he shut the door behind him.

"Listen," Winger said, pulling on a faded field jacket. "You can hang out here until you're ready to head down to the Village."

"Thanks," Dartt said, figuring he would take Winger up on his offer. He had a good four hours to kill before he was due at the Golden Bull.

"There's food in the refrigerator, help yourself," Winger said. He pulled on a pair of Gore-Tex street boots before sticking a flat-handled throwing knife into a scabbard that had been sewn on the inside of the left boot. Rolling his pants down over the top of the boot, he patted the slight bulge. "There," he said, smiling at Dartt, "my mama always told me to take good care of my feet. Don't forget to lock the door." Winger waved to Dartt as he walked out of the apartment.

Dartt got up and went to the kitchen area. He was pretty pleased with the way things had been going lately. Horn and Winger had become more than just a source of income for him; he considered them friends and trusted their judgment. They were also honest, which was a virtue Dartt had been little exposed to during his life. He took a fresh beer from the refrigerator and took a long swallow. Setting the bottle on the counter, he stared at his ruddy face in a cracked mirror that hung over the sink.

Dartt's life had been a series of ups and downs, but mostly downs. He'd worked as a roughneck on a geothermal crew in Oklahoma for ten years after dropping out of high school. His wife had left him for the crew boss, who in turn fired him, saying he couldn't be trusted. Dartt had gone to Reno and lived with a drug-addicted brother for several years, working as a dive bouncer and collection artist for the loan sharks who fed on the gambling addicts.

Working collections required Dartt to use his muscle and attain some measure of finesse with a handgun. It also demanded that he develop skill at tracking down those who tried to disappear. He found out he was good at man-tracking and developed his own sort of underground consulting service: advertising by word of mouth to a clientele that preferred to keep their profiles low. While the pay was good, the job had a down side, as Dartt found himself increasingly drawn into the low end of life. He'd been offered death contracts on several occasions and had always refused. One of his customers had kidded him, razzing him with the old cliché, *How can you be in it, but not of it?* Dartt took the question to heart and had begun to wonder how long it would be before he started taking lives for money. The more he thought about it, the more he'd become withdrawn.

It was Dartt's other claim to competence, his ability to *drive the hell out of anything that rolls or flies,* as he liked to put it, that eventually gave him a way out. It was his driving skill that had gotten him hooked up with the two cops on the Outland Strip—pure coincidence, but Dartt wasn't about to look a gift horse in the mouth.

Horn and Winger had sort of taken him under their wing and had gotten him work in New York, for which Dartt was grateful. He knew he was going nowhere and had jumped at their offer to follow them to the city. In spite of the long, irregular hours and continual dangers, Dartt found that he was getting a rough version of a *new start*. He'd even considered asking Horn about the possibilities of joining the NYPD.

"You, a cop?" Dartt laughed at himself in the mirror and smiled, noticing the exaggerated crow's-feet that spread out from the corners of his eyes. He shook his head and opened the refrigerator again, rummaging around, finally pulling out a plastic dish covered with foil. He peeled it back, revealing what looked like lasagna.

Dartt stuck the dish into an old microwave and set the timer for two minutes. He pulled open one of the drawers under the counter, fishing around until he came up with a plastic fork. "Winger's not much of a homemaker," he chuckled, opening a door on the cabinets above the counter. He stared at the odd contents before grabbing a cardboard can of processed Parmesan cheese next to a plastic container of gun-cleaning solvent. He noticed the label on the cheese said Refrigerate After Opening and it had been opened. Twirling the plastic lid, he stuck the can under his nose and sniffed. It smelled all right.

The buzzer on the microwave went off, and Dartt removed the dish, juggling it in his hands before dropping it on the counter. "Now I know what Pavlov's dog went through," he said, shaking out a thick layer of the cheese onto the steaming lasagna. Tearing a paper towel from a roll next to the sink, he carried the dish to the card table and swept an area clear with his left arm before setting it down. He stepped back to the counter and grabbed his beer and the plastic fork. "I'd give a hundred credits for a big slice of garlic bread," he said, sitting down at the table.

He was just getting ready to fork a large piece of pasta into his mouth when a soft scratching sound caused him to turn his head toward the door. He set the fork into the dish and got up. "Who's there?" he said, standing. The sound came again, reminding Dartt of a dog or cat scratching to get into a room. "Who's there?" he repeated, walking toward the door.

A weird, helpless sensation ran like electricity across Dartt's spine and down his back as he watched the door blow off its hinges in a strange sort of slow motion. It was as though the apartment had sucked it inward violently as the jamb splintered and blew apart, pieces of wood flying across the room like shrapnel. Dartt had a brief vision that a tornado was tearing through the apartment. He raised his arms just as the door struck the upper part of his body and knocked him backward in a violent cartwheel over the card table.

"Goddamn!" Dartt looked up and saw two figures in the doorway—one of them was aiming an odd-looking weapon at him.

Dartt did a sloppy somersault and rolled behind the couch just as the weapon fired, its report sounding like an explosion of compressed air. He pulled the .44 from his holster and stuck it over the back of the couch, firing blind two times, the big weapon kicking back against his bent wrist so hard that Dartt thought he might lose his grip.

"Did you hit him?" a voice near the door yelled.

"Hell, no!" someone with a wheezing voice answered. "Flush him out from behind that goddamn couch so I can get a clear shot at the son of a bitch."

Dartt took a deep breath and rose from behind the couch and aimed toward the doorway. Trying to find a target, he turned to a short man who was on one knee, fiddling with his weapon, then to a taller figure who was holding an advanced Uzi. Both men jerked their heads up as Dartt fired.

The taller man jerked back around the door just as the .44 cooked off, its recoil bouncing Dartt's arms back over his head. A football-sized chunk of the door jamb blew out into the hallway as the guy who had been kneeling dived back into the hall and rolled out of sight.

Dartt barely had time to duck as the man with the Uzi appeared in the doorway, spraying the apartment with a stream of lead.

"Damn," Dartt breathed as pieces of plaster and wood rained down from the walls and ceiling. He knew he was going to be in a world of hurt real soon unless he returned fire. Crawling to the edge of the couch, Dartt was about to risk another blind shot when he saw a round little miracle on the floor, a foot from his face. "Bless you, Stu Winger," he said, grabbing the concussion grenade. Pulling the pin, he flung it toward the doorway and yelled, "Suck on this, assholes!"

There was a long uncomfortable silence before the grenade went off, sounding like a nuke inside the tiny apartment. The place shook violently and the window blew out as though it had been hit with a sledgehammer.

His ears ringing, Dartt moved toward the doorway, holding the .44 in front of him with two hands. The hall had filled with smoke. Listening for movement, he heard nothing save the ringing from the explosion. "Here goes nothing," he breathed before jumping into the hallway, firing the big Magnum in both directions as though expecting an apparition to leap out of the smoke. His attackers had vanished.

Dartt moved cautiously toward the stairs. Plaster crunched beneath his boots as he moved past several other apartments. Dartt hoped someone had called the police.

Swallowing hard, he moved to the landing of the stairs and peered down toward the front door of the apartment building. A door opened behind him, and he turned. The next thing he knew, he was slammed against the wall and a Uzi was jammed under his chin, choking the hell out of him.

Dartt tried to raise the .44, but the man with the Uzi brought up his knee and rammed it square into his crotch. The blow caused him to jerk forward, knocking his attacker momentarily off balance. Dartt managed to bring the Magnum up in a swinging motion and deliver a glancing blow across his adversary's temple.

"Shit!" the man yelled, and grabbed the wrist of Dartt's gun hand. "Toad! Where are you?"

Dartt leaned his head back and slammed his forehead into his attacker's face. He heard cartilage snap as blood poured from the man's nose.

"You son of a bitch!" the man yelled, spraying blood into Dartt's face. He dropped the Uzi and grabbed Dartt's neck, jerking him sideways.

Dartt felt the weapon land at his feet as the man grabbed him. The next thing he knew, they were rolling head over heels down the narrow stairs. As they landed in a heap in front of a glass door, Dartt was aware that he'd lost his Magnum. He looked around and saw it on one of the stairs. "Damn," he breathed, and lunged for it, but fell back as something struck the back of his head.

"Not so goddamn fast," the man hissed.

Dartt rolled over just as his attacker was bringing his clasped hands down for another blow. He brought one of his boots up and pumped it straight into the man's chest, knocking him back. Rage welled up in Dartt as he rose and delivered a swinging kick to the side of the man's face. Blood and spit splattered as the stranger's head snapped sideways.

"Want some more?" Dartt snarled, moving in and catching the man with a right cross to the jaw, flooring him like an animal in a slaughterhouse.

"Excuse me."

The voice sounded like sandpaper on rusting metal. Dartt turned toward the smaller man he'd seen earlier. He cringed at the sight of the odd-looking weapon that was being aimed straight at his chest. Fear pumped through his veins like ice water, and Dartt cursed himself for having forgotten about the gnome-like man.

"That's right," the man said. "Go ahead and shit your pants."

The weapon jumped in the man's hands. Two dart-like probes, trailing thin wires, sailed out of the end of the contraption and found their mark just above Dartt's left breast. Something like fire exploded inside his brain, and he found himself on the floor, flopping around uncontrollably like a fish just hauled into the boat.

"Pull them out, quick! Don't kill the son of a bitch!"

Dartt was vaguely aware of the men standing over him. The shorter man put his foot on his chest and wrapped the thin wires around his hand before jerking the probes out of his body. The fire in his brain was immediately replaced with a warm comfort that Dartt realized was the absence of pain. He watched the little man lean down, and for the first time noticed he was wearing mirrored sunglasses. Dartt could see his reflection in the glasses and, as the man moved closer, he was amazed that his skin looked so white. He closed his eyes and wondered if he was about to die.

CHAPTER THIRTEEN

HORN ARRIVED at the Chelsea Street Tavern on time, but didn't see the assistant DA anywhere. That didn't really surprise him, even though Service didn't seem like the type of woman who believed in being fashionably late. He took a seat at the brass-and-oak bar, in sight of the front door, and ordered a beer. Looking around, Horn figured most of the bar's clientele were lawyers, investment bankers or other white-collar professional types who earned big wafers and liked to talk about it. The men were dressed as if they'd just stepped out of a fashion magazine, and the women were dressed to kill in five-hundred-credit dresses and heels. Horn looked down at his street uniform—safari-style jacket, bush pants, jump boots—and instantly felt out of place. He shrugged and took a long pull from the mug the bartender had set in front of him.

It wasn't long before a cab pulled up in front of the bar and Service emerged and walked toward the door. Horn noticed that she was wearing a dark gray business suit and had her blond hair pulled back into a librarian's bun. She was carrying a trench-style coat draped over a simple, brown leather folder. She entered the bar and immediately spied Horn, nodded once and walked over.

"Max," she said, draping her coat over the back of a bar stool. "I'm glad you could make it." Placing her folder on the bar, she rubbed her hands together. "I think it's going to snow, no kidding."

Horn enjoyed the warmth in her smile. She looked genuinely happy to see him.

"I'm glad I could make it, too," he said. "You're looking good."

Service smiled again, only this time her face seemed to radiate. Horn was glad. He had wondered how she was going to react around him after their last meeting in her apartment.

"Thanks, Max," she said. "After today I needed that."

"What's the matter, bad day in court?" Horn waved at the bartender.

"You could say that," she answered, turning the bar stool around and climbing into its upholstered seat. "My star witness in the case we'd made against the Thompson brothers flew the coop. Two of the biggest crooks in Manhattan will be on the street in time for dinner."

Horn was familiar with the Thompson brothers' case. He'd been involved in the surveillance of their exporting business, which was actually a front for the illegal shipments of toxic and radioactive waste to Third World countries. "Sorry to hear that," he said. "What would you like to drink?"

"Gin and tonic," she replied, crossing her legs.

Horn couldn't help glancing at her legs, which were exposed to the thigh as Christina's skirt rode up on her stockings. He placed a credit wafer on the bar and picked up the drink, handing it to her.

"Thanks," she said, taking a sip.

"I didn't know you were into the brass-and-plant scene," Horn said, gesturing across the semicrowded room.

"Where did you want to meet, a pool hall?" She touched his arm. "The place is convenient."

A tall man in a classic pinstripe suit approached. He was holding a drink and had a beer bottle in his pants pocket.

"Hello, Christina," the man said, smiling flashily.

"Oh, hi, Larry," she said, turning. "This is Max Horn." She nodded at Horn. "Larry Bishop."

Horn held out his hand and noticed that the man stared at his glove momentarily before taking his hand out of his pocket and consummating the greeting.

"Well, Christina," Larry said, turning his back to Horn, "I tried to call you earlier in the week. Did you get my message?"

"Yes," Christina answered, "but you know how it goes. It's the end of the year and the devil is beating his wife. But that's no excuse. What did you want?"

Christina glanced at Horn over Larry's shoulder, the look in her eyes saying she was trying to hurry the conversation. Smiling, he picked up his beer and tried to ignore their conversation.

"I've got two tickets for the opening of *Santa Fe* tomorrow night and I was wondering if you'd like to go." Larry maneuvered himself farther between Horn and Service.

"I don't think so, Larry," Christina said graciously. "Max and I have plans."

"Huh?" Larry studied Horn coldly.

"Yeah," Horn said, trying to keep from smiling. "We're going bowling." He raised the mug of beer in a mock toast and took a drink.

"Bowling?" Larry's jaw dropped open for a moment before he recovered and cleared his throat. He looked at Christina, who shrugged her shoulders and smiled. "Well," he said, glancing at Horn, "I've got to get back to my group."

When he was gone, Christina looked at Horn and broke out laughing. *"Bowling?"* She covered her mouth in an attempt to stifle her laughter.

"Hell, I'm serious," Horn said, keeping a straight face. "You used me to get yourself off the hook with Larry. Now you have to pay the price."

For a second Christina looked worried. Then she caught on. "Really, Max," she said. "If you knew Larry, you'd know why you said the perfect thing. He probably showers with a tie on."

Horn realized he was enjoying Christina's company.

"Now, tell me what really went on in L.A.," she said seriously.

Horn was caught a little off guard. "You read my report," he said bluntly. He signaled the bartender for two more drinks.

"I read your report." Christina nodded. "But let's face it, Max. There's generally more information on the back of a cereal box than there is in one of your reports."

Horn chuckled. "You know, they call L.A. the city of fallen angels," he said. For some reason he felt like seeing how long he could kid Service around before she put her foot down. "What do you think they should call New York City?"

"I don't know," she answered impatiently. "How about the city of dead angels? Now cut the crap, will you?"

"Okay," he said. "What do you want to know?"

"What did this fellow Latch tell you other than the techno-garp about the droid and the fact that they were tied in on the Merrifield thing?" Service flipped open her folder and looked at her notes.

The bartender set fresh drinks in front of them. "He gave me a confirm on the UN *demonstration*, as you called it."

"As Kindu called it," Christina corrected.

"He said it's going to happen soon," Horn said.

"How soon?" Her voice had dropped to a whisper.

"He said two weeks."

"And that was last week," she said. "Why didn't you tell me?"

"I've been doing some checking," Horn replied. "I'm sure you know the General Assembly is supposed to be on recess until early December. However, they've scheduled a special session for the twenty-ninth to try and resolve the Pakistan thing."

"You think that's when it will happen?"

"Has to," Horn answered. "If the timetable Latch gave me is correct."

"What should we do?"

"If we can't get them to call it off, I need to be there with an assault team."

"What are the other alternatives?"

"Find Ticket," Horn answered. "I'm also hoping August can come up with some sort of weapon we can use against the droids. Stu is supposedly checking on that as we speak."

Christina's eyes bored into him. "Who's August?"

Shit, Horn thought, wondering how long he'd have to talk to the woman before he stripped naked and totally spilled his guts. He thought about trying to bullshit his way out of his slip of the tongue, but figured she'd see right through him.

"August is my friend in the Bronx," he answered. "It's a private relationship, and I'd prefer to keep it that way."

Service glanced at his right arm, then his right eye. "Certainly," she said simply. "By the way, how did you get that cut across your cheek?"

Horn subconsciously raised his hand to the white scar he'd carried as long as he'd worn his mods, then dropped his fingers to the bruise and contusion Toad had left him. "Oh, this?" he asked, feeling his face flush slightly.

Service nodded. "Did Latch do that to you?"

"No," Horn answered. "It was one of his henchmen, a guy he called Toad."

"Toad?" Service looked a little disgusted.

Horn laughed lightly, amused by the woman's expression. "If you saw him, you'd know how he got the name."

"Listen, Max," Christina said, glancing at her watch. "You want to get a bite to eat?"

"Sure," Horn answered, looking toward the dining area. "Here?"

"No." Christina laughed. "Not here. If you don't mind, we could go to my place and I'll fix us something."

"I'd like that," Horn answered. He helped Christina on with her coat and tossed another credit wafer onto the bar. Fifteen minutes later they were in her apartment and she was hanging his jacket on the rack next to the door. "That, too," she said, nodding at Horn's shoulder holster.

Horn peeled it off and held it out, watching her arm sag when she took it.

"The damn thing's heavy," she said, hanging it over a hook next to his jacket. "Come in here. I'll pour you some wine, and we can talk while I fix dinner."

Horn felt a little naked without the automatic and said so as he followed Christina into a combination dining-and-kitchen area.

"Maybe that means you've been wearing it too long," Christina said, removing a large bottle of white wine from the refrigerator.

Horn laughed. "You sound like Dr. Locke," he said, referring to his precinct's resident psychiatrist.

"God, I hope not," Christina said, joining in his laughter. "I had to use her as an expert witness once, and by the time she'd finished her spiel, two members of the jury were asleep! No kidding."

"That's her." Horn took the glass of wine Christina held out. "Every time there's an EF, I have to pay her a visit," he said, referring to the routine departmental investigation following any use of excessive force. "She always asks if I had some sort of problem with my mother when I was growing up."

"Why don't you have a seat," Christina invited, taking off her suit coat and hanging it on the back of one of the chairs grouped around the dining room table.

"Thanks," Horn said, but he didn't sit down. He looked at several photos on the divider that separated the dining from the living area. One photo of a younger Christina, probably in her early twenties, caught his eye. It showed her standing on a beach, her blond hair blowing in the wind. Something about the photo, however, struck him as odd. At first he thought it was because he was viewing it normally with his left eye and in video with his modified right eye. It gave the color print a sort of stereoscopic quality, but that wasn't what Horn found different about it. The woman in the photo didn't look exactly like Christina. Horn couldn't tell if it was her hair, skin or what, but something was slightly off center. He turned toward Christina and held up the frame.

"When was that taken?" Horn asked.

Service finished slicing a tomato and dumped the pieces into a bowl. Seeing what Horn held, her expression changed as if she'd been reminded of something sad. "That was taken in Pensacola, Florida," she answered.

Her reaction made Horn feel as though he were treading into some secret or private place. He started to put the photo back on the divider, but something made him ask, "How old were you then?"

Christina appeared as though she wanted to say something but couldn't get her thoughts hooked up with her voice.

Horn placed the photo back on the polished wood and took a sip of the wine, figuring he'd let the question slide.

"That's not me," Christina said, "that's my sister."

Horn, surprised by the revelation, wondered why she seemed so guarded about it. He sat down and watched Christina continue with the preparation of a salad.

"She's very beautiful," Horn said. "She looks just like you."

"She should," Christina replied, her voice dry and emotionless. "She's my twin sister."

"I didn't know you had a sister, let alone a twin," Horn said. "Where does she live?"

"She doesn't," Christina answered. "She's dead."

A dull pain struck Horn in his chest. "I'm sorry," he said. Horn looked up and saw she was crying, a towel stuck to her face, chest heaving.

He started to rise but she held up a hand. "No, don't," she said without looking around. "I'll be fine."

"Want to talk about it?" Horn cursed himself as soon as he'd asked the question. He didn't know why he'd asked. Horn prayed she'd decline; he had enough of his own ghosts without bringing new ones into the fold. His heart sank as she turned and began to speak.

"She was killed fifteen years ago, right here in the city. Strangled, raped and murdered while jogging around Central Park at ten in the morning." Christina picked up her wine and downed half the glass.

Something stuck in his throat. He shut his eyes and held on for the grim ride he knew was coming.

She told him how her sister had been brutally molested and murdered by a street gang whose six members ranged in age from thirteen to seventeen. They had gone to trial, but one by one the few witnesses had died or simply dropped out of the picture as the city's case became increasingly weakened by a dilapidated judicial system that had long ago erased the word *swift* from its mandate to execute the law.

"My sister's the real reason I went to law school and joined the DA's office," Christina said. "The fact that those six lowlifes never served a day for her death is probably why I'm such a hard-ass." She smiled weakly, as though recounting what had happened to her sister had rejuvenated her.

"They call you the Barracuda," Horn said, glad she was done with the recollection.

"I'm aware of that," she said. "Max, I appreciate you listening to that. You're one of the very few people I've told since it happened."

Horn figured she tended to guard the secret places in her life and wondered why he was the one sitting there hearing it. It had to be one of the most private and emotional episodes of her life. "Is there more wine?" he asked.

"You sure?" Christina glanced at his glass, which was still two-thirds full.

Horn downed its contents in one swallow, enjoying the instant warmth it brought to his stomach. "Let me," he said, motioning for Christina's glass. He poured them both more wine while she set the table.

"Excuse me," Christina said, reaching around Horn and into the refrigerator. She retrieved a plate covered with half a salmon and a jar of blue-cheese dressing. "I hope cold salmon and a salad is okay," she said, putting the food on the table.

"I'll get the salad," Horn said, walking to the counter.

"Get the loaf of French bread, too, please." Christina pointed at a waxed paper sack on the end of the counter.

"Cold salmon and salad is a feast compared to what I'm used to," Horn said as he placed the bread on the table.

"For some reason I have this vision of cops eating apples all the time," Christina said, placing a butter tray on the table. She sat down and served Horn a healthy portion of salad.

"Thanks," he said, taking his seat. "Actually, egg rolls have replaced apples. We eat a lot of egg rolls and wash them down with gallons of coffee."

Christina laughed as Horn dug into his food. He was hungrier than he'd thought and asked for seconds in a matter of minutes. The two laughed and joked as they ate, Horn telling her about Lenny, one of Winger's snitches, who carried around a cordless electric razor and would use it at the oddest times. When they finished eating, Christina poured them brandy and they moved into the living room. She put some soft swing music on the digital stereo and sat down on the couch next to Horn, kicking off her shoes.

"Your story about Lenny was funny," Christina said, reaching back and undoing her hair. She shook her head and it fell down around her shoulders, casting her face in a sort of golden halo.

"Yeah, every day on the street you meet a hundred Lennys," Horn said, suddenly feeling awkward. "I don't know why you find that sort of thing interesting." He shook his head and took a sip of the brandy. "Being a cop is mostly hours of sheer dragged-out boredom. People like Lenny add a little color to an otherwise dull job."

"Yeah, right," Christina said. "I wanted to be a cop before I wanted to be a lawyer."

"You've got to be kidding," he said.

"No," she answered, shaking her head. "I know I give you guys a hard time, but I really admire you."

Christina bent over and kissed Horn on the mouth, grabbing his head with both hands. He felt an instant jolt of excitement run down his spine and felt his arm flex slightly. Christina apparently felt it, too, and looked down briefly as she broke the kiss.

"Is that for being a cop?" he asked.

"That's just for being you, Max," she said, moving closer and kissing him again, probing his mouth with her tongue.

Horn returned the kiss and breathed in her perfume, the combination of her touch and the smell creating the sensation that his head was floating somewhere near the ceiling. He knew that he wanted her but sensed there was something more than sex she was trying to communicate to him.

Opening his eyes, Horn was met by Christina's own ice blue orbs. He had missed her breaking the kiss and wondered how long he'd drifted there, content to be lost in her soft embrace. Horn knew he wanted to love this woman who could break his heart just by looking at him. An old, old feeling had been awakened behind a long-locked door in his past, and he could hear it begging to be let out.

"I could love you, Max," she said in a low voice. "I could love you like no other. You're the only man I've ever met who made me feel like this."

Horn wanted to tell Christina to love him and he would love her back with the same, if not greater, intensity. Something held him back. It was as though he sensed something sinister hiding in the narrow gap between them, waiting to swallow him up and destroy her in the process. He tried to put his finger on what it was, and his mods glitched, not as they had in the past; they actually *moved,* sending him a signal, saying, we're a part of this equation. Suddenly he felt distant and alone.

Christina seemed to sense the change in him. "Are you okay, Max?"

There was a cold sweat forming across his forehead. His skin felt clammy. When he tried to swallow, he realized his mouth had dried up.

"Are you okay, Max?" Christina repeated.

"I'm all right," Horn answered hoarsely, knowing he was lying.

"I felt your body sort of jump, and then you...went away." She moved her hand up and wiped the perspiration from his forehead.

"Listen, it's late," Horn said, the odd, alien sensation hanging open in his brain like a window to another world. "I should probably be heading home."

"Spend the night here," Christina said. "There's no sense in you trying to go across town at this hour."

As if it were a reflex, Horn glanced toward the door he knew led to her bedroom. A strange nervousness added to the mild paranoia his mods had created.

Christina laughed. "I mean on the couch, here," she said, patting one of the cushions. "It folds out. You'll sleep like a baby, I promise."

"All right," Horn said, standing shakily. He helped Christina move the coffee table and take off the cushions and unfold the hide-a-bed.

"Why don't you go ahead and take care of your business in the bathroom," she said. "There's a couple of new toothbrushes in the cabinet next to the sink. Help yourself."

Horn brushed his teeth and splashed cold water on his face before chancing a look at himself in the mirror. One word came to mind as he stared at his face: *ragged*.

On his return to the living room, the hide-a-bed was made up with clean sheets and a comforter. Christina appeared from the kitchen.

"Listen, Max," she said, turning off the light in the dining area. "About tonight...." Horn figured she was about to say something to the effect that she was sorry it happened; or it must have been the wine; or some other reason that would let her off the hook.

"I'd like to pick up where we were a while ago when you're feeling a little better." She walked over to Horn and kissed him softly on the lips before turning off the lights and disappearing down the hall.

Horn felt numb. He leaned back on the bed and closed his eyes, blinking off the video and, in effect, shutting down the right half of his vision. The smell of her perfume seemed to be enhanced by the darkness. Horn didn't know how long he lay there before getting up. Taking extra pains to be quiet, he let himself out.

CHAPTER FOURTEEN

"WHICH ONE ARE we working on now?" Latch asked, wiping the sweat from his brow. "I've lost count." He looked across the table at Ticket, who was hooking synthetic blood supply to a droid's titanium spinal tube.

Ticket looked up, obviously annoyed. His face was drawn and pale, and dark bags hung under his eyes. "Why the hell don't you count them?" he snapped, gesturing toward the eight droids they'd already completed.

Latch counted the Neuroids, which were lined against a wall of the spacious laboratory, their lifeless eyes staring straight ahead, ready to receive a high-voltage jolt to their temples. "This is almost the last one," he said, gesturing at the droid beside him on the stainless-steel table.

Ticket peeled off his gloves and placed them on the back of the droid's head. He went to a long counter covered with electronic parts, equipment and instruments, picked up a pack of cigarettes and shook one out. Lighting it, he turned toward Latch and leaned against the counter.

"The last one is reserved for you, Jack," Ticket said. He took a long drag on the cigarette and blew smoke toward the ceiling in one big cloud.

Latch had been mulling over whether he would opt for the droid body or ask for a sizable paycheck from Ticket and take his chances with the cancer that was chewing his insides. As well, Latch wasn't keen on winding up like Number 24, following Ticket around like a drugged Doberman.

"Having second thoughts?" Ticket raised his eyebrows.

"We have had problems," Latch said.

"*What* problems?"

Latch figured it would be best to lay his cards on the table. He gestured toward the droids. "We've had to perform your reset technique on six systems so far. When we activate them, are they going to be like Number 24?"

"What the hell is wrong with Number 24?" Ticket's voice had lost its calm facade.

"Look at it," Latch said, pointing to the droid who was standing next to the door, staring into space. "The thing seems *lethargic,* or something. I'd bet if you hooked it up to the bus analyzer, you'd find a lag of at least four seconds."

"There's nothing wrong with Number 24," Ticket said. "Any lag is merely a reflection of the state of the neural system when I plugged it in."

Latch nodded slowly, knowing from experience that it wouldn't do any good to argue.

"I'm glad you agree," Ticket said.

"Still," Latch said, "I think I'll forego the droid and take the money we'd originally talked about."

"Jack," Ticket said. "I thought you had your heart set on letting me extend your life, so to speak."

"Well, I changed my mind," he replied. "After we finish this I think I'll head down to Australia and get lost."

Ticket spoke in a soft voice. "How much time do they say you have left, Jack?"

"A year. Maybe less."

"Think you can spend a couple of million in that short a time?"

"I won't know until I try," Latch answered cautiously.

"Are you ready for another system?"

Both men turned toward Toad, who had just walked through the door. His hair was tied back in a thick ponytail, and he was wearing a white apron covered with bits of flesh, hair and blood.

"Not just yet," Ticket said, grinding out his cigarette. He returned to the operating table and pulled on his gloves. "We've got to finish this one first."

Latch wiped his forehead and moved a cart holding an electroencephaloscope next to the table. He hooked a lead into a receptacle built into the base of the droid's titanium skull and looked up at the scope.

"Normalize it," Ticket said, turning up the gain on the pump that was circulating the synthetic blood through the droid's neural system.

Latch adjusted several knobs until a straight flat line ran horizontally across the pale blue screen. "Ready," he said, nodding at Ticket.

Grabbing a small hand-held device, Ticket stuck two short probes against the back of the droid's skull. "Stand clear," he ordered, glancing up at Latch.

Latch backed away from the table and watched the droid bounce violently as Ticket pushed a red button on the instrument in his hand.

"There we go," Ticket said, his voice a mixture of relief and satisfaction.

Latch looked up at the scope and saw that the line had changed into a sine wave that ran across the small screen. "That doesn't look that good," he said, moving back to the table.

"What the hell are you talking about?" Ticket raised his voice defensively. "The son of a bitch is up, *isn't he?*"

But the line suddenly went flat.

"Goddammit!" Ticket yelled, waving Latch away. He jammed the hand-held device against the base of the droid's skull and hit the red button again, causing the body to jump, though not as much as it had the first time. The line on the scope changed into a weak wave form for a couple of seconds before dying.

"Goddammit!" Ticket repeated, flinging the little probe across the room. It hit the front of a metal storage cabinet and broke into several pieces.

"We lost him," Latch said as Ticket pounded the table next to the droid's head with his fists.

"I know we lost him," Ticket snapped, glaring at Latch. He walked to the counter and poured Scotch from a quart bottle into a water glass.

"Should he be drinking that shit and doing this sort of thing?" Toad asked Latch in a hushed tone. Toad smelled like he'd just come off the line of a meat-packing plant.

"Probably not," Latch answered, "but why don't you be the one to tell him to cut it out?"

"Screw you," Toad wheezed. "That son of a bitch's fuse is double short."

"No shit," Latch said. He watched Ticket tilt back the glass and guzzle down booze as though it were iced tea. Ticket turned toward him, the liquor appearing to have calmed him.

"We'll have to do another reset," Latch said, anticipating what Ticket was going to say.

"That's correct." Ticket lit a cigarette. "Is the probe loaded?"

"Not yet," Latch answered, motioning Toad toward a tray of instruments on the table. "Load the probe," he ordered.

Toad charged the thin, wirelike end of the probe with anesthetic from a small glass vial. Ticket took the probe.

"You want to assist?" Ticket asked, looking at Toad.

"You sure you want to do that?" Latch interrupted, knowing Toad wasn't that skilled when it came to detail work.

"Shut up!" Ticket barked. "You're the son of a bitch worried about how many resets we've done, so if it bothers you that much, don't watch."

Latch, shocked by Ticket's outburst, said, "Fine," and peeled off his gloves and walked to the counter. "At least have him put on gloves." He pointed at Toad.

Ticket looked down at Toad's hands and nodded toward the tray that held a box of disposable rubber gloves. "You've seen Jack spread the seam," he said, picking up the spreading instrument and handing it to Toad. "Go ahead and give it a try."

Latch poured a healthy shot of the Scotch into a disposable cup and slammed it back. Toad stood on his toes in order to be able to lean into the droid's body cavity. "Don't force it," Ticket said calmly as Toad worked the knifelike edges of the instrument into the seam of the titanium sheath.

Latch figured Ticket was entrusting Toad with such important tasks because he was going to need a new lackey once he left. He watched Ticket glue his eye to the probe's rubber cup and bend over the droid.

A moment later Ticket lifted his head and smiled. "There," he said. "First time, every time."

"Did you get it?" Toad asked, his stubby hands still clamped on to the spreading device.

"Of course I got it," Ticket answered, pulling out the end of the probe. He flashed Latch a smile. "I invented the process, didn't I?"

Toad let out a patronizing laugh. "That's right," he said, releasing the jaws of the spreader and allowing the seam to close. "Piece of cake."

"There it is," Ticket said, pulling the shocking device away from the droid's skull as the E-scope lit up with a nice healthy sine wave. "You think you can close him up?" he asked, looking down at Toad, who was grinning like a fool.

"Sure, Dr. Ticket," Toad answered.

Ticket walked over to where Latch was standing and drank the rest of the Scotch in his glass. He picked up the still-smoldering butt from the ashtray and lit a fresh cigarette with it. He turned to Latch.

"Sorry I snapped at you, Jack," he said, pouring more Scotch. "Another drink?"

Latch shook his head, unsure if the liquor he'd already swallowed was going to stay down. His stomach felt like the sink in an autopsy room.

"I can have your money for you in twelve hours," Ticket said. "You want gold or blue script?"

"How about half and half," Latch grinned, the thought of the money making him feel a hell of a lot better.

"No problem." Ticket drank more Scotch. "We'll do the next droid and then, hell, you can take off once I get your money. There's no reason why you should stick around for the little party Kindu is cooking up, unless you want to spend some time with the fat bastard."

As Ticket knew, the thought of Kindu made Latch's skin crawl. "No thanks," Latch said, his stomach churning.

"What about the cop?" Toad asked, peeling off the gloves. "When are we going to plug his system into Number 1?"

Ticket's face lit up. "It's a little too late for that now, isn't it?" Latch said, not wanting to take the time to screw with any more mods than necessary.

Ticket turned to Latch. "What do you mean?"

Latch felt as if he'd just swallowed a cup of drain cleaner. "I mean the guy's partner hasn't found us by now. What's the sense in slowing him down? In two days all this shit will be history." He motioned about the room.

Ticket gave Latch a quizzical look. "Are you saying forget about the cop?"

"Yeah," Latch answered. "We should have brought the droid up the night we snatched the cop's partner."

"If I remember correctly," Ticket chuckled, "you weren't in such great shape the night you brought the guy in. As a matter of fact, you looked like you'd been run down by a truck." Ticket's chuckling turned into chest-heaving laughter, and he slapped Latch on the back. Ticket's laughter suddenly stopped. "I was thinking about introducing Number 1 to Mr. Toftoy."

"Let's go ahead and do the cop's partner," Toad interjected enthusiastically. "Want me to gather his system?"

"Why not?" Ticket said, opening a drawer on the counter. He reached in and pulled out a brown bottle of amphetamines. "Go get him, Mr. Toad," he said, shaking two of the white pills into his hand. "Gather his system over there on the spare table." Nodding at a bare operating table in a corner of the room, he slid the pills into his mouth and downed them with a swallow of Scotch.

Latch felt uncomfortable when Ticket held out the pill bottle. For some reason he took two pills and popped them into his mouth, swallowing them dry.

"Go on, get in there." Toad's voice came from outside the door. Seconds later he shoved Dartt's body over the threshold. Dartt's hands were fastened behind his back with a plastic strip normally used to bundle wire, and he was blindfolded with a wide strip of silver tape.

Ticket took a hypo from the counter and stabbed Dartt in the left shoulder. Almost immediately Dartt fell to his knees and began to shake his head slowly.

"I hope you're not putting him under," Latch said, pouring a shot of Scotch. He drank it down and realized he was starting to feel a whole lot better. The speed was starting to sweep the fuzziness out of his brain and now, as he looked at the cop's kneeling form, he knew he was going to enjoy administering his own special form of payback.

"Don't worry," Ticket answered, tossing the syringe into a plastic barrel. "He should come out of this in time to feel Toad cut his spine out of his back."

"I'm ready to do him now," Toad said.

"Not yet," Ticket said, putting a hand on Toad's shoulder. "Take a stretcher downstairs and get Number 1's shell. We'll do the implant without freezing the system—take it out of the cop and plug it straight into the droid."

When Toad was gone, Ticket motioned for Latch. "Give me a hand here," he said, rolling over the Neuroid on the table, then spinning it around so its feet hung toward the floor.

Latch grabbed an arm and helped Ticket carry the droid across the room, where they stood it up next to Number 31.

"I'm kind of anxious to see how Number 1 functions," Ticket said, lighting another cigarette. "He has some interesting features."

"Like what?"

"Well, besides the rather ugly device on his arm—" Ticket made the shape of a pincer with his thumb and forefinger "—his other appendages were built with servos and actuators that are used mostly in machines that crush rocks and bend metal. Unlike these other Neuroids, Number 1 is what you might call *industrial strength*." Ticket chuckled. "Did you notice that his hand and legs and other body parts are oversized?"

Latch recalled seeing that the droid's appendages were large, like those of a weight lifter who'd taken too many steroids. "Yeah," he answered. "Now that you mention it, they did seem abnormal."

"Number 1 is a crude bastard," Ticket said. "But I'll lay you odds he'll be hard to stop."

Just then, Toad wheeled the gurney bearing the droid's shell through the door. The two men helped Toad lift the droid's body onto the operating table, then donned fresh gloves as the little man took the gurney away. To Latch, Toad looked like a kid on Christmas morning.

"Can I gather the cop now?" Toad asked, grabbing some gloves from the tray. He looked from Ticket to Latch, then back to Ticket.

"Ask your boss," Ticket said, laughing. He gestured at Latch, walked to the counter and poured more Scotch.

"Let me see if he's awake enough," Latch said, turning to Dartt. He grabbed an edge of the tape and ripped it from his eyes. The action didn't seem to affect Dartt, who continued swinging his head from side to side like a stunned cow.

"Come on, wake up," Latch said, slapping Dartt several times across the face.

"You want to give him a shot of something to counteract the tranquilizer?" Ticket asked.

"Sure," Latch answered. "Go get it, will you, Toad?"

Toad brought back a syringe. "Where do you want me to stab him?" he asked, holding the dripping needle next to his head as if it were a gun.

"In the butt," Latch ordered. He watched Dartt's eyes as Toad administered the hypo, and in less than twenty seconds they fixed on Latch with amazing clarity. "Hello, asshole," Latch said, grinning madly.

Latch started to turn to Ticket, but instead felt his heart stop momentarily as Dartt spit square in his face. For several seconds Latch couldn't move. He stared at Dartt until rage finally replaced the surprise he felt.

"You son of a bitch!" Latch screamed. He grabbed Dartt by the hair and slapped him as hard as he could. Then Latch cocked his leg and drove the toe of his shoe into Dartt's midsection so hard that his momentum caused him to trip and fall across his victim's body.

"Goddammit," he swore as Toad helped him to his feet. Latch could feel the speed pumping his body up and knew it was fueling his anger to the point where he might kill the man with his bare hands. He jumped on top of Dartt and started beating his head against the floor.

"Here, here!" Ticket cautioned, grabbing him by the shoulder. He and Toad pulled Latch from Dartt. "Don't break his skull, for chrissakes," Ticket said, his hand pressed against Latch's chest.

"Sorry," Latch said. "The bastard spit in my face." He wiped Dartt's saliva off his face, using the tail of his smock.

"At least I think he's awake enough to feel what Toad is going to do to him, right?" Ticket dropped his hand away from Latch.

Latch and Toad grabbed Dartt's arms, dragged him to the empty table and hoisted his body onto the stainless-steel slab. "Get a goddamn hypo," Latch growled as he turned Dartt onto his side. "We're getting ready to make you a new man, cop," he said, staring into Dartt's green eyes. Latch was shocked and chilled to hear Dartt emit a bloodcurdling laugh, a sign that he'd abandoned himself to his fate.

"I'm not a cop," Dartt said, his maniacal howling trailing off as his chest heaved. "My name's Dartt, Les Dartt."

Latch did a double take. "You're Horn's partner, right?" he asked, an odd sensation jumping from his mind straight into the pit of his stomach.

"Sorry," Dartt answered, shaking his head. "You got the wrong guy."

Latch sensed he was hearing the truth. "Then who the hell are you?"

"I'm the guy who serviced your mother when your old man was out of town," Dartt answered.

"You stupid bastard," Latch hissed. "Where's that goddamn hypo?"

"Here," Toad said, slapping the plastic syringe in his hand.

Latch stuck the needle in Dartt's shoulder by his neck. Almost immediately Dartt's body went limp.

"Come on," Latch growled, turning Dartt onto his stomach. "Cut his hands loose and get rid of his shirt."

Toad grabbed a pair of surgical scissors and clipped the plastic band from Dartt's wrists. As if on a prearranged cue, Dartt jumped up on his knees and rolled off the table, knocking Toad backward into a cart filled with surgical instruments. The cart fell over and the equipment scattered across the floor.

"What the hell!" Latch stumbled backward in shock. Across the room, Ticket grabbed a vial on the counter and threw it to Latch.

"The son of a bitch gave him another shot of adrenaline!" Ticket screamed.

Latch turned back toward Dartt, who had Toad cornered and was in the process of slamming his fists into the little man's body. "Shoot him!" he yelled, figuring Toad was carrying a pistol.

"I can't, goddammit!" Toad managed to yell between blows. He found a scalpel on the floor and swung it at Dartt, who retreated several steps. "I don't have my gun! Help me, goddammit!"

"I'll help you," Dartt uttered. He picked up a cordless oscillating bone saw and held it menacingly over his head, its high-pitched whine sounding like a swarm of angry bees.

"Oh, shit!" was all Toad could say as Dartt swung the saw down on the front of his head. Toad squealed like a pig, and his glasses flew off as the gash opened up, spilling blood down his face in a crimson flood.

Latch looked around for a weapon, cursing for not packing his own handgun. Grabbing a stainless-steel set of rib spreaders, he slammed them across the back of Dartt's head just as the saw was being raised for another swipe at Toad's head.

"Damn!" Dartt screamed. He turned quickly and swung the saw in a wild arc, causing Latch to jump backward.

"Oh, no, you don't!" Dartt said, suddenly bolting for the door where Ticket was about to exit the room. Dartt grabbed him by the collar of his smock and rammed his head into the side of the operating table that held Number 1. Ticket collapsed like a house of cards in a windstorm.

"Goddammit," Latch said. He wondered why the hell Number 24 hadn't turned on Dartt. He didn't figure the damn thing would respond to him, but he gave it a try. "Number 24!" he yelled, "take him out!" He waved and pointed at Dartt, who stared at him, surprised. The droid didn't move and continued to stare blankly across the room.

"What the hell are you doing?" Dartt asked, glancing at Number 24, then Latch. "This son of a bitch is one of your killer droids?" He grunted and glanced at the Neuroid again. "You better trade him in or give him a shot of that shit you gave me, because right now he seems pretty docile." Dartt suddenly broke into a crazy laughter that echoed in the room.

Toad was leaning against the wall moaning and clutching the wound on his head. Latch caught movement out of the corner of one eye and was surprised to see Ticket crawling back toward the counter. He didn't know what he was up to, but he hoped it was something that would stop the lunatic with the buzz saw. Latch moved away from the counter, hoping to distract Dartt.

"So what the hell happened to the cop?" Latch asked, thinking he'd try to keep Dartt talking. Ticket was screwing with something on the counter.

Dartt was flipping the saw's switch on and off, causing an intermittent buzzing that was driving Latch crazy. "What do you mean, what happened to the cop? Nothing happened to the cop. *Both* cops are probably looking for my ass right now."

"Both cops?" Latch repeated, parrying Dartt's sweeping thrust. "You mean Horn and his partner?"

Dartt nodded. "That's right. And I guess you and the gnome over there thought I was Horn's partner, right?"

"You got it, ace," Latch answered, grinning. "But you know, you got a little problem now. You got no place to go."

"Hell, I figure I can get past the guards downstairs," Dartt said, returning the smile. "Then I'll have so many cops crawling over this garbage pile, they'll look like rats."

"Think so?" Ticket interrupted. He was standing some four feet behind Dartt, holding an open beaker filled with a clear liquid.

Dartt swung around and was met in the face by the contents of the beaker. "What! Shit!" He screamed in agony and dropped the saw as the liquid began to smoke on his face and down the front of his shirt.

Ticket moved in quickly with a hypo and jabbed it into Dartt's midsection, hitting the plunger hard.

Dartt screams faded and he collapsed, his burned face smacking into the floor with a sickening thud.

"Hurry up and get Toad," Ticket ordered. "I gave this bastard enough dope to kill a horse, now hurry up!" He grabbed one of Dartt's legs and started dragging him toward the operating table.

Latch was astonished. "You want us to go ahead and gather his system after all this shit?"

"You're smarter than you look sometimes, Jack," Ticket said, dropping Dartt's leg. "Now, get this son of a bitch on the table, now!"

Latch grabbed Toad. "You're not hurt that bad," he said, shoving him toward the table. The two assistants lifted Dartt's body onto the table as Ticket returned to the counter for a long pull of Scotch straight from the bottle.

Thirty minutes later Latch was hooking up Number 1's synthetic blood pump to Dartt's spine while Ticket was implanting his microcontroller into the brain's cerebellum.

"Cap this for me, will you?" Ticket requested, pulling off the electron glasses. "I'll bet you he'll come up like that." Ticket snapped his fingers.

Latch grabbed the curved piece of titanium that formed the back of the droid's skull, fitted it into place and tightened the machined screws with a torque screwdriver. Wiping the sweat from his forehead, he glanced at Toad, who was smoking a cigarette and holding a compress over the gash on his head.

"I'm just about ready," Latch told Ticket. He hooked up the electroencephaloscope and nodded at Ticket, who was holding a new jump-start device in one hand.

"Sure you don't want to bet?" Ticket grinned.

Latch shook his head, suddenly feeling very tired. Figuring the speed was wearing off, he knew he'd probably end up taking more. "No, I don't want to bet, go ahead," he said.

Ticket stuck the probe at the back of Number 1's skull and punched the red button. The droid jumped, and a good healthy sine wave appeared on the screen.

"What'd I tell you?" Ticket said, pointing to the scope. "You know, I really think it makes a big difference when we don't freeze the neural systems. In the future I think we should try to bring in the donors, you know, ambulatory, before we do the mod. What do you think?"

Latch was thinking of an Australian beach. He looked over at Number 24 and asked, "You think that's what's wrong with him? Brain damage because of the cryogenics?''

Ticket nodded undefensively. "Could be. But he's worse than any we've done so far. It could be a combination of the freezing and a donor problem. Remember, that was the system you gathered on short notice before you went to L.A.''

"That's right,'' Latch admitted. He tried to remember the particular donor from whom he'd gathered the system, but there had been so *many* and he usually tried to block their faces and personal characteristics out of his mind.

"Mr. Toad," Ticket said. "Close Number 1 up, please.''

"Yes, sir," Toad replied, snuffing out his cigarette and returning to the table. He had taped the compress to his head, the blood-soaked bandage making him look like the victim of an earthquake or some other natural disaster.

"You want a drink?'' Ticket asked as Latch pulled a set of heavily insulated electrodes from under the table.

"No, thanks,'' Latch answered. "I'd like to get the next droid finished so I can get my shit together and get the hell out of here. No offense,'' he said, holding up a hand, "but I don't have a whole hell of a lot of time to waste.''

"No offense taken,'' Ticket said, lighting a cigarette. "I understand perfectly. And this is it,'' he said, gesturing toward the Neuroids lined up against the far wall. "These are Kindu's nine droids. There aren't any more."

Latch was confused. Why did he think there was still one more droid to do? The pills and liquor had clouded his mind. He shrugged indifferently. He felt relieved and happy that he didn't have to make himself stomach another insert.

"As a matter of fact," Ticket said, pausing briefly to blow a lungful of smoke toward the ceiling, "I'll get Toad to help me give these the big jolt. But at least stick around for a couple of minutes. I'd like you to see how Number 1 looks when he's animated."

"Sure," Latch said, feeling better by the second.

"There," Toad said, grunting loudly as he heaved the droid onto its back. "Let me," he offered, taking the electrodes out of Latch's hands. "Is this right?" he asked, placing one on each temple.

"Close enough," Latch said, walking to a switch panel on the wall near the head of the table. "Make sure you're holding the handles."

"I'm ready," Toad said excitedly.

Latch pressed a button labeled Charge and watched the big droid go instantly stiff and begin to shake. A relay snapped and the droid relaxed. Toad pulled the electrodes away from the strange-looking head and suddenly jumped back, gasping in fright, as the droid sat up straighter on the table.

"Good!" Ticket said, walking in front of the droid. "You are Number 1," he said, speaking directly to the Neuroid. "You will fix on my voice and follow direction from no other pattern. Now please get off the table and stand so we can have a look at you." Ticket's voice was almost gleeful. He turned to Latch.

Latch watched the droid get down from the table, its servos and linear actuators making the room sound like an automated assembly line. He was amazed at how agile the thing seemed to be as it stood, its body slightly bent at the waist. "The son of a bitch is noisy, isn't it?" he commented.

"What can I say?" Ticket smiled, obviously proud of his creation. "I told you he wasn't built for show. Number 1," he said, turning toward the droid, "I want you to give us a demonstration of your physical strength." The droid turned toward Ticket, and the camera lens in its eye socket moved out several centimeters as it focused on his face. "I want you to crush that man's skull using the pincers on your right hand." Ticket turned and pointed directly at Latch.

Latch couldn't believe what he'd heard. "This is a joke, right?" he stammered, but the lump of wet cement that had replaced his heart told him Ticket wasn't joking.

Number 1's motor drives whirred and squealed. An instant later Latch found himself lying on his back with lights flashing before his eyes like strobes. The pain across his right temple told him he'd been blindsided. Panic rose up in Latch's chest as his sight returned. The horrible Frankenstein monster that was Number 1 had straddled him like a wild animal that had just downed its prey.

As the droid clamped its pincers on to his head, Latch opened his mouth to scream but nothing came out. He felt a growing painful pressure, and the last thing he heard was Toad's insane laughter ringing like a funeral bell.

CHAPTER FIFTEEN

HORN STOOD at the end of the run-down pier and watched the gray light of morning spread across the choppy water of the East River. A winter storm was blowing in from the Atlantic, and the smell of snow was in the air. Turning his collar up in an attempt to protect himself from the freezing wind, he swung around and watched a car pull off the frontage road and drive up the pier toward him. Seconds later Winger was motioning for him to get into the Chrysler, waving a gloved hand as he unlocked the passenger door.

"You picked a hell of a place to have a meeting, partner," the young cop said as Horn pulled the door closed. He reached into a white paper sack on the floor and pulled out a covered disposable cup. "Here," he said, holding it out. "I brought you some coffee."

"Thanks," Horn said, taking the cup. He peeled off the lid and sipped the steaming liquid.

"Any word on Dartt?" Winger asked, pulling another cup from the sack.

"No," Horn answered. "They put out an APB, but I doubt it'll do any good. Have you been back to your apartment?"

"Yeah," Winger grunted, "it looks like a war zone." He took a drink of his coffee. "You think he's dead?"

Horn felt a sinking feeling in his gut. "I don't know," he finally answered. "If they were going to kill him, I'd have figured his body would've been there."

"You think it was Latch?" Winger asked, fiddling with the digital heater controls on the dashboard.

"I don't know. Could be whoever made the hit was after you. If that's the case, it could have been any number of people. We aren't exactly popular when it comes to the lowlifes in this city."

"Yeah, that's true," Winger said, "but the fact that he's gone . . . missing, is too damn strange."

Strange is the right word for it, Horn thought. "As soon as this UN thing is over, we'll find out what happened to him, you can bet on it." He knew his words were cheap, but it was all he could come up with. The sinking feeling in his gut was telling him that something bad had happened to Dartt.

"Right," Winger said simply, looking out the window.

"What's with August and this weapon he was supposed to come up with?" Horn asked, wanting to get down to the business at hand.

"It's not ready yet," Winger answered. "He's having a problem with the power source. Apparently the thing uses a shit-load of juice, and he was trying to modify some sort of power supply from a satellite or something so you wouldn't have to carry around a thousand pounds of crap just to fire the damn thing."

"How does it work?" Horn wondered.

"It uses EMP, according to August," Winger answered. "The damn thing is actually a directional antenna hooked up to something called a Marx generator that you gotta carry in a pack on your back. The EMP disrupts the droid's electrical system, gives it a sort of high-grade nervous breakdown." Winger grinned.

"What the hell is EMP?" Horn asked, impressed by Winger's technical knowledge of what August was supposedly putting together for them.

"Electromagnetic pulse," Winger answered. "According to August, it's the same shit generated when a nuke goes off."

Horn looked at his watch. "Well, the damn thing isn't going to do us much good unless we have it in our hands, is it?" he said.

"August was going to work on it all night," Winger replied. "He told me to come by at nine this morning, and he'd give me a quick lesson on how to fire it."

"Nine is when the delegates start arriving," Horn said. "That's less than two hours from now."

"I can't help it," Winger said, holding up a hand. "August said he was lucky he had all the parts he needed to put the damn thing together. I told him I needed it first thing this morning, and he jumped all over my ass."

"Sorry. I forgot how touchy August could be."

"By the way," Winger said, pointing to a thin tubelike device curving up from the inside of the collar of Horn's jacket and ending just below his lower lip. "What the hell is that?"

"It's a commo link," Horn answered, turning his head and pointing to a small device behind his right ear. "This is how I hear, and this is how I talk." He pointed at the tube below in front of his chin. "It's how I'm going to talk to the commander of the assault team."

"How many men did they give you?"

"Forty. Plus a dozen uniforms."

"Forty?" Winger reacted as if the number was either surprising or appalling. "Goddamn, Horn. You saw what *one* of the droids did in that hotel downtown. Forty guys doesn't sound like much."

Horn agreed but didn't say so. "If something does come down," he said, placing the empty cup in the sack, "we're going to evacuate the entire assembly off the helipad. That's how they're coming in, that's how we'll get them out. None of them will ever set foot on the street."

"That's smart," Winger said, nodding his approval. "But what happens to you and the rest of the cops if the shit hits the fan? I'm sure they're not going to have enough helicopters on top of the goddamn building to get *everyone* out of there."

"You're probably right," Horn said. "And if that happens, we'll do what cops always do—survive. Now, get your ass up to August's." Horn opened the door. "Tell him to do me a favor and skip your little firing lesson. Just have him show you how to pull the trigger."

"I'll see what I can do," Winger said as Horn climbed out of the car.

Horn headed across the cracked concrete toward the new United Nations building, which sat like a giant tombstone on a section of Stuyvesant Town facing the East River. The twenty-story steel-and-glass structure was new, having replaced the old United Nations Headquarters, whose burned-out shell a mile and a half up Franklin Roosevelt Drive served as a home for rats and other forms of New York City street life. Horn vaguely remembered when an obscure terrorist group had wiped out the old headquarters with a fuel-air bomb, taking off the top half of the building, as well as leveling most of the other structures in a quarter-mile radius.

As Horn jogged across Roosevelt, he hoped his prediction that the Libyan's "demonstration" would take place that day wouldn't come true, even though he, as well as Service, would look like fools. He knew the assistant DA had stuck her neck out to get him support and had busted her butt to convince the State Department to let them occupy the UN building during the special session.

Horn walked up the front steps and was met just inside the main entrance by Sergeant Raece, who was talking into a hand-held radio and directing a number of other bluesuiters who were roping off the lobby and putting up signs saying the building was closed to visitors.

"Have the PATs guys shown up yet?" Horn asked, referring to the gentlemen of the Police Assault Team.

"They sure have, Detective Horn," Raece answered, turning off the radio and hanging it by a special clip to his belt. "They got here about twenty minutes ago and started setting up their positions from the fifteenth floor down, just like you ordered." The police sergeant took a small notebook out of his shirt pocket and flipped it open. "Lieutenant Bearden is commanding the team and they're using this frequency." He tore a sheet from the notebook and handed it to Horn.

"Here," Horn said, pulling his jacket away from his body, revealing a small radio strapped to the small of his back. "Set the frequency, will you? Whoever designed this thing sure as hell wasn't a human-factors engineer."

"They're a pain in the ass," Raece said, bending over. He punched the frequency into a small keypad on the radio. "There you are."

"Thanks," Horn said, pulling his jacket back in place. "You said Joe Bearden is commanding the PATs team?"

"That's right," Raece answered, the tone of his voice adding, *I'm sorry to say.*

Horn had never worked with Bearden and, based on the man's reputation, was glad he hadn't. The cocky little lieutenant was known for being overly aggressive and had earned the dubious nickname of "Quickdraw." He wasn't exactly the kind of guy you wanted around when a situation was delicate.

"Well, Bearden's orders are to follow my orders," Horn said, adjusting a switch on the device behind his ear. "The plan is to shut down the lobby the first sign of a problem."

"Right," Raece said, flipping through his notebook. "The place is fitted with quarter-inch-steel blast shields that close off the entire front here." He pointed at a long slot that ran completely across the front of the building, just inside the ten sets of glass doors. "I'll control them from over there." Raece turned and pointed toward a combination receptionist-and-guard station that served as a checkpoint between the expansive lobby and the rest of the building. "As soon as you give me the word, I'll shut them down. But..."

"But what?" Horn asked.

"If we're going to close the building to the public, why don't we go ahead and drop the blast shields?"

"Apparently it takes three or four days to reset them once they're dropped," Horn answered. "Anyway, we had a hard enough time just convincing the UN to let us come in here and *protect* them."

"Sort of hard to force your benevolence on them, hey?" Raece laughed heartily. Horn waited quietly for his merriment to finish.

"Anyway," Horn said, "you don't have to wait for me to give you the go-ahead to drop the shields. If you see somebody spit on the sidewalk funny, go ahead and drop them. Use your own judgment.''

"Yes, sir," Raece acknowledged.

"Are the snipers in place?"

"Yes, sir," Raece repeated. "We've got four guys from our precinct spread out on those buildings over there." He pointed out the front doors toward several neighboring office buildings. "But the range and the placement is bad. I really don't think they'll do much good if something happens."

"You're probably right," Horn said.

"Where's the meeting going to take place?"

"On the nineteenth floor," Horn answered, looking at his watch. The delegates were scheduled to begin arriving in less than fifteen minutes. "That's where I'll be. There's a guard station up there, and I'll keep the telemonitor linked directly with the one down here." He pointed to the receptionist's desk. "Also, we're going to take the elevators out of commission. The only way up or down will be the stairs. The helipad is considered the twentieth floor, so if something does go down, we should have plenty of time to clear the assembly members before anyone could hoof it up the stairs. Speaking of which—" Horn slapped Raece on the back "—I better get up there unless I want to walk up nineteen flights."

"Don't worry about a thing, Detective Horn," Raece said. "I don't know who the hell these guys are you might be expecting, but we can take care of them."

Horn thought of the bodies stacked up around the suite in which they'd found Merrifield's corpse, and shivered slightly. "Sure thing," he said before turning and walking toward the elevators.

Stopping on the fifteenth floor, Horn was greeted at the elevator by Police Assault Team Commander, Lieutenant Joe Bearden. "Detective Horn," Bearden said, holding out his hand, "I understand I'm to coordinate my activities with you."

Horn looked at the man called Quickdraw and nodded, purposely not extending his hand. He'd noticed the lieutenant had said "coordinate" and figured he'd better let him know who was running the show before the guy tried to reverse their roles, as he had a reputation for doing.

Bearden stood no taller than five-four and was dressed in a black jumpsuit whose built-in body armor made him look almost muscular. An all-composite Browning assault rifle hung by a sling over his shoulder. It was fitted with a special folding clip that nearly tripled the number of rounds the weapon could fire without a reload. Horn thought the little man looked like a polished bullet.

"That's not quite right, Lieutenant," Horn said, making eye contact with the gung ho cop. He watched Bearden's face turn red and could see the veins standing out on his neck.

"You want to elaborate on that statement, Detective?" Bearden asked between clinched teeth.

"Sure," Horn said sternly. "I'm in charge of this little operation, so you don't *coordinate* your goddamn activities with me. As a matter of fact, you don't do shit unless I tell you, got it?"

Bearden looked as though he were about to have a stroke, and for a moment Horn thought he'd try to buck his authority.

"I got it," Bearden finally said, his expression saying he didn't like it a damn bit. "Where do you want my men?"

"Where are they now?" Horn asked.

"They're spread out in the two main stairwells from here down to the fourth floor," Bearden answered.

"Are there only two stairwells?"

"That's all the floor plans show. There's a couple of outside fire escapes, but they're like ladders. We've got a couple of men outside wiring them with plastique. If somebody tries to use them, we'll blow them off the sides of the building."

"Good work," Horn said. "If something happens, I want your men to go into a regressive bounding overwatch. The objective will be to slow down the perpetrators."

Bearden seemed surprised by Horn's use of tactics-type terminology. "Why don't you just let me take out whoever may be dumb enough to try coming up the stairs?" he asked. "There's no way anyone can get by my men."

Horn sighed. "Just do what I tell you, when I tell you. Understood?"

"Understood," Bearden said as Horn turned and got back on the elevator.

Horn switched his radio on. "Keep the talk on the net down to only what's necessary," he said, punching the nineteenth-floor button.

"Yes, sir," said Bearden as the elevator closed.

Horn walked out of the elevator into a small lobby that served as a focal point for the nineteenth floor. A uniformed cop from his own precinct greeted him from behind a U-shaped guard station. "Go ahead and tell them to shut down the elevators," Horn said as he walked around behind the polished-wood counter. "Have the delegates arrived?"

"Yes, sir," the cop answered as he keyed in a code on one of six telemonitors built into the counter. Horn heard him tell someone to take the elevators off-line.

"Are you finished?" Horn asked, walking to the telemonitor. The cop nodded and backed away. He punched in the main lobby, and Raece's face came up on the screen. Horn could tell something was wrong— the grizzled sergeant was fidgeting and his eyes were everywhere else but on the sensor relaying his image.

"What's going on down there?"

"Probably nothing. A moving van has pulled up outside. I sent two of the uniforms to check it out."

Horn switched another monitor to an outside camera that took in the main driveway. Sure enough, a bright orange semi was parked directly in front of the main steps. He watched as one of the uniforms walked around to the front of the tractor-trailer and was met by a man in an orange jumpsuit who had climbed down from the cab of the truck.

"Was there some sort of delivery scheduled for to-day?" Horn asked, turning toward the cop who was studying a monitor at the far end of the counter.

"No, sir," the cop answered without looking up. "We canceled all business and all deliveries today. Maybe somebody didn't get the message."

Horn looked back at the screen and was stunned to see the orange-suited man grab the cop in a headlock and throw him violently. The only thing missing was the sound of his spine breaking. Shifting to the screen Raece was on, Horn yelled, "Shut it down, now!" He watched Raece fumbling with some controls. "There," Raece said, sweat running down his face. "They're closed."

"Turn your sharpshooters loose," Horn ordered, "I'm going to evacuate the delegates."

"Right," the police sergeant responded, bringing the hand-held up next to his head.

"Who's in charge of the helipad?" Horn asked, pushing a button on his earpiece that would allow him to have a hot mike.

"Ah, Kirkmeyer, sir," Raece answered, punching in a code on his own radio.

"Kirkmeyer," Horn immediately spoke into the end of the tube in front of his chin. "This is Detective Horn. We're going to evacuate the delegates. Put the pilots on hot standby."

"Roger," a voice came through the earpiece, surprising Horn with its clarity. He remembered the little radio was multiplexed, which supposedly allowed several people to communicate on the same channel without interfering with one another.

"Okay," Horn said, turning to the cop. "Get the delegates upstairs. You know the procedure."

The cop disappeared through a set of double doors as Horn turned back to the telemonitor feed from the lobby.

"Take a look at what they've got going outside," Raece said, his voice strained.

Horn glanced at the other monitor and saw that something resembling a small bulldozer was being driven down a ramp from the back of the van. Instead of a blade, it had a huge steel wedge sticking out from its nose.

"Can you guess what they intend to do with that son of a bitch?" Raece asked.

Horn hoped Raece wouldn't panic. "How about the sharpshooters? Did they do any good?"

Raece looked into the screen and laughed crazily. "Shit!" he retorted. "Either my guys are firing blanks or these motherfuckers are built from the same prints as the guy downtown."

Horn knew Raece was talking about the droid who'd wiped out Merrifield and his entourage. "How many of them have you seen?" he asked, glancing at the other screen.

"Four or five," Raece answered. "It's hard to tell. They're all wearing the same thing and they all look alike."

"You and your men head upstairs," Horn ordered. "If you've got anybody outside, tell them to beat it the hell away from there."

"Got it," Raece said, a measure of relief in his voice.

Horn could hear something in the background that sounded like a wrecking ball slamming into the side of the building. The monitor showed the tracked dozer backing up to make another run at the blast shields. Pieces of glass and twisted steel door-frames were scattered across the sidewalk and driveway. A dent the size of a small car had been made in the thick steel, and Horn figured it wouldn't take many more runs with the battering ram before the droids would be inside.

"Bearden, this is Horn," he spoke into the tiny mouthpiece. "Are you copying this?"

"This is Bearden," the lieutenant's voice came back. "I've been monitoring the net, and we can see what's going on outside."

"Raece and his uniforms are going to be coming up the stairs," Horn said, thinking they could blow the stairwells if they had to. "Once they're by, expect—"

"Like I said," Bearden interrupted, "we're aware of what's going on. We can handle it."

"I hope so," Horn said, wondering how the cocky lieutenant would react the first time he faced a droid.

"Kirkmeyer," Horn barked. "How's the evac going?"

"We got a problem," the cop's voice poured into the earpiece.

The familiar air-slapping sound of the blades of several helicopters made it somewhat difficult for Horn to understand the cop. "What kind of problem?" he asked, raising his voice as the distinct sound of automatic-weapons firing mixed in with the noise.

"Some kind of gunship..." Kirkmeyer said before his voice trailed off into the din pouring in through the earpiece.

"Shit." Horn bolted through the double doors and sprinted up the carpeted stairs leading to the helipad.

The first thing Horn saw on the roof was an old MH-80 helicopter with a single gun-pod mounted between its skids. The bird swung out over the East River, banking back around, apparently setting up to make another pass. Horn swung around to the three Aerospatiale transporters still on the pad. Two had their blades turning, and one was shut down, smoke pouring out of the engine cowling, a ragged line of bullet holes stitched across its slick skin.

Horn quickly approached a man whom he assumed was Kirkmeyer, crouched next to a large vent. He dived down next to him just as the MH-80 made another pass, tearing up the roof as its chain gun screamed out a thick stream of lead. The bullets ran up the side of the smoldering helicopter and blew off its rotor hub in a shower of sparks and flying metal.

Horn grabbed the Colt autorifle Kirkmeyer had in his hands and emptied its clip at the gunship as it banked away from the roof. "What the hell is wrong with you?" he screamed in Kirkmeyer's face, and shoved the weapon against the cop's chest. "Get your ass over there and get the goddamn delegates off that bird before it blows!" He pointed to the damaged aircraft.

"What then?" Kirkmeyer stammered, his eyes wide with fear.

"Put them on the other two," Horn ordered, shoving the cop toward the helicopters.

Standing, Horn pulled his 9 mm from its holster and blinked on the weapons mode in his right eye as the gunship banked around over the river, its exhaust leaving a trail of white vapor in the cold gray sky. He walked toward the edge of the building, stepping over the shredded body of the cop who'd been at the guard station with him just minutes earlier. The big automatic felt good in his hand; it felt *right*. Horn felt a chill climb up his back, but knew it wasn't from the cold. The gun, the confidence he was now feeling, was being generated by his mods. Without willing it, the 9 mm came up in his hand and drew a rough bead on the gunship, which had gone nose-down and was coming in for another pass.

Horn had the feeling he was an innocent bystander and watched with a strange fascination as the cross hairs in his eye locked onto a green-visored helmet in the left seat of the attacking aircraft. He could hear yelling and screaming behind him as the gun pod opened up, flashes of orange flame lighting up the front of the helicopter like a bizarre strobe.

Horn waited for his finger to pull the trigger and suddenly felt the chill run up his back again like the edge of a straight razor. He realized he was waiting for his E-mod to pull the trigger and watched as the aircraft burned in over Franklin Roosevelt Drive, filling his field of vision like a high-speed dream. A bucking sensation ran down his arm, and Horn watched the slide of the automatic jack back several times, spent brass flying out of its breech.

Everything seemed to be moving in a jerking stop-and-go, as though Horn were watching the scene unfold frame by frame. He saw the windshield of the helicopter break apart like an eggshell, and a milli-second later the green-helmeted pilot was blown backward in a fantastic blur of colors and motion.

Horn ducked as the inside of the MH-80 exploded, ejecting fire and debris as it flew overhead, its rotor blades sounding hollow and out of balance. Shielding his face and turning, he watched the helicopter disappear over the edge of the building, trailing smoke and fire forty yards behind its broken carcass.

"Can you hear me, Kirkmeyer?" Horn spoke into the tube as an explosion erupted from the place where the helicopter had gone down. He looked across the roof. The cop was helping another uniform close one of the undamaged birds.

"What is it?" Kirkmeyer asked.

Horn noticed by the tone of the man's voice that he seemed more in control. "You got all the delegates loaded?" he asked, watching Kirkmeyer run from beneath the spinning rotor blades.

"We've got two dead and two or three wounded," the cop answered. "I got the wounded on, but there's no room for the dead."

"Launch them," Horn ordered. "Then get ahold of central dispatch and tell them to get some birds in here."

"Roger," the cop came back. Seconds later the two aircraft lifted off and banked down over the river, their turbines screaming from the loads they were carrying.

Horn sprinted toward the stairwell. Stopping just inside the doors, he punched the spent clip from the handle of the 9 mm and reached inside his jacket, pulling out a full one. "Bearden," he spoke calmly, jamming the fresh clip into the butt of the weapon. "What's the status down there?"

"Not good," Bearden answered, sounding anxious. "I've got at least a dozen men dead and half as many wounded. What the hell are we fighting, anyway?"

"What floor are they on?"

"The fifteenth," Bearden answered. "We've moved up to the seventeenth."

Horn moved down the stairs, wondering if Bearden had tried to fight it out with the droids instead of simply evacuating as he had been told. By the number of men Bearden reported dead, he figured the idiot had tried to fight. "Are they coming up both stairwells?" he asked.

"No, just on the north side," Bearden answered. "We blew the other one. It's jammed up with a ton of shit, believe me."

"Blow the one you're in now," Horn ordered, hoping it wasn't too late.

"We can't," Bearden answered.

"Why the hell not?" Horn asked, stepping into the stairwell and staring at Bearden's sweaty face.

The lieutenant's jaw dropped. "Because," he said, jerking around and gazing down the stairs, "we lost the demo package."

"What do you mean?"

"Miller was carrying the goddamn package," Bearden answered, his face drawn and flushed. "And one of those goddamn *things* nailed his ass." He nodded down the stairs.

"Are they using weapons?"

"Who?"

Horn felt his patience slipping. "The guys in the orange jumpsuits. The droids."

"Droids, huh?" Bearden shook his head. "We weren't told anything in the briefing about no goddamn robots."

Horn grabbed Bearden by the front of his body armor, shoved him against the wall and clasped his jaw. "Listen, you asshole," he said, his face within inches of Bearden's. "When I ask a question, I want a straight answer. And when I tell you to do something, I want it done without any of your editorials, understand?'' Horn shook Bearden's head up and down, resisting the urge to slam his head against the wall. He released his grip, but didn't back away. ''Now, were the droids using any weapons?''

''Yeah, yeah,'' Bearden answered, rubbing his pained jaw. ''Automatics mostly, though someone said they heard a shotgun.''

''Where's Raece?'' Horn asked. The sound of weapons firing floated up from the stairwell.

''He's down on fifteen trying to slow them down,'' Bearden answered.

''Is that where the rest of your men are?''

''Yes, sir. I was just on my way down there.''

''Then go.'' Horn gestured toward the stairs with the 9 mm.

A flash of fear crossed Bearden's face as he glanced down the stairway. ''What do you want us to do?'' he asked nervously.

''Whatever the hell you can,'' Horn answered. He grabbed Bearden and shoved him toward the stairs. ''Just be ready to pull your men out and head for the roof when I call.''

Bearden nodded and swallowed hard. ''Got it,'' he answered before heading down the stairs.

''Kirkmeyer,'' Horn spoke into the microphone. Leaning against the wall, he noticed he was sweating profusely and wiped his forehead.

''This is Kirkmeyer.''

"What's the status on getting us a way off the roof?"

"The status is that there ain't no status," Kirkmeyer answered.

"It'll be at least half an hour before they can get us a bird. Even then—" he paused "—dispatch says they can only spare one."

"Shit," Horn breathed. "What about the two goddamn helicopters we just launched? Why don't they drop their load somewhere and come back?"

"Let me check on that," Kirkmeyer answered.

"And where the hell is Winger?" Horn spoke to himself and looked at his watch. It was 10:30.

Horn realized there wasn't much he could do to slow the droids. He thought about barricading the stairwell, but figured it would take more than a bunch of desks and file cabinets to create anything more than a minor inconvenience for the Neuroids.

"Bearden," he said, dropping his head slightly so the end of the mike was in front of his mouth.

"What is it?"

"What floor did you blow the other stairwell on?"

"If you're thinking about cutting back under them, forget it," Bearden answered. "We blew the fifteenth floor, and the whole damn structure collapsed, above and below. You can't go up and you can't go down. Sorry."

"Shit," Horn said, his gut churning. Suddenly he remembered that the fire escape was a ladder on the outside of the building. He turned and walked through a door into the fifteenth floor. Across the open office area he saw a red arrow-shaped sign over a window, which read Emergency Use Only.

Horn grabbed the vertical blinds covering the window, ripping them from the wall as though tearing a sheet of paper from a pad. He found himself staring straight into the emotionless face of one of the Neuroids. One arm hooked over a rung of the ladder, it was in the process of ripping the locking mechanism from the base of the window.

"Goddamn!" Horn gasped, stumbling back. The droid lunged through the plate glass and hit the floor rolling as glass showered all around. It came up in front of Horn on its feet. It swung around and aimed one of its boots straight for Horn's face, the huge leg unfolding like a switchblade.

Horn swung his right arm up and across, diverting the droid's kick enough that it only caused a glancing blow on the side of his head. He thrust forward and swung his modified arm in a backhanded slice, aiming for the droid's throat. A shock wave jolted up the titanium as his hand slammed into the droid's thick neck and stopped cold, as though he'd hit a concrete piling.

"Damn!" Horn cursed, thinking he should have known better. The droid came at him with amazing speed, its arms churning through the air like two pistons, swinging at Horn's head every time the range was close. He managed to fend off two or three blows by knocking them away with his E-mod, a dull, metallic ringing echoing in the empty office like the sound of a medieval sword fight.

Sidestepping, Horn raised his arm to counter another one of the droid's swings and found himself falling over a pushcart filled with mail. He felt a fist slam into his side and screamed, surprised that he didn't hear his ribs breaking. Forcing himself to roll, he managed to stagger to his feet just as the Neuroid brought both hands down in a single fist straight for his head. Horn jerked sideways, and the blow slammed into his right shoulder, knocking him backward onto the floor next to a copier.

Something red and shiny caught Horn's eye as the droid moved toward him, cocking its arm over its head for another blow. Grabbing a fire extinguisher that was hanging from a bracket on the end of the copier, he kicked his right leg in a sweeping motion, flexing his modified knee with as much power as he could muster. The droid was upended, crashing sideways into the copy machine before falling on its barrel-shaped chest next to Horn.

"You son of a bitch!" Horn gasped as he struggled to his feet. He swung the heavy extinguisher up over his head and brought it down directly on the back of the droid's skull. The sound rang out like a hammer striking an anvil.

The droid lifted its head and shook it before rising to its feet. Horn backed away and threw the extinguisher into the droid's chest, watching it bounce off harmlessly.

Using his 9 mm pistol, Horn fired three times between the droid's eyes, even though he knew it wasn't going to do much good. The droid's head jerked back with each shot, and it brushed a hand in front of its face as though trying to shoo an annoying insect.

"Shit," Horn breathed, figuring to move around the droid and back to the stairs. If he got the thing to follow him up to the roof, he could try to make it take the big dive. It was thin, but better than nothing.

Horn turned and felt a trapdoor in his stomach swing wide open, dropping his heart into free-fall. Another droid stood blocking his escape route, staring at him with lifeless eyes.

Raising the 9 mm, Horn emptied the rest of the clip, alternating shots between the two droids. He didn't intend to go down without a fight. He launched a flying kick into the nearest droid's chest and managed to knock it backward against a row of bookshelves. He made a dash for the opening and felt himself jerked off his feet as the second droid wrapped its thick arm around his neck like a python.

Horn saw stars as the droid applied pressure, and knew he was about to go under. He cocked his mod and swung his elbow into the droid's midsection, but all that happened was that the droid squeezed tighter.

"Can't leave you alone for a goddamn minute, can I?"

At first Horn thought he was dreaming. The sound of Winger's voice was followed by a loud electrical snapping, like a circuit shorting out. Then the droid fell from around his neck as though it were a leech stabbed with the glowing end of a cigarette.

Horn staggered forward, clutching his throat. He heard Winger's voice telling him to get the hell out of his way. He felt a hand grab his arm and jerk him to one side, followed by the sound of a circuit shorting out again.

"Got the son of a bitch," Winger said as Horn took several deep breaths. "You all right, partner?"

The vision returned to Horn's left eye, but his right was still changing modes like someone flipping through the channels of a television. He closed his eyelid over the lens and looked around with his natural sight. The two droids were curled up in fetal positions on the floor, their bodies twitching uncontrollably. Winger, grinning, was holding a device that resembled an electric charcoal starter. It was hooked by a thick cable to a coil-shaped object hanging from a strap over his back.

"Let's help the others," Horn said, picking up his 9 mm from the floor. He motioned for Winger to follow, and started for the door.

"Hold it." Winger grabbed Horn by the sleeve. "I already took care of them."

"All of them?" Horn raised his eyebrows, conscious that his heart was beating in his chest like a bass drum.

"Even the ones that were in the helicopter that crashed," Winger said, releasing his partner. "Believe it or not, three of those bastards came out of the wreckage like nothing had happened." The young cop laughed and shook his head. "Their clothes and hair were burned off. They looked pretty damn bizarre."

"How many were there, total?"

"Nine, counting these two." Winger nodded at the droids on the floor, whose bodies had finally grown still.

"You sure you got them all?" Horn cocked his head slightly to one side.

"I'm sure." Winger led Horn toward the door. "Come on," he said. "There should be a chopper on the roof by now."

"What's going on?" Horn asked, trying his right eye and finding with some relief that it had normalized. He blinked it in and out of each mode a couple of times before leaving it in video.

"The Barracuda sent the bird," Winger answered as he motioned Horn upstairs. "She said to have you call her as soon as we're airborne."

"Wonderful," Horn said as he stuck the 9 mm in its holster and mounted the steps.

CHAPTER SIXTEEN

As soon as the helicopter was airborne, Horn used the telemonitor behind the pilot's seat and keyed in Christina Service's office number. Seconds later a tight-lipped brunette, whom Horn recognized as the DA's office receptionist, came on the screen.

"Ms. Service, please," Horn said, sliding as the pilot banked hard-over and headed east.

"Is she expecting your call?"

Resisting the urge to give a snappy and impertinent answer, Horn said, "Why don't you ask her?"

The receptionist glared at Horn before switching the screen to standby. Almost immediately the flashing red letters were replaced with Service's image. Her arms were folded across the desk, and she was leaning forward, her face filling the screen.

"I've been trying to get a hold of you for an hour," she said.

"I've been kind of tied up," Horn said, glancing at Winger, who was cramped into the copilot's seat. The young cop grinned crazily, rolling his eyes.

"I hate to tell you this," Service said, "but two of the wounded delegates you managed to evacuate died."

"I doubt anyone could have prevented it," Horn said, wondering how many would have bought it if Service hadn't convinced the State Department to let them chaperon the meeting. "Nobody expected them to use an armed aircraft."

"I suppose you're right," Service said. "Are you wondering where you're headed?"

"The thought had crossed my mind."

"Julius Ticket's compound," Service said. "We tracked him down to the old LaSalle Academy out on Long Island. You should be there in a matter of minutes."

"How did you figure out where to find him?"

"I've got my sources," Service answered, using the line he had used so many times with her.

"Okay," he said, smiling.

"Ask her if she's arranged for some backup," Winger said, leaning backward and tapping Horn on the leg. He repeated the question to Service.

"Right now that's a small problem," she replied, a worried expression crossing her face. "There's a major labor union riot going on down in Brooklyn. Every available bluesuit is there or on the way there. As I understand it, they're even sending the PATs team that was supporting you."

"You mean what's left of them," Horn said, wondering if Raece had survived the battle in the stairwell. "Any word on Dartt?"

"Sorry." Service shook her head.

Horn felt sorrowful and angry as he thought about Dartt. "Get me some backup as soon as you can," he said. "In the meantime, we'll make do with what we've got."

"Listen, Max," Service said. "We've got word that Kindu's in the country. There's a good chance he'll be at Ticket's. If he is, the State Department would like to have our assurance that he'll be taken into custody...ah..." She puckered her lips, seemingly unsure how to finish the sentence.

"Alive," Winger said, leaning toward Horn. He reached over and pressed the Mute button on the keypad. "She wants to make sure we give our word that we won't kill the son of a bitch."

"She said the *State Department* wants assurance, not her," Horn said, knocking Winger's hand away. "Now, keep your goddamn hands off this panel." It suddenly struck him as funny that he was defending something Service had said. He looked at Winger, who held both of his hands up as if to say, *Give me a break*.

"What the hell is going on there?"

"Nothing," Horn answered. Winger had turned around and was staring out the windshield.

"Listen, Max," Service said quietly. "I still want to get together with you again, you know."

Horn was surprised, given the circumstances. He leaned back, realizing he didn't know what to say. He looked up at Winger, whose expression was neutral.

"Sure, Christina," he said. Horn felt his mods sort of ripple and admitted to himself that he shared the doubt reflected in her expression. "You don't even know me," he said, dropping his voice.

"I'm sure you're right, Max," she said, and the screen blinked off.

Damn, Horn thought, feeling his mods glitch for real. Nothing seemed to make sense when it came to the woman. Nothing made much sense when it came to *anything*. Horn looked up as Winger slapped him on the leg.

"Let's take care of this Ticket joker, then find Dartt," the young cop said, his patented grin returning to his face.

"Right," Horn said, folding the telemonitor into the back of the seat. At least what Winger said made sense. The thought of Dartt hung like a dark shadow in his mind. He had a feeling Latch had something to do with their friend's disappearance and he remembered what August had said: *Find Latch and you'll find Ticket.* Now he hoped the opposite was true.

It had begun to snow as the helicopter came down in a slow spiral over the old LaSalle compound. "Where do you want me to land?" the pilot asked Winger.

The small four-seater helicopter was being buffeted wildly in the heavy wind as Winger searched for a suitable landing site. Twice, in leaning forward, his forehead slammed into the Plexiglas bubble. "There," he finally said, pointing to a circular driveway near the largest of several buildings.

"You know they'll hear us when we land," the pilot said, holding one of his earphones away from his head.

Winger looked back at Horn as if to say, *Do you care?* Horn shrugged and pulled out his 9 mm. He popped out the clip and popped in another and jacked a shell into the chamber.

"Go ahead and land," Winger told the pilot. "They've probably heard us already."

The pilot put the bird on the ground. When the back of the skids hit the ground, the craft pitched forward violently.

"Holy shit!" Winger yelled as the machine skidded to a stop, its spinning rotor blades inches from a flagpole.

Horn was reaching for his seat belt when the pilot's door swung open, admitting a blast of cold air and swirling snow. A big arm hooked around the pilot's head, pulling him a foot out of the vehicle before his shoulder straps unreeled to the Stop position.

"Goddammit!"

Winger pulled his machine pistol from his coat and fired over the pilot, who was twisted sideways.

Horn tried the door to his left but something outside had jammed it closed. He smashed a fist through the fogged-over Plexiglas. Whover or whatever had grabbed the pilot around the neck was blocking the door by jamming a hip against it. Horn punched the thing's kidney area as the pilot screamed, sounding as though he was getting his arms torn off. The blow didn't faze whoever was outside the bird, and Horn knew immediately it had to be a droid. He looked at Winger, who had apparently realized it, too, and was trying to reach August's weapon in the seat next to Horn.

"Give it to me!" Winger yelled, firing another burst over the writhing pilot.

The pilot screamed again, then suddenly went silent. A loud snap filled the inside of the helicopter.

"Give me the son of a bitch, hurry!" Winger implored again. "Turn it on for me!"

Horn grabbed the handle of the weapon and shoved it into Winger's waiting hand. "Switch on the coil!" Winger yelled, pointing the fan-shaped antenna past Horn's head toward the door.

Horn saw what Winger was talking about just as the door next to him jerked open. He placed his hand over the switch just as a pair of ice-cold hands wrapped around his throat and jerked him from the aircraft. He hit the snow-covered ground and bounced violently as the droid whipped him back and forth like a dog shaking a rag. Reaching up, Horn grabbed the droid by the head and tried to throw it over his shoulder. He might as well have been trying to rip one of the faces off Mount Rushmore.

The droid suddenly stopped shaking him and began to squeeze his neck in a slow, almost deliberate manner. For some reason it struck him as odd; it was as though the droid couldn't do more than one thing at a time. "Winger!" he managed to gasp as his modified eye began to blink uncontrollably.

"I'm afraid to shoot!" Winger shouted. Horn could see him standing next to the helicopter, aiming August's weapon at the droid. "I don't know what this son of a bitch will do to you!"

"Shoot!" Horn managed to croak, thinking he'd rather take his chances getting zapped with the weapon than get choked to death by a dumb droid.

Horn, his consciousness slipping away, glimpsed his partner pulling a small lever on the device that obviously served as the trigger. At first he felt nothing, just more pressure from the droid's crushing hands. In the next instant the droid had flipped forward and was kicking and bucking as though every component in its electrical system was shorting out.

Coughing like crazy, Horn tried to roll away from the thrashing droid. Suddenly he thought he'd been struck by lightning as his arm and knee went berserk, kicking and swinging as if they were possessed by some spastic demon. The violent action propelled Horn facedown in the snow, where he watched a bizarre light show as his right eye flipped modes like the tail of a nervous cat.

"Horn!" Winger yelled, crouching down next to him. "Are you all right, partner?"

Horn felt his mods wind down. One second he was flopping around crazily, and the next he was calm, save for some minor twitching like the aftershocks of an earthquake. "I'm fine," he said. He pushed himself to his knees. The droid was still jerking around, though not as violently as it had when first hit.

"You think it's dead?" Winger asked.

Horn thought about the young cop's question a moment before answering. "What do you mean, *dead?*"

"I mean like him," said Winger, nodding at the pilot, who was hanging from the helicopter, his neck twisted savagely.

"That evil bastard." Horn turned to the droid, which had finally come to a dead stop. "Let's get moving."

Winger nodded.

"Why don't you check out the building over there," Horn said. He pointed toward a two-story boxlike structure across a narrow road. "I'll check out this one." Horn jerked his head, indicating the larger building in front of them.

Winger started to protest. Horn was taking the building in which they'd most likely find someone or something.

"Just make a quick pass through it," Horn said, "then come back here and find a back way into the place. I should have stirred up enough shit by then that you'll be needed."

"Like at the UN?"

"Don't wait that long." Horn grinned and waved Winger away. He went to the double glass doors of what had to have once been the headquarters of the old LaSalle Military Academy. He figured he may as well stick with his normal approach, which was to try to find a shorter distance between two points than even a straight line.

He stepped into a polished tile hallway. Two uniformed guards behind a walnut counter stared at him as though he were the President making a surprise visit.

"How the hell did you get by—"

"My name's Max Horn." He stuck his right elbow on the counter, holding his gloved hand out toward the nearer guard. "I've got an appointment with Dr. Ticket. You see, I've been having a little problem with my right arm here. I can't seem to—" he suddenly backhanded the guard square on the nose, knocking him back into the wall "—control it sometimes." The guard slid down the wall, his eyes looking like frosted glass.

"Shit!" The other guard struggled to pull a big-handled Magnum from his belt.

"Oh, no, you don't," Horn said, grabbing the man's wrist. He twisted and squeezed, not bothering to restrain his mods. The wrist snapped like a piece of dry kindling, and Horn jerked the howling attendant forward, his chest slamming into the counter. His face smacked into the tabletop like the flat of an oar hitting water. Releasing the arm, Horn watched the guard's body slide to the floor in a crumpled heap.

He went to the bottom of a wide stairwell, sensing that whatever or whoever he was looking for would be at the top. Pulling the 9 mm from its holster, he moved up cautiously, blinking his eye into its IR and weapons modes.

The first door at the top of the stairs was locked. It was marked Unauthorized Personnel Keep Out. He thought about breaking it down, but instead he continued down the hall. The next door was a large swinging door stenciled with the words Operating Room. This time something told him there were warm bodies inside.

Pushing the door open just enough to admit him, Horn slipped in, moving quickly to his left and crouching along the wall. It was pitch-black. Almost immediately he inhaled a sickening smell that made him gag. He forced himself to choke down the contents of his stomach, which had moved up into his throat.

Horn picked up the IR image of someone across the room, behind some sort of partition, pointing a pistol toward the door through which he'd just entered. Suddenly the weapon erupted in a brilliant flash of light, and everything he'd been viewing in the familiar IR green went white. Hearing the bullet slam into the wall by the door, Horn rolled to his left, blinking his eye into video.

"Shit." Horn immediately recognized the wheezing voice as Toad's. His mods twitched mildly as he remembered the mirror-faced, neckless man in the hangar in Burbank.

The low-light video gave him enough vision to pick out his target. Just before Horn activated the laser sight, however, Toad walked to the door, apparently thinking Horn had never entered. He pushed the door open slightly and peered into the hall.

Not wasting any time, Horn moved up and swung the 9 mm and cracked the barrel of the big weapon across Toad's gun hand, knocking the pistol from his grip. It hit the floor and Toad screamed. Bringing the automatic up into Toad's face, Horn shoved him back and heard a loud grunt as he struck the hard floor.

The lights in the large room suddenly came on. Crouching, Horn saw a man in a white lab coat standing by a row of switches, his hands in the air, smiling strangely.

"Dr. Julius Ticket, I presume?" Horn said, shoving the struggling Toad back to the floor.

"That's correct. And you must be Maxwell Horn," Ticket said, approaching him, his watery eyes twinkling in the bright light.

"That's far enough," Horn said when Ticket was ten feet away. He noticed his 9 mm was already aimed at the middle of Ticket's chest.

"No problem," Ticket said calmly. "I see you've met Toad."

"This is the one I was telling you about," Toad wheezed. It was hard for him to talk because Horn's foot was planted firmly on his short neck.

"So I've deduced," Ticket said.

Horn shifted, placing his right knee on Toad's chest and the barrel of the 9 mm against the side of Toad's head. "Toad and I have met," he said, ignoring the little man beneath his knee. "Where's your Libyan friend, Hindu?" he asked, watching Ticket's face for a reaction.

"*Hindu?* That's funny." Ticket chuckled lightly. "Mr. *Kindu* and his dubious entourage left about four hours ago." He started to reach into the pocket of his lab coat, but stopped. "May I?" he asked. "I assure you I'm not armed."

"Go ahead," Horn answered.

Ticket pulled out a pack of cigarettes and a disposable lighter. "It's too bad we had to meet under such ugly circumstances. I was told you carried some rather unique—how shall I say it?—*body armor.*" He lit one of the smokes.

Horn felt the short hairs on the back of his neck bristle. He turned to gain a better view of the doorway.

"Oh," Ticket said as if he could read Horn's mind. "Don't worry about Mr. Latch. He's on what you might call an extended business trip." He took a long drag from the cigarette. Smoke poured heavily from his nose and mouth. "Since you are up here, can you tell me how you got past Number 24?" Ticket sounded genuinely curious.

"Number 24?" Horn didn't have an idea what he was talking about.

"The droid downstairs. The one that greeted you."

"Your guards asked the same question," Horn replied. "Let's just say he was a little slow." He squirmed as he thought of the dead pilot.

"I told you we shouldn't rely on—"

"Shut up!" Ticket snapped before Toad could finish.

Horn stood up, pointing the 9 mm directly at Toad's head. The beam of his laser sight reflected off the mirrored glasses in flashes of red. "Your little contingent of Neuroids at the UN didn't fare much better," he said, addressing Ticket.

Ticket looked momentarily stunned. "That's impossible," he said, smiling stiffly. "The last report we got had the droids *mopping up.*"

"Mopping up might be one thing they're good at," Horn said. "By the way," he said, bringing the 9 mm up and painting a red swatch on Ticket's forehead with the weapon's sight, "you haven't happened to run across a friend of mine, have you? A guy named Les Dartt?"

Toad's laughter sounded like an animal being run down on the highway. Ticket smiled. Smoke curled up in front of his face, framing it in a hazy veil.

Horn didn't know if it was Toad's hellish laughter or the look in Ticket's eyes that caused him to *split.* Something triggered a transformation in him that he'd never experienced before. His mind was perfectly clear and calm, almost as if it were set apart from his body, which was poised on the delicate edge of violence. He felt no *spirit.* It was as though he'd stepped, or been pushed, over a thin invisible line. He wondered if he were experiencing what August was talking about when he'd said he would make him a total *weapons* system. He suddenly felt clean and unencumbered by a nagging conscience; decisions were easy, driven by the immediate situation only. There was no need for moral reasoning. Horn liked the sensation; it had the instant effect of making his job easier.

"Where's Dartt?" he asked, the pencil beam of the laser sight still pegged on Ticket's forehead.

Ticket watched Horn as though he had seen the change. His expression was a cross between curiosity and grave concern. "I...I don't know," he finally answered.

"But you'll find out," Toad said from his prone position on the floor. Laughter gurgled out of his throat like sewage in a backed-up drain.

Horn looked down at Toad as though he'd forgotten the man was there. In a motion that was almost *casual,* he swung the 9 mm down and fired a single shot directly between Toad's eyes.

Ticket screamed and crouched in panic as the explosive sound filled the room. Toad's head bounced as though it had been struck with a sledgehammer, then blew apart, splattering blood and pieces of his brain in a gruesome mess.

Horn raised the automatic to Ticket. "Don't make me ask you a second time where Dartt is," he said calmly.

Ticket cleared his throat and straightened up, seeming to regain some of his composure. "So you want to know where this *Dartt* is," he said, tossing his cigarette butt to the floor. "To tell you the truth, we thought he was your partner."

Horn squeezed the trigger just enough to activate the laser sight and automatically fine-aimed the 9 mm. Ticket jerked his head down, stared at the red dot that appeared just over his left breast and sucked in his breath. "No, wait," he said immediately, holding up his hands. "You want Dartt? I'll give you Dartt. Number 1!" Ticket turned his head and yelled over his shoulder. "Enter now!"

The droid came through the door slowly, slightly bent at the waist. Horn looked at it, but nothing registered. He returned his gaze to Ticket, who was smiling grimly as the droid moved beside him and stopped.

"You've got less than ten seconds to tell me where Dartt is," Horn said, ignoring the droid.

"This *is* Dartt," Ticket said, motioning toward Number 1. "At least, this is his neural system." He moved around behind the droid, laughing strangely.

Horn stared at the droid as the shock ran through his system. He watched the camera lens spin in and out of the *machine* side of the thing's head as if it were sizing him up. Horn realized he'd dropped out of the weapons mode and felt a stab of anxiety in addition to the shock. "Les?" he said tentatively, focusing on the side of the droid's face that resembled a human's.

"Don't waste your breath, Mr. Horn," Ticket said, peering over the Neuroid's shoulder. "This one won't respond to your voiceprint."

"Les, is that *you?*" Horn said, ignoring Ticket.

"I told you, the droid—"

Ticket's speech was cut off in midsentence as Number 1 emitted a guttural, almost primal groan. The droid tilted its head back and swung it slowly from side to side as if it were in great pain.

"Goddamn!" Ticket jumped away from the droid and looked ready to take off in a run.

"Les," Horn implored. "It's me, Max."

"Listen, goddammit," Ticket addressed the Neuroid. "Kill him! I order you!" He pointed to Horn.

Number 1 moved toward Horn, its metallic right arm moving up from its side, its steel pincers opening like the jaws of some giant mutant insect.

"Don't, Les," Horn said, holding up his hand. "We can get August. He can help you."

The droid stopped four feet from Horn and cranked its head toward Ticket, who looked horrified.

"Kill him!" Ticket shouted, stomping his foot.

Number 1 turned back toward Horn and opened its hideous mouth. "Max." The name came out in a strained and synthesized voice that sounded like the echo of someone who had fallen into a well.

Horn felt as though his heart had been stabbed with a spire of ice. "Oh, Les," he half whispered, realizing that Dartt was actually a part of the hideous machine standing in front of him.

"Kill him," Ticket repeated, his voice reflecting forced restraint. "Kill the son of a bitch now."

Horn took a step toward the droid and reached out with his left hand. "Come on, Les, I'll take you to August's. He'll help us."

Number 1 jerked its head halfway around in Ticket's direction and emitted another sound. This time it was a scream straight from the depths of some ungodly machine hell.

Horn felt the hair on the back of his neck stiffen as he imagined what it was like to be trapped inside the mutated machine. "Come on, Les," he said, touching the metal appendage that served as the droid's right arm.

The droid's move was so sudden that Horn didn't have a chance to react. It brought its left arm up and around in a blur and cracked the palm of its humanoid-shaped hand across the side of Horn's face, knocking him sideways off his feet as though he'd been hit by a speeding truck.

"That's it!" Ticket almost cheered. "Finish the job." He turned and headed for the door that opened into the main hallway.

Horn thought for a moment that he'd been shot, and half expected to open his eyes in the world of the dead. Instead, he saw a crazy burst of stars as he shook his head in an attempt to clear it, the pain feeling like the clamp of ice tongs on his temples. His vision cleared and he watched Number 1 turn toward him, then stop as if it were contemplating its next move.

"Damn!" Ticket yelled as the door through which he was about to exit suddenly swung inward and struck him on the shoulder. Winger shoved his way into the operating room, knocking Ticket backward several steps. "Hold that son of a bitch!" Horn yelled, pointing the 9 mm at Ticket, surprised the weapon was still in his hand.

Winger turned. "Watch it! Goddamn!"

Horn turned as the droid's steel pincers came straight for his face like the fangs of a mechanical cobra. He jerked away and felt the cold steel against the side of his head. The Neuroid's legs rammed into Horn's upper body and sent him sprawling backward.

Scrambling to his feet, Horn sidestepped just as the droid came at him again. This time he was ready. He jammed his right foot down in front of the droid's legs, flexing his modified knee as they collided. It felt as though his leg had been hit by a steel ram. Still, he managed to bring his modified arm around in a sloppy sort of backswing and slam his elbow into the droid's back, knocking it onto its face, its body sliding forward several feet on the slick floor.

"Here!" Winger yelled.

Horn turned toward his partner, who had managed to wrestle Ticket to the floor. He was holding the man facedown and had one knee resting on his back. Horn watched the young cop heft the coil of August's EMP weapon from around his shoulder and swing it by its strap, sliding it to him across the floor.

The droid whirred as it struggled to get up. Horn looked down at the ugly weapon at his feet. He watched Number 1 rise and turn toward him.

Winger yelled at him to pick up the weapon. The young cop's voice sounded as if it were coming from a million miles away. Horn was aware of his 9 mm being shoved into its holster and felt himself bend down and flip the switch on the coil before grabbing the gun portion of the weapon. He never took his eyes off the droid moving toward him, its pincers opening wide.

"Les, don't make me do this," Horn whispered. He aimed the directional antenna straight at the Neuroid as Winger yelled from some other dimension for him to shoot.

Horn thought of Dartt, the human, his friend. The crazy bastard had saved his ass more than once and here he was about to kill him. Horn had his finger on the lever, but couldn't bring himself to trip it. He felt sadness come over him as the droid stopped less than six feet away, staring, looking almost as if it were *waiting*. Horn tried to *see* Dartt in the machine that was standing in front of him, but all he saw was something ugly, cold and bred to kill.

A shock ran down Horn's spine as the droid moved toward him again. It wasn't fear he felt jolting his nervous system. It was the realization that the droid was telling him, forcing him to fire the device and put it out of its misery. "Goddammit," he said, aware that

tears were forming in his eyes. "So long, friend."
Horn flipped the lever, and the scaled-down Marx
generator snapped out its electronic death message.

Horn watched as the droid's nervous system caved
in on itself and instantly ran its electromechanical shell
amok. As the Neuroid's body literally beat itself to
death, Horn walked over to Winger and dropped the
EMP device on the floor.

"Goddamit, Max," Winger barked. "The next time
I tell you to—"

"Shut up," Horn interjected.

"What?" Winger looked up, confused and surprised.

"Shut up and get the hell out of here." Horn turned
to Ticket, who had shifted his head and was looking
up at him.

"What?" Winger rose and faced Horn. "I don't
know what the hell you've got in mind, Max, but forget it. I'm not going to let you do something you'll be
sorry for later."

Horn looked Winger in the eye, remembering what
Ticket had said about them thinking Dartt was his
partner. "If you stay, you're not going to like what
you see," he said simply.

Winger looked down at Ticket, then turned back to
Horn. The two cops locked eyes for several seconds.
Then Winger sort of nodded and shrugged at the same
time. "I'll wait for you downstairs," he said, turning
and leaving the room.

A numbness crawled into Horn's mind, and he welcomed the absence of any human feelings. Looking down at Ticket's body, he willed his mods to take control.

Be sure not to miss Book 2 of the new action-packed series
TIME WARRIORS.

FORBIDDEN REGION
David North
THE BROTHERHOOD PACT

TEXAS—Workers at a uranium-processing
plant die suddenly, inexplicably... and in agony.
The town is declared a nuclear disaster area.
Evacuation is immediate.

THE FORBIDDEN ZONE—In a desolate area
in a parallel dimension, strange glowing rocks
have come to light. The nearby inhabitants are
dwindling in numbers.

THE AEGEAN—A mysterious figure heads
a sinister operation to depopulate
many worlds. Only two men can thwart
him: Black Jack Hogan and Brom,
Lord of Kalabria.

Destiny has joined these modern and ancient
warriors to battle a sinister power in
two worlds.
